NO TIME TO HIDE

A LEGAL THRILLER
FEATURING MICHAEL COLLINS

J.D. Trafford

Publisher's Note: This is a work of fiction. Names, characters, places, and incidents are a product of the author's imagination. Locales and public names are sometimes used for atmospheric purposes. Any resemblance to actual people, living or dead, or to businesses, companies, events, institutions, or locales is completely coincidental.

Book Layout ©2013 BookDesignTemplates.com

Ordering Information:
Quantity sales. Special discounts are available on quantity purchases by cor-porations, associations, and others. For details, contact the "Special Sales Department" at JDTrafford01@gmail.com.

No Time To Hide/ J.D. Trafford. -- 1st ed.
ISBN-13: 978-1496043733
Book cover design by Scarlett Rugers Design www.ScarlettRugers.com

Other Books By J.D. Trafford:

No Time To Run

No Time To Die

No Time To Hide

To my readers. Thank you for your patience and support.

—J.D.

PART ONE: THE HIDDEN

"Man is not what he thinks he is, he is what he hides."
— *Andre Malraux*

CHAPTER ONE

He sat in his car across the street from the church and watched, holding a cell phone to his ear.

He wasn't talking to anyone. The phone, in fact, wasn't even on.

Nervous, he tried to look normal. If a late-night dog walker or a curious neighbor saw him, there needed to be a reason why he was there. The phone offered a logical explanation.

He looked down at his watch. It wasn't much later than the last time he had checked. Scanning the street, he felt a knot of nerves. Adrenaline tightened inside of him. It was a little after 1:30 am. He shouldn't have to wait much longer.

The subway station was about four blocks away. That's where Father Stiles should get off, and then start his last, lonely walk back to the rectory.

Two months earlier, Father Stiles had gotten a regular Thursday night gig at The Coney.

Burlesque shows were now popular amongst the Park Slope hipster crowd, especially if they featured a few overweight dancers as well as specials on Pabst Blue Ribbon. The hipsters came in their skinny jeans, received odd titillation for an hour, and then the ultimate irony: an Elvis impersonator who had taken a vow of celibacy.

1

He had heard Father Stiles preach about his new Elvis act in a Saturday mass.

"Jesus often hung out with tax collectors and prostitutes," the priest had said, "so spending one evening a week in an Elvis costume with a smutty mime and a few unemployed actresses practicing for the next revival of Gypsy couldn't be all too bad in the eyes of the Lord."

He lifted the blue sweatshirt in the passenger seat, wondering if he should give up for the night. He didn't *have* to kill the priest. But the crowd wanted him to do it. They talked about it all the time. They shouted at him, even when he was tired and needed sleep. The crowd wanted to strip Michael Collins of everything that the lawyer loved. It was revenge. What goes around comes around.

He looked underneath the sweatshirt. There was a seven-inch straightedge knife. It was old, but still good. He had found it in a Hoboken antiques shop amidst a table filled with WWII memorabilia and supplies.

Initially he was going to buy a gun. That just seemed like the right thing to do, but then he was asked to fill out the forms. The sales clerk had started to ask questions. The crowd didn't like that. Too complicated. The crowd told him to keep it simple, don't trust anyone. They liked the knife. They told him that the knife was good, but he had his doubts. The gun had advantages. Perhaps he'd revisit the matter later.

He took a moment and ran the tips of his fingers along the blade. The edge didn't cut, but he could tell the blade was sharp. Then he covered the knife back up with his sweatshirt and waited.

Ten more minutes passed.

He saw a flicker in the streetlight and shadows. The crowd became excited. They chattered.

Sliding lower in his seat, his heart pounded. He scolded the voices. He told the crowd to be quiet. He needed to think, but it was hard. The cackle was constant.

His hand slipped under the sweatshirt and his fingers wrapped around the worn leather grip.

The plan was to wait until Father Stiles unlocked the side door. Then he'd get out of the car and cross the street as fast as possible.

It needed to happen.

After years of delay, the foreign banks had finally complied with the government's subpoenas. He'd been told by Agent Vatch that Michael Collins would soon be arrested.

This information created urgency. The crowd didn't want Collins to go to jail. The crowd wanted Collins dead along with everybody else.

But Father Stiles wasn't alone. Two women and another man were with him, wandering down the sidewalk in a group.

He swore under his breath. The crowd grumbled. The voices disagreed. He wasn't sure what he should do. The additional people created a complication. It was the first time the priest had come home with others. There was indecision.

A few voices began to jeer, heckling him to go forward. They called him a coward and a fool.

He fidgeted. His anxiety rose. He flicked the blade, back and forth; nervous.

The knife's tip made tiny cuts in the passenger seat as he thought through his choices.

His eyes widened as he watched Father Stiles and his friends stumble toward the church. They were all intoxicated, although Father Stiles handled the liquor better than the others.

He contemplated killing all four of them. Why not? The voices in his head didn't give a clear answer. He looked down at the knife in his hand, and he wished that he had bought the gun.

He watched Father Stiles and the others stop in front of the church's side door. He inched up in his seat, ready to charge. Then he heard one of the women giggle good-night.

They were leaving, he thought. The priest would be alone. He just needed to be patient, wait a few more seconds.

He watched as they hugged each other farewell. Father Stiles turned away from them and toward the side door. The priest took a step, but then stopped. More words were exchanged, and after some back and forth, they all apparently decided to go inside the church for a nightcap.

Another complication, and the crowd went crazy.

When the church's side door closed, the street went quiet. He sat in the darkness for a minute, then he decided to move. He couldn't wait. If he had to kill all of them, he would. He didn't care.

"Do it," the crowd said. "Kill them all."

He jumped out of the car and sprinted toward the door with the knife in hand. He moved as quickly and quietly as he could.

Falling into the doorway's shadow, he looked for a place to hide and wait. When Father Stiles and his friends had finished for the night, he wanted to be there. He wanted to be in a position to catch them from behind.

There was a mid-sized hedge that lined the outside of the church. He decided that would be a good place to hide.

The crowd agreed, and the crowd was content for the moment.

His heart pumped as he took a breath. He tried to slow down his system. He needed to be in control. He knew the chatter would come back, louder. He had to resist the crowd. They needed to stop shouting at him. The crowd needed to stop torturing him.

He made a small cut on the back of his hand. Blood rolled down his fingers. He felt a wave of relief. His system cooled and he closed his eyes for a second. He took a deep breath. He enjoyed the release and the moment of silence.

The crowd would be happy soon, he thought. They just needed to wait, just like him.

He opened his eyes and took a step further behind the hedge, then stopped himself.

A smile crept over his face. It was a strange idea, and it was certainly possible. There was little harm in trying. Why not?

"See what happens when you let me think?" he scolded the crowd. "See what happens when you give me space?"

He wiped the blood off of his hand and onto his pants, and then walked up to the heavy church door. He reached out, gripped the knob, and gave it a turn. The hundred-year-old mechanicals squeaked. The knob and latch moved, and the door swung open. He was now inside.

The drunk priest had forgotten to lock it.

Another hour passed before the two women and the man came down the stairs. From a dark corner in the unlit hallway, he watched them leave. The crowd screamed at him to jump.

When he resisted, the crowd let loose a string of expletives. He ignored them, but he couldn't stop his hands from shaking.

Father Stiles opened the side door to the street. He and his guests exchanged their good-byes, and then Father Stiles came back inside. The priest paused, looking around as though he sensed that something was not right, and then he locked the door.

From the dark corner, he watched the priest. He listened to the priest's footsteps as the priest walked up the steps to the rectory. He decided to wait a little longer. It'd be easier if the priest was asleep, although it would be a less exciting kill.

The crowd didn't like that decision at all.

It was still night, but morning was coming. He needed to move.

He unfolded his body, standing. His back was sore from sitting for so long, he forced one foot forward and then he started to climb the steps.

He stayed on his toes. He took one step at a time, pausing every third step and listening. He didn't hear anything, so he continued.

At the top of the steps, he opened the rectory door that led into the priest's study. Father Stiles had left a small desk lamp on, which provided just enough light to navigate the cluttered space. He walked around the piles of books to another door.

He turned the knob, hoping it wasn't locked, and it wasn't. The door opened and he walked into the priest's main living area.

A few in the crowd started to chant, and then the others picked up on it. In unison, the voices drove him forward.

They chanted for revenge to the steady beat of his heart, a beat that kept getting faster the further he went inside the house.

He had never been in the space before, but all homes had a certain logical design. He figured that a bedroom was nearby. He walked down the hallway and the crowd's chant continued.

He looked into one doorway and discovered the bathroom. He looked into another small room. There was a single bed, but it was empty. The crowd pushed him on.

"Revenge. Revenge. Revenge."

Then he went to the last room on the corridor.

This had to be it, he thought.

He opened the door. It was pitch black, but felt right. This was the master bedroom. Father Stiles had to be inside.

The chant broke, and the individual voices in the crowd started screaming, disjointed high-pitched screams. "Do it."

A bolt of energy shot through his body. He turned on the light and jumped toward the bed with the knife held high, yelling.

It took just a second to get there. He brought the knife down, and it sliced through the sheets into the lump underneath. But, there wasn't enough resistance. It was too soft. The bed was empty. The lump was just a pillow.

He swore, again, as he looked around. "Find him," said a voice in the crowd, and then others joined.

Panic.

The lights were on. He was exposed.

He turned around, scanning the empty room. He decided that Father Stiles must sleep someplace else, maybe on the main level.

He moved away from the bed, leaving. He wondered if Father Stiles had escaped. He wondered if the police were on their way.

"Find him," the crowd shouted. "Hunt."

He got to the door, and he reached for the light switch.

About to turn the lights off, he saw something out of the corner of his eye. It was a bare foot on the floor. The foot was in a small space between the bed and the room's outside wall.

He walked back. The foot wasn't moving.

He crouched down, examining the body. It was Father Stiles.

The priest wore only a t-shirt and boxer shorts. Father Stiles had obviously been about to go to bed, but had never made it. He watched the priest for a minute, waiting for Father Stiles' chest to rise, but there were no breaths taken.

He crouched lower, reached out, and felt the priest's forehead. It was cold.

He felt for a pulse, waited, and then took his hand away. There was nothing.

He stood up and walked out the door.

The crowd was disappointed. The crowd voiced its displeasure with him for waiting so long. They taunted him, but there was nothing he could do. There was no revenge to be taken.

The priest was already dead.

CHAPTER TWO

Too many people were in his bed. Michael Collins felt it, even before he had opened his eyes.

Michael was in the middle. On one side, Andie Larone was still asleep. On the other side, Kermit Guillardo stared at him.

"Dude." Kermit's eyes bugged out a little wider. "You gotta wake up, man."

Michael didn't move.

"Seriously?" Michael's head was cloudy.

Kermit had never respected the personal boundaries of others, but this was the first time Kermit had snuck into Michael's bed while he was with a woman.

"I have no choice, mi amigo." Kermit kept his voice to a whisper. "This is important, yo, like, crazy important."

Michael turned to him.

"If you tell me we're out of limes again, and you need some petty cash for the market, then I'm going to have to hurt you."

Kermit shook his head. He remained focused as his gray dreadlocks bounced.

"No, man. I'm sans humor at the momento." Kermit rubbed his ratted beard. "This is like, related to the you-know-what, which happened way back you-know-when and got you-know-who all up in your business."

Kermit waited, but Michael didn't respond. It wasn't the first time Michael did not get as excited as Kermit about a new revelation.

Kermit cocked his head to the side.

"So you gonna like hit me or listen to me?" Kermit leaned back. "Looks like you could go either way."

"I'm listening." Michael glanced over at Andie. "But keep your voice down." She was still asleep, having drunk well past her limit the night before.

Kermit nodded and moved back into Michael's personal space, sincere. "Big brother has landed."

"What?" Michael was confused, so Kermit moved even closer.

Inches away, Kermit whispered. "They invaded the beach, my man. They are here."

"Who?"

"Government agents, mi amigo." Kermit's voice rose, as if it was obvious, and Michael felt his stomach turn.

Michael had known they were getting closer. One of his bankers had tipped him off about a new subpoena. Agent Vatch wasn't letting the investigation drop and Michael's residence at the Sunset Resort's Hut No. 7 was quite possibly the worst kept secret in the history of white-collar crime. A few months ago he had even been quoted in the cover article of "High Times" magazine as the manager of one of Mexico's top ten resorts to get "sun baked."

While Michael thought about the end, Kermit filled the silence with a chant of synonyms.

"The federales, the men in black, the gestapo," he said. "The po-po, the man, the pigs, the spooks, the fuzz, the 5-oh." Kermit paused for a breath. "The forces of darkness 'tis upon our humble encampment, sayeth your majesty's humble servant."

Kermit nodded, satisfied with his superb communication skills, then concluded, "In summary and as stated earlier, they … are … here … dude-e-o."

Kermit's eyes opened wider. "Like now."

Michael looked at the door. "How do you know this?"

"Not too many tourists come in a helicopter, land on the beach, and then get out wearing dark suits and sunglasses, muchacho." Kermit rolled over, got out of the bed, and stood up.

"You want me to light your hut on fire to distract them?"

Michael shook his head. "No." He closed his eyes trying to figure out his options, but his mind worked too slowly in the morning. It was tarred by alcohol and whatever other abuse he had inflicted upon himself the night before.

Kermit became impatient. His feet began to tap. "I think I got a little flame thrower in here." He fished around for a lighter in the pockets of his ripped cargo shorts.

"Please don't set any fires." Michael sat up.

This wasn't how Michael had imagined it. Someday he was probably going to get caught, he figured, but he had gotten away so many times in the past. He had almost allowed himself to believe it was never going to happen.

Michael looked at the door, and then back to Kermit. "When did they get here?"

"A few minutes ago." Kermit walked over to the window and peeked outside. "I figure you can probably sneak out the back, run to the road, and then I can get the ol' El Camino and we can make a run to Brazil, maybe Colombia. That wouldn't be too bad. I could come back here in a few months when the buzz dies down and fetch Andie."

Kermit clapped his hands, excited. "Then start the whole thing over. Start fresh with a new name on a new beach." Kermit nodded, agreeing with his plan. "I could call you Roger Smiles. That's a cool name —Roger Smiles — and I know a doctor who could give you a nose like Barbra Streisand and ears like Dumbo. Nobody would recognize you, bro-ha, like nobody."

Michael started to respond, but there was a knock at the door.

Kermit finally located his lighter, took it out of his pocket, and pressed the button. A flame flicked out the top.

"Put that away." Michael swung his legs over the side of the bed, stood up and walked toward the door. "Who is it?"

"Mr.   Collins,   I'd   like   to   talk   with   you." Michael saw the knob turn a little, but the man on the other side of the door didn't turn it all the way. He didn't come in. He was just getting ready.

"Give me a second." Michael looked back at Kermit who had walked over to the curtains and appeared to be figuring out whether the curtains were flame retardant. Then Michael looked at Andie. She was starting to wake up, but still half asleep. Michael wondered whether this was the last time he'd see her as a free man.

"Just let me throw on a shirt," Michael shouted.

He walked over to his dresser. He glanced at the picture of his revolutionary namesake on the wall, and then he forced a sticky drawer open. Michael grabbed a wrinkled Flogging Molly T-shirt and put it on.

"We gonna make a run?" Kermit was now in his ready position. He was crouched low with his arms out wide.

Michael shook his head. "No." He walked back toward the bed. He grabbed his keys and sunglasses off of his nightstand. Then Michael kissed Andie's forehead.

"I'm done with running." Michael had said it softly, more to himself than to anyone else. "No more hiding."

CHAPTER THREE

Michael looked at the man. He was in his early-fifties with slicked hair that was graying at the temples. He wore a dark blue, pinstriped suit. His teeth were unnatural, glow-in-the-dark white. He held a large leather briefcase in his hand, but Michael didn't see a gun. There was no badge attached to his belt. There was no holster for a firearm, either.

A younger version of the older man stood behind him wearing the same outfit. He was an assistant of some sort, but he wasn't paying attention. He had an iPhone, and was hypnotized by the screen.

Kermit was right about the two visitors being trouble, Michael thought, but they weren't government. They smelled more like lawyers.

"You can talk, and I'll listen. Let's start with that."

Michael began walking over to the Sunset's largest thatch hut. It was the resort's bar and main office. It was the place where, years earlier, he had arrived with nothing but a backpack, a few paperbacks, and a sheet of paper with the account numbers and passwords for a half-dozen foreign bank accounts.

15

Andie Larone had greeted him with a soft smile and an ice-cold Corona (the foundation of any romantic relationship), and soon he had signed an overpriced lease agreement for Hut No. 7. He'd found a home among the losers and drop-outs and he didn't ever want to leave.

"It'd be nice if the boy wonder stayed behind." Michael gestured toward the young associate. "He kind of freaks me out with that phone."

"Any other requests?"

Michael nodded. "If you're sticking around, I'd like you to change your clothes before the rest of the resort wakes up. White guys in suits are bad for business."

Michael thought for a moment. "Or better, yet, I'd rather you just leave as soon as we're done. Don't bother changing your clothes."

Michael walked up three steps to the large, thatch-roofed hut at the end of the path. He found the right key, and then unlocked the door to the bar.

"Follow me." Michael went inside. "We serve the best Bloody Mary in Mexico."

There weren't many early risers at the Sunset Resort and Hostel, and so the beachfront bar didn't typically open for brunch until eleven. If people got up before then, they made some coffee in their hut and ate a granola bar or biked into San Corana to have breakfast at one of the cafes that lined the small city square.

"Have a seat." Michael pointed to a chair at a table with a nice view.

It was early and the sun was still low in the sky. Its light bounced off the blue Caribbean water. Seagulls alternated between chasing the waves and chasing each other above the rocky point that jutted out into the water in front of the resort.

"Want anything to drink? Coffee? I was also serious about the Bloody Mary. They're good." Michael walked toward the back of the bar. He tried to play it cool, but he knew that whatever the lawyer wanted to talk about was going to be bad.

The man shook his head. "I really would just like your full attention for a moment," he said. "I need to get back as soon as possible."

"No complaints about that." Michael opened a small refrigerator under the bar, grabbed a bottle of water, and then walked back over to the man and sat down at the table. "Why don't you start by introducing yourself?"

The man extended his hand, and they shook. "Tad Garvin." He smiled, expecting Michael to recognize him or the name. There was an awkward pause, and then Garvin added, "I'm a senior partner at Franklin and Uckley in New York."

Michael shrugged his shoulders. "I've heard of it." He unscrewed the top of his water bottle. Michael took a sip, continuing to keep an outward appearance of calm.

Franklin and Uckley merged with two other major international law firms when the housing market crashed and took the global economy into a recession. The firm had laid off hundreds of "dead weight" partners as part of the merger, but, despite the layoffs, Franklin and Uckley became the third largest law firm in the world and, more importantly to its remaining partners, Franklin and Uckley was the most profitable law firm.

Size matters, but money matters more.

When Michael had been an associate at Wabash, Kramer and Moore, they had referred to Franklin and Uckley by its nickname: F U

It was a nickname and attitude that the firm embraced, even going so far as to acquire the domain name www.fu.com from an Eastern European pornography company in the late 1990s. That's how they rolled at Franklin and Uckley: F U

CHAPTER FOUR

Garvin leaned back, taking a deep breath to inflate himself. "In short, my client wants to meet with you." He smiled, displaying his perfect teeth. An aura of confidence radiated from his orange, fake tan. "But it needs to be done privately. I am not involved, and I, quite frankly, don't want to be involved any further."

Michael smiled back at Garvin. "Great," he said, sarcastically. "Where is he?" Michael looked around the room, feigning eagerness.

"My client is not a 'he.' Brea Krane is Joshua Krane's daughter." The reference to Joshua Krane hit Michael like a quick jab to his stomach. He winced, but Garvin continued. "She says it's urgent."

Michael took a sip of water, trying to recover. He hoped that his discomfort wasn't obvious.

He thought back to the corrupt businessman and the night that changed his life. Michael's hand, reflexively, touched the scar on his cheek. "I didn't know Krane had a daughter."

"He had a daughter and a son," Garvin said. Michael's mind raced as Garvin continued to prattle on.

It had been years since Michael had burned his suits and ties in a glorious back alley bonfire. After being shot on the

19

same night that Joshua Krane had been killed, Michael had left New York with no plans other than to never practice law again. It was a plan that was greatly assisted by the funds in Joshua Krane's off-shore bank accounts. Money didn't buy happiness, Michael's mother used to say, but it was a pretty good down payment.

Michael had never thought of Krane as a father. He had never really thought of Krane as a person, much less a family man. Krane was just another billable hour. A rich chump that his law firm was going to charge massive amounts of exorbitant legal fees until the client was either broke or in prison, whichever came first.

Michael took a drink. He put the cap back on the water bottle.

"What does she want to talk about?"

"Like I said earlier," Garvin lifted his briefcase off the ground, opened it, and removed a large, thin envelope. "I don't know the details and I do not want to know. Brea Krane has sent me here to make contact with you. She was quite insistent."

"And the client is always right."

Garvin smiled. "And the client is always right." It was every lawyer's mantra.

Garvin put the briefcase back by his feet and slid the envelope across the table to Michael. He pointed at it.

"Please, take a look. Her contact information is inside."

Michael looked down at the envelope. Then he pushed it back toward Garvin.

"I'm not interested in anything she has to say." Michael stood up. "Why don't you get back in your helicopter or whatever it is and go home. I only came out here because ..." Michael's voice trailed off, but Garvin knew where Michael was going.

"You only came out here because you thought I was going to arrest you." Garvin smiled.

Michael stared back at Garvin. He already hated the man. Michael had just met him, and yet, he knew that Tad Garvin was more arrogant than all the senior partners at Michael's old law firm, but dumber.

"You can see yourself out." Michael turned and started walking toward the door.

"Mr. Collins," Garvin said. "Did you know that Agent Frank Vatch is testifying in front of a grand jury this morning?"

Michael stopped, but didn't turn around. So, Garvin continued.

"My client has already testified. Your various bank accounts are already flagged and likely frozen, and the United States Attorney will get the indictment today or tomorrow."

Garvin paused, letting the information sink in for a moment. Information was power, and Garvin leveraged it.

"You need to be smart." Garvin tapped the envelope sitting on the table. His voice now carried an edge. "Brea Krane just might be the only person in the world who can get you the one thing that you need."

"And what's that, Tad?" Michael said with disdain. "What's the one thing I need?"

Garvin smiled, smug.

"Your freedom, son. You need freedom from your past."

CHAPTER FIVE

Frank Vatch studied the documents that had just been hand-ed to him. "These are bank records that I received a month ago."

United States Attorney Brenda Gadd nodded her head and walked back toward counsel table. A few of the jurors were looking at the clock, but most of them leaned forward in their seats. They were now engaged.

It had been two days, and they wanted to see the evidence that had been hinted at from the beginning. Like all juries, there was also a desire to just get the job done — hang the bastard and go home.

"And how did you obtain these bank records?" Gadd sat down. She picked up a pen and made a checkmark by one of the questions typed on her sheet of paper.

"It wasn't easy." Vatch forced his narrow slit of a mouth into a bent smile. He attempted to seem normal and friendly, but it didn't work. When he made eye contact with a few of the jurors, they looked away. Since he was a child, Vatch simply gave off a bad vibe. He was an asshole, and anybody who spent more than thirty seconds in his presence quickly figured that out.

"Michael Collins' story didn't seem right to me. I always treated him like a suspect, because it would be stupid not to."

Vatch paused, and then continued. "He had opportunity and he took it."

"Explain," said Gadd, and Vatch obliged.

"On the night Joshua Krane was murdered, Krane and Mr. Collins went to get the account numbers and passwords from a safe deposit box as part of a potential settlement agreement with the Justice Department."

"Why?" Gadd asked, just as they had rehearsed the night before.

"Krane had been accused of bribery and various other bad acts while securing very large contracts from the Defense Department. We are talking billions of dollars. The money in those accounts was going to be used by Krane to pay back some of what had been stolen and also as a penalty."

Vatch paused and waited. Gadd nodded her head and he continued.

"In the confusion that night, either before or after Krane was killed and Mr. Collins was shot, Michael Collins got those bank account numbers and then later illegally transferred the money to his personal accounts."

"And Michael Collins had no authority to make those wire transfers, true?"

"That's true." Vatch spoke directly to the grand jurors. "That money either belonged to Krane, Krane's family, Krane's company or the victims who had been defrauded by Joshua Krane. I don't know who it belonged to, exactly; I'll leave that to the lawyers. I just know that the money didn't belong to Michael Collins."

Gadd nodded earnestly, allowing the jurors a few moments to process the information.

"And to you, as a trained law enforcement officer, what did this mean?"

"It means that Michael Collins committed wire fraud."

Gadd nodded, making sure to give the jurors time to write down the words "wire fraud" in their notebooks. She liked the term 'wire fraud.' It sounded like Michael Collins was an old-time mobster. "And then?"

"And then motive wasn't too hard to figure out." Vatch leaned forward. "Michael Collins had grown up pretty poor, and the temptation to get rich quick isn't unusual for his type. Then he disappeared. People don't normally ditch all of their belongings and move to Mexico," Vatch smirked. "It made him look very suspicious to me."

"Are you saying that Michael Collins arranged to have Joshua Krane murdered?"

Vatch shook his head.

"I can't say that. It's possible, but I can't say that for sure. There were others who also wanted to kill Krane and take the money." Vatch paused, unsure of how much detail he should provide. "I just know that Michael Collins took the money and ran."

Vatch caught the eye of a few jurors. They nodded at him, despite their dislike. Then, Vatch nodded back. His honesty had apparently just scored a few points.

"A few years ago," Vatch continued. "Collins had come back to New York. His girlfriend was in trouble, and we had an opportunity to make an arrest. But things got complicated."

"How so?" Gadd knew that Agent Vatch was going to talk about Lowell Moore, Patty Bernice and the *Maltow* file. It was complicated testimony that she would try to avoid at the actual trial, but in the safety of a grand jury room, Gadd wanted to see how it would play out. She wanted to practice, just in case Vatch had to testify about it at the actual trial. Without a judge or defense attorney in a grand jury proceeding, there wasn't any better place to test Agent Vatch.

"Well, I had been focused on Michael Collins from the beginning. But, it appears that there were multiple people who knew about these bank accounts and wanted to take the money from Krane. A den of thieves, so to speak." Vatch paused. He smirked, hoping that somebody would find him humorous, but nobody laughed. He was back to being an asshole.

"The law firm where Collins worked had mishandled a case, called *Maltow*. The firm had missed a major deadline, which resulted in the case being dismissed. Rather than come clean, the senior partner, Mr. Lowell Moore and his assistant, Patty Bernice, tried to cover it up. They didn't tell their client. They faked a settlement agreement, and then paid for the *Maltow* settlement from the escrow accounts of other clients of the law firm, and this started a domino effect."

"What does that mean?" Gadd interrupted, sensing that the jurors were getting confused.

"*Maltow* was a huge case," Vatch said. "To avoid a malpractice claim and tarnish the law firm's reputation, they faked the settlement and the law firm issued a large settlement check to their client. Although the settlement was fake, the check was real and so Lowell Moore and Patty Bernice started constantly shifting money among the law firm's various client escrow accounts. Like a pyramid scheme or a Ponzi scheme. The law firm's books were never in balance, because they were always short the amount the firm paid out in *Maltow*. Ultimately, by stealing Joshua Krane's money, Lowell Moore and Patty Bernice believed that they would be able to cover up the faked settlement. The money would replenish the escrow accounts and bring the law firm's books into balance and nobody would be the wiser."

Vatch stopped himself, knowing that his testimony was getting too detailed.

"And why does all that matter in this case against Mr. Collins?" asked Gadd, giving Vatch an opportunity to get back on track. Vatch took a breath, and then refocused.

"In short," Vatch said, "I believe Lowell Moore and Patty Bernice were likely involved in Joshua Krane's murder. When this information came to light, it became unclear whether Lowell Moore and Patty Bernice had taken Joshua Krane's money, whether Michael Collins was working with them, or whether Lowell Moore and Patty Bernice intended to take Joshua Krane's money but Michael Collins snatched it first."

"So then what happened?" Gadd asked.

"I had to back off." Vatch turned to the jurors and puffed up his chest. "My job is to get the right perpetrator and build a rock solid case."

A few of the female jurors rolled their eyes, but Vatch didn't stop. "As long as there were other people out there who were just as likely to have stolen the money, a prosecution couldn't move forward. We needed proof beyond a reasonable doubt."

"And then what?" Gadd liked how Vatch had handled the question. She scanned the grand jurors, looking for any sign of confusion. She saw none.

"We had to wait for the banks to provide the information," Vatch continued. "The only way to get the truth was to follow the money trail to Michael Collins. We needed proof beyond a reasonable doubt, and we couldn't do that without clear evidence that Michael Collins had Joshua Krane's money."

"So you sent the subpoenas to these banks right away?" Gadd made a checkmark next to another question on her sheet of paper.

"No." Vatch shook his head. "First we had to figure out where Joshua Krane had hidden the money. Due to the plea negotiations, we knew there were secret, foreign accounts. But at the time, the government didn't know where the accounts were located. There are hundreds, if not thousands, of banks where people can hide assets."

Vatch took a breath and waited to see if Gadd was going to ask another question or wanted him to proceed. She didn't say anything, so he continued his story.

In an actual criminal trial, a witness was not allowed to talk without a specific question. A good defense attorney would object and a judge would sustain the objection, stopping the narrative. But this was an initial grand jury proceeding. There was nobody to object. There was simply United States Attorney Brenda Gadd, alone in a room with a witness and the grand jurors. The playing field was so tilted in the government's favor that most attorneys are unable to remember a time when a grand jury had refused to indict the accused. So here, Gadd wanted Agent Vatch to tell this part of the story uninterrupted and that was exactly what happened.

"It took about six months of reviewing computer files and paper files before our forensic accountants could identify where the bank accounts were located," Vatch said. "Once they were located, we had to force these banks to respond to our subpoenas, which was not easy, and then the process had to be repeated every time the money was moved."

"The money moved?"

"Many times," Vatch said. "We found the original accounts, but they all had minimal funds or were closed by the time we had located them and the banks released the information."

Gadd went back to her table and turned on a projector. It was time to move forward. She also didn't want Vatch talking about his little debacle in Florida after the botched arrest in New York.

A small fan inside the projector whirled to life, and the jurors turned toward the screen. A chart showed a diagram of how Michael Collins had purportedly transferred over $500 million from Krane's accounts to a series of other foreign bank accounts throughout the world. There were dozens of boxes with arrows to other sets of boxes, and then another series of arrows and boxes and then another.

Brenda Gadd allowed the jurors a moment to review the complex chart on their own, and then she got up, walked to the witness stand, and handed Agent Frank Vatch a laser pointer.

"Tell us how the money got from Krane to Michael Collins."

Vatch closed his eyes for a second, remembering the numerous times he had rehearsed this testimony with Gadd in the last month. Testifying felt good, but the actual criminal trial would feel even better. He opened his eyes.

"Perhaps it's easier to work backwards." Vatch pressed a small button on the device in his hand. He pointed it at the bottom of the screen.

"Do you see down here?" Vatch bounced the red dot from the laser pointer between two large boxes.

Gadd nodded her head. "Yes."

"These are two major withdrawals that were made by Michael Collins. The first is a rather large donation to his parish here in New York. He is very close to the priest there. Then we have another withdrawal when he purchased the Sunset Resort and Hostel in Mexico through a shell company. There's no dispute that this donation and the acquisition of the resort were done by Mr. Collins with Joshua Krane's assets."

Vatch pointed at the series of boxes directly above these two itemized withdrawals.

"These are the accounts where that money came from." Vatch moved the laser pointer to the next series of boxes and then to the next. "As you can see, the money was transferred multiple times, but the trail clearly goes from Joshua Krane's original foreign bank accounts to Michael Collins."

"And you have copies of every money transfer and purchase made from these accounts, which provide the foundation for the chart that we are now looking at?"

Vatch set the laser pointer down and nodded.

"Absolutely." Vatch pointed at a large stack of documents sitting next to the projector. "They're right there. Every receipt. Every account statement. There are also emails between the bank and Michael Collins that discuss the transactions. There is no doubt in my mind that Michael Collins stole this money from his law firm's client, Joshua Krane."

The cab stopped in front of Vatch's apartment. The cabbie got out, popped the trunk, and removed Vatch's collapsed wheelchair. He fiddled with the lever. Eventually the wheelchair opened and the cabbie set it on the sidewalk near the open passenger side door.

Vatch grabbed the small handle above the door. He pulled himself out of the back seat and into the wheelchair. "How much?"

The cabbie looked through the window at the meter. "Thirteen twenty."

Vatch nodded. He got out his wallet and handed the cabbie a ten dollar bill and four ones.

The cabbie looked at the cash in his hand.

"That's it?" he said. "No tip. I haul that wheelchair around and get no tip from you?"

Vatch's face sharpened. "You got a tip." Vatch's tongue flicked out of his mouth as he pointed at the cab's meter. "You owe me eighty cents, according to that thing, and I'm letting you keep it." Vatch undid the wheel lock and turned, while the cab-bie started yelling at him.

After Vatch had rolled ten feet, he turned around.

The red-faced cab driver continued to rant.

"Hey," Vatch pointed. "Quiet down, you're disturbing my neighborhood."

This began a new line of insults as a random group of neigh-bors emerged to watch the commotion. After another ten feet, Vatch stopped and turned.

"Okay, here's an additional tip of the non-monetary variety: Next time don't take the scenic route like I'm a tourist. You wasted five minutes of my life, padding that meter."

The watchers burst out laughing. They heckled the cab driv-er as he left. For Vatch, it was a small triumph. It added to the larger triumph earlier in the grand jury room.

This was a good day, thought Vatch, and he wanted to share it with one of his only friends.

"Seen Anthony?" Vatch asked the largest woman in the crowd. She lived down the hall from him, known for wearing a small amount of tight clothing to show off her "curves."

"Up with Spider."

She pointed to a group of teenagers hanging out on the cor-ner about a half-block away. There were seven of them, ranging in age from eleven to nineteen. Spider was easy to pick out. Spider was the tallest, more than six-feet tall with long arms, and even from a distance, Vatch caught the reflection of his gold teeth. All of the group's energy was directed at him. Spider was the leader, a magnet. He was the guy that the others want-ed to impress.

Vatch saw Anthony standing a little off to the side, clearly not one of the gang, but trying to be included. Vatch wanted to go down there, grab Anthony, and disperse the group of thugs-in-training. But, he knew that wouldn't work. It would only push Anthony further away.

"Thanks for keeping an eye on him," Vatch said to the woman.

"Watching him ain't hard." The big woman shook her head. "Keeping him outta trouble is hard. Ms. Finkel's purse got stoled yesterday. Nobody seen it, but Anthony was around."

Vatch nodded, taking it in. The information wasn't surprising. He had heard a growing number of similar allegations recently.

"I'll talk to his mom." Vatch looked back down the street to the corner, suddenly feeling less victorious. "Maybe his mom can talk to him about getting Ms. Finkel's purse back."

"Better." The big woman put her hands on her ample hips. "She was packing in that purse."

"Old Ms. Finkel was carrying a gun?"

The big woman pointed at Vatch's belt where he holstered his government-issued Glock 22.

"Don't everybody?"

CHAPTER SIX

Michael watched the security video of Garvin coming into the Sunset's bar. He had bought the camera six months ago. Andie hated it, but Michael had been feeling more paranoid than usual at the time. The camera calmed him, a security totem.

He clicked a few buttons on the computer, saved the images, and then emailed himself a copy of the files. Could be helpful later, thought Michael.

He walked over to the resort's credit card machine and slid his card through. He'd already done it before. Michael knew what was going to happen, but he hoped for something different this time.

He hunched over the machine and waited. The word "PROCESSING" flashed at him. Then Michael glanced impatiently around the small back office. The desk was cluttered. It was surrounded with boxes of toilet paper, towels, and cleaning supplies. Behind it, there was also a sad, rusted, rarely used filing cabinet.

Michael looked down at the screen, again. A different word had appeared during the seconds that he had looked away: DECLINED.

Michael felt his muscles tighten. Tad Garvin was telling the truth. His bank accounts were frozen.

"What's going on?" She stood in the doorway.

Michael turned and saw Andie Larone.

"How long have you been there?"

Andie came toward him.

"Long enough to be worried." She looked at the credit card machine, and then at the bank card in Michael's hand.

He followed her eyes. For a moment, Michael thought about telling her about Garvin and the indictment, but he held back.

"Nothing's going on." Michael picked his wallet up off of the desk, opened it, and put the card away.

Andie's expression fell.

"Come on, Michael." She put her hand on his shoulder. "I thought we were past this."

"It's fine." Michael brushed her hand away and started to walk out of the room. He didn't want to talk. "I just need some time alone to figure some stuff out."

"That's what you always want." She became irritated. "That's always been the problem." Andie followed him. "What happened this morning? I woke up and you were gone."

"It's nothing."

"You're lying, Michael." Andie waited for him to deny it, but Michael said nothing. "I'm not an idiot," she said. "I saw the man who you were talking to get into a helicopter. He didn't exactly fit in. His assistant was asking some of the guests about getting to the nearest Starbucks."

Michael let her comments pass. He walked out of the office and through the lobby while Andie continued.

"When are you going to trust me, Michael?"

Michael stopped at the front door, ready to go outside. The bright sun cast half his face in shadow.

"I tried that before and you left, remember?" It was cruel, but it was true. Although they had worked hard to patch their relationship together since Andie had come back to the Sunset, their past was still unresolved. She was gone for almost two years, after accepting and then rejecting his proposal to be married. It was a record for the world's shortest engagement. No letter. No phone call for two years. It still hurt.

Michael turned away. He took a step out the door and then stopped.

"I love you." Michael was unable to meet her eyes. "I just need a day or two, okay? Then we can talk."

"Promise?" Andie asked as Michael starting walking away.

"I'll try."

###

It was a two-hour bike ride from the Sunset Resort to the dirt path.

He stopped and looked up at the bright, cloudless sky. Michael breathed hard. Sweat beaded and rolled down his face. It felt good.

There weren't any signs, and the path didn't appear on any official maps. For archaeologists and locals, however, it was well known. The path was one of the easiest ways into the Sian Ka'an Reserve.

The name of the reserve, roughly translated from Mayan, meant "where the sky was born."

It was a 1.3 million-acre oasis of forests, wetlands, and coastline, protected from the constant onslaught of developers and land speculators. The Sian Ka'an Reserve was also one of the few places in the Yucatan that hadn't dramatically changed in the past thirty years, and arguably it hadn't changed much in the last ten thousand.

The path led away from Highway 304 about five kilometers through a prairie savannah and then to the more densely vegetated portion of the reserve. All of the Sian Ka'an was wild, but this part was the wildest.

As Michael biked further, it was more likely that he'd see the foundation of a 1,200 year old Mayan structure than another person.

After twenty minutes, the path faded and the ground softened. It was no longer possible to peddle, and so Michael stopped.

He laid the bike down. He took his pack off the bike's rear wheel rack. Then Michael removed his GPS from the pack's front pocket and recorded his location. If he didn't preserve his coordinates, it was unlikely he'd ever find the mountain bike again.

Then Michael drank half his bottle of water. He paused when he was done, listened and looked for anything that was out of place. He stared behind him, searching to see if anybody had followed. Then, Michael loosened two straps, put the straps over his shoulders and the pack on his back.

Michael paused, took a deep breath of the heavy air, and started hiking even deeper into the reserve.

After his mother had died, Michael had moved from Boston to New York. He spent the rest of his teen years in the rectory with Father Stiles or alone, wandering the streets. These were not the typical activities of a teenage boy, but nothing about Michael's life was typical and he figured nothing about his future would be typical, either.

During one of his walks through Manhattan, Michael had discovered the Gotham Book Mart. A rusted metal sign hung over its large black awning. The sign depicted three men in a fishing boat trying to reel in a book from the sea. Underneath, in large block letters were the words, "WISE MEN FISH HERE."

Inside the red brick building, old and new books filled shelves and were piled high on top of tables. A literary critic once said it was "a place filled with observations."

Its owner tried to nudge the masses toward new writers with different voices, but over time the masses didn't want to be nudged anymore. They were more interested in books with large stickers on the cover proclaiming 30% off. Sales dropped as people bought books elsewhere, bad financial decisions were made, and the store eventually closed.

While it was still open, however, Michael had found a self-published 'zine dedicated to the New York Underground. It was filled with black and white photographs, sketches, and maps interspersed with stories about the thousands of "mole" people who had lived beneath the city. There were poems about abandoned subway stations decorated with elaborate mosaics and reviews of secret nightclubs far underneath Broadway that had been built during Prohibition.

Most were myth, but some of the maps were real. Michael would go out late at night and sneak into the sewer system, exploring the tunnels and caves and letting his imagination take him to a better place.

His knowledge of the underground had helped him escape Agent Vatch once before, maybe it would work, again.

Like subterranean Manhattan, the Sian Ka'an was a world that had been left behind. Rather than sewers and subways, the Sian Ka'an had old Mayan aqueducts, caves, and ponds.

Michael checked his GPS, cut north-east for fifty yards and stopped at a large sinkhole. It was about one hundred yards wide, filled with crystal clear water and no apparent tributaries.

Michael took off his backpack and laid it on the ground. Then he stripped down to nothing. He tossed his sweaty t-shirt, shorts, and boxers to the side and jumped in with goggles in hand.

The water was cool, and it sent a shock through his naked body as his temperature dropped. Although the water's salt stung some of the superficial scrapes he'd endured on the hike, it was worth it.

He came up for air, feeling alive and free.

Michael put the goggles on, and then he swam back and forth. He reached his arms out as far as they could go, and then scooped them back. He dipped under the surface of the water, making shallow dives at first, and then diving deeper.

He was weightless. The underwater world was a large room of filtered light. He tried to stay submerged as long as he could.

Michael returned to the top of the water. The Caribbean sun instantly dried his face, then he took a breath and dove back into the peace as soon as he could.

Michael lazed in the water for awhile, but he had a purpose. This wasn't a pleasure trip. Michael got out and walked over to the pack amidst the pile of his clothes.

He opened the top, and then got his GPS, the same one that had recorded the location of his bike and had guided him to the sinkhole. He pressed a button on the GPS's bright yellow plastic casing, waited for it to power on, and then he used a Velcro strap to attach the device to his wrist.

Finally, Michael reached into the pack's largest compartment. He grabbed a long rope with a carabiner clip attached to the end.

With rope in hand, he ran a few yards and jumped back into the water.

He swam out toward the middle of the sinkhole, checked the GPS on his wrist, and then swam another ten yards to the left.

Michael dove down, pushing himself deep into the hole. The water was still clear, and he could see schools of brightly colored fish darting away from him while larger fish jerked past with a few turns of their tails.

He looked, but didn't see it.

Michael returned to the surface. He caught his breath, and then dove back down into the hole, deeper this time, holding the rope with the carabiner tight in his hand.

He felt the pressure building in his lungs, but he didn't want to return to the top. He was close. He knew it was there. He just couldn't see it. When he couldn't hold his breath any longer, Michael started to swim back to the surface, and it was then that he saw an unnatural block of square, plastic foam hiding in a narrow shadow.

There was relief, but there wasn't time to celebrate.

Michael was a second behind. He took in some water as he reached the surface, and he emerged in a fit of coughs. Michael tried to recover. The water burned his lungs and made him gag.

It took some time to recuperate, but Michael dove again. He knew where he was going this time. He had direction.

Michael swam toward the white floater. It was an innocent object. If anybody else had seen it, they would have assumed it was a piece of garbage left by an ugly tourist. The white plastic foam rode the subtle underwater movements, but it didn't stray too far. A weight held it in place, tethering it to the sinkhole's bottom.

Michael swam to the foam block, attached the carabiner, and shot to the surface with the long rope in his hand.

He swam to the edge of the sinkhole and lifted himself out. Then Michel sat down, and started pulling. The rope snagged a few times, but within a minute his prize came to the surface.

Wise men fish here, he thought as a small waterproof box came to shore. The box had been the weight attached to the end of the rope, tethering the foam to the bottom of the sinkhole.

Michael examined the box. It was covered with moss, but the inside was going to be dry. And, that was all that mattered.

CHAPTER SEVEN

Michael had to retrieve his bike, get back to the highway, and then ride north to a rough dirt road that led to Punta Allen. With a population of 400, it was the largest village in the area.

It was dusk by the time Michael made it. He was tired and hungry. The trip had been hotter and more grueling than the last time, probably because he was that much older and more out of shape.

The actual name of the village was Javier Rojo Gómez, but nearly everybody called it Punta Allen for reasons that Michael never understood. His best guess was that Punta Allen was just easier to say. It also sounded like a village. Javier Rojo Gomez was too long. It sounded more like an actor on one of Mexico's telenovelas than a place where people live.

Michael biked into town. He turned left, and then went further south for another three blocks and stopped in front of a dirty, white, one-story building. He set his bike down and walked inside through the open door.

The bartender looked up at him. It took a moment to register, but then a smile crossed the bartender's face.

"Look what the cat dragged in." He shook his head. "You look old."

"I feel old." Michael walked up to the bar, and then feigned inspection of the place. "Still living off your dubiously obtained disability benefits from the State of Louisiana?"

"Of course, wouldn't have it any other way." The bartender bent over, pulled a Corona out of a cooler and took the bottle cap off. He put the open bottle down in front of Michael.

"What the hell you been doin' to yourself?"

Michael took a drink of the cold beer. It was one of the best beers he had ever tasted. Michael savored it for a moment while also thinking about the question.

"Now that's a fair inquiry. You want the truth or something more philosophical?"

The bartender scratched his stubbled chin.

"The truth is usually interesting, but philosophy is more useful to me in my day-to-day life."

"Nietzsche or Camus?"

"Nietzsche." The bartender extracted another Corona from under the bar. He set it on the bar, removed the bottle cap, and then raised the bottle high. "Camus was a pussy," he declared, then took a sip.

Michael laughed. "And Nietzsche had a better mustache."

"Not fair." The bartender smiled. "Camus didn't have a mustache."

Michael nodded. "Exactly." Then the two outcasts clinked their bottles and chugged them down.

###

The bartender, Timmy Driscoll, was another drop-out. He had been a high school guidance counselor for twenty years in New Orleans, twice divorced.

In middle age, his life had mostly entailed being abused by idiot teenagers during the day and caring for his three-legged dog in the evening. The three-legged dog was named Sparky. He loved that dog and figured that they would grow old together in New Orleans. Then Hurricane Katrina hit. His little house was washed away along with his school and the job.

He was evacuated by bus to Texas.

Timmy had snuck Sparky on board in a duffle bag. They made it an hour short of Houston when Sparky was discovered by the bus driver. Timmy and the dog were dropped off at a Greyhound bus station in Beaumont.

Timmy didn't have much cash, but he had a credit card. He bought a ticket on the next bus and paid an extra fee for Sparky. From Beaumont, Timmy went to San Antonio, and from there, Timmy and Sparky went to Matamoros on the Texas-Mexico border and then down the coast. They kept going south until he and the dog made a long pit stop at the Sunset Resort, and then eventually moved on to Punta Allen.

After a few months of living in Punta Allen, Timmy decided to liquidate his 401k and buy the "The Salty Sands" bar.

Timmy wasn't a good bartender, but it was the only bar in town. The bedroom in the back of the bar also gave him a place to sleep and the soft pulse of the waves coming to shore gave him a little peace. The sound reminded him of the good parts of living in New Orleans without the bad.

Michael and Timmy sat across from one another, laughing. They exchanged stories of the most recent attempts by the federales to shake down local businesses with new permit fees as well as the latest travails of tourists who drifted in and out of their lives.

In the meantime, Sparky, the three-legged dog, searched for stray pieces of popcorn on the floor.

Michael finished his beer, and Timmy gave him another. Then Timmy started in with the third installment of his trilogy, "The American Gringos and The Salty Sands."

"So this blonde chick comes in here from Alabama or someplace like that with her husband, and they're arguing about the name, 'Punta Allen' and how to pronounce it correctly. She wants to be all ethnic, and so she's pronouncing it like Pawntwa Al-onge, and her husband is telling her its Punt-a Allen, 'like your cousin Allen, not Al-onge. Al-onge is like French. It's Allen, like your cousin.'"

Timmy paused so that Michael could appreciate the mental ability of the blonde and her husband.

"So eventually this lady comes over to me and says, real slow and loud like I'm cognitively deficient and half deaf, 'Excuse me. Can you tell me where we are and how you pronounce it?'"

Timmy laughed in anticipation of the punchline.

"So I played along. I went all glassy eyed and nodded my head at her without saying a word. And then she says to me, 'Good. Just pronounce it real slow-like because me and my husband don't really speak Mexican.'

"Then she turned to her husband, and says, 'Earl, you listen up, this man is going to tell us where we are.' "

Timmy picked up a handful of popcorn. He shoved it into his mouth, and then continued after a beat and a swallow.

"So I did what she asked and I told her where she was real slow, stretching out each syllable so that she got the pronunciation just right. I told her, 'You....Are....In....A.....Bar.'"

###

When they were done. Timmy led Michael into the back. He pointed out a bathroom with the smallest shower that Michael had ever seen.

"You're free to use it, if you can fit in it." Timmy shook his head. "It was designed by skinny Germans. I have to stand on the outside and just stick one body part in there at a time."

After the bathroom tour, they walked out the back door.

There was a ladder propped up against the building. Timmy pointed to it.

"There you go, my friend. Just climb up to the penthouse and I'll see you in the morning. I'll bring your bike inside and get it locked up. Not much action here at night, but you never know."

Michael thanked him. He slung his pack over his shoulder and started to climb.

CHAPTER EIGHT

On the roof, there was a large white hammock strung from rusted poles cemented into opposite corners of the building. On the ground next to the hammock, there was a stack of bedding, consisting of a thin sheet, pillow and mosquito net.

Two small kerosene lanterns had already been lit and cast everything in an orange light, but the light from the lanterns didn't dim the thousands of stars above.

The setup was beautiful and serene. It was marred only by the sight of Kermit Guillardo smoking a large joint and engaging in one of his new hobbies: naked yoga.

Kermit took a deep breath.

He untangled himself from the lotus position and stood.

"We gotta build one of these rooftop pleasure centers at the Sunset, yo." Kermit looked up at the stars and stretched, then took a long drag off his joint and released. "My core is totally ripped right now." Kermit checked out his abs and nodded. "Plus, I'm like centered, like totally centered and ripped at the same time. Just call me Rip Van Centered."

Michael looked at Kermit's abs. They looked a little more like a beer pooch than a six-pack, but he didn't say anything. He set down his backpack, then he sat on the hammock.

"It's a nice spot."

"A nice spot to glow." Kermit reached his arms to the sky, stretching. "Are you catching my glow?"

"Totally." Michael laid back in the hammock. "Just being near you has changed the color of my aura." Michael closed his eyes. "Rip Van Center has engulfed me in a totally mellow magnetic field."

Kermit nodded, not catching the sarcasm.

"It always does, my man. That's what I done-did-do."

After Kermit explained to Michael how he was grossly over-worked and underpaid, he managed to guilt Michael into letting him sleep in the hammock.

Michael blew up his Therm-A-Rest mattress and laid down on the roof a few feet away.

"What are you going to tell Andie?" Kermit swung a little bit in the hammock, allowing one of his long legs to dangle over the side. "Gotta tell her something."

Michael listened to a pick-up truck bounce by on the street below.

"I know," he paused. "She obviously knows what's going on, but it's just that …"

"It's just that you don't want the cookie to crumble another time."

"Sort of." Michael rolled onto his back, looking up at the sky. "We've been piecing it together slowly, getting to know each other, again. But I just have a bad feeling."

"You think she's a snitch?" Kermit whistled, shaking his head. "No way, mi amigo, not my Andie. She's a lotta things but she wouldn't —"

"I know. I know," Michael cut him off. "But she almost did before and the timing is off. That's all. She comes back and now, lo and behold, the indictment follows."

Kermit sat up, his expression serious.

"The government's had enough evidence to get you for a long time, muchacho. You said it yourself a hundred times. It happened in New York, and then they dropped it. It coulda happened in Miami, and somehow they let you go. The clock just ran out, like you thought it would."

Kermit looked up at the sky.

"Some spy satellites probably peeping down on us right now. Andie's got nothing to do with it. She just made a couple mistakes." Kermit paused. "Just like you, man. Just like anybody."

Michael rolled over onto his side. "She's just been acting weird lately, more needy." Michael closed his eyes. "Something just feels off."

CHAPTER NINE

Michael was up at sunrise, a time when the air was cool and the sky was still a muddle of dark blues and oranges.

He rolled off of his thin air mattress and stood. Michael was sore from the bike ride. Sleeping on concrete didn't help. His joints creaked as he walked over to the edge of the roof. A gentle breeze came off the water. A cruise ship coasted north in the distance. It was headed toward Cozumel, an island whose sole apparent function was to separate tourists from their money.

Michael knelt. He glanced back at Kermit, who appeared to still be sleeping, and then picked up his backpack. He unzipped it, removed the waterproof box that he had retrieved from the sinkhole, and set the backpack down.

The box was roughly the length and size of a shoe box. It was constructed of a hard polycarbonate plastic. It was purportedly crushproof, waterproof, and airtight. We'll see, Michael thought.

He unfastened two latches and flipped open the top.

Black foam lined the interior of the box, and Michael stared at the large plastic zipper-lock bag that was nestled in the base. It was his second lifeline.

His first lifeline had been at Hoa Bahns in Chinatown. Hoa Bahns was half speakeasy, half unregulated, unlicensed bank. He had used that lifeline when Andie was in trouble and he had been forced to go back to New York and defend her. Now he had this.

Michael took the bag, unzipped it, and checked the contents: $10,000 in cash; five rolls of fifteen gold South African Krugerrand coins, each coin worth about $1,700 and totaling just under $130,000; a fake Canadian passport; four disposable pre-paid cell phones; and the list.

The list was a one-page spreadsheet, last updated after the purchase of the Sunset. It identified the names of a dozen off-shore bank accounts where he had stashed money, bank contact information, the account numbers, and passwords. Of course, Michael had used a simple cipher to encrypt the account numbers, just in case somebody discovered the dry box. He would now have to contact each bank, hoping that there were one or two accounts that the government had not found and frozen.

Michael put two of the cell phones in his pocket. He removed ten one-hundred-dollar bills and put them in his wallet, and then he returned the remaining cash and the rest of the items to the bag.

"You're a damn good planner, muchacho."

Michael jumped. He turned toward the voice and saw Kermit sitting in the lotus position on his yoga mat, smiling.

"You're going to give me a heart attack."

Kermit laughed. "Doubtful, but Timmy's famous bacon might clog one or two of your heart highways."

"Hungry?" Michael put the zipped bag back in the dry box and latched it shut.

"Always hungry, yo." Kermit stood and stretched. "Got the passion of a lion and the metabolism of a hummingbird."

"Timmy's probably not up yet." Michael put the dry box into his backpack, and then slung the pack over his shoulder. "So let's go break into his kitchen and get something to eat."

"That's the spirit." Kermit rubbed his hands together. "Free the bacon."

###

Timmy came through the back in his boxers and a white T-shirt that was a size too small. Sparky hopped behind him. "Y'all are paying for all that stuff?"

"I thought it was free for locals, like a neighborhood food-share." Michael took a bite of his omelet and winked at him.

Then Kermit turned to Timmy. He was holding a gigantic breakfast burrito a few inches from his face.

"Your eggs are mighty nice, mi amigo, but your swine is mighty fine." Kermit put the burrito down on his plate and picked up a piece of bacon. He waved it around. "As always, your bac-o didn't shrivel in the skizzle. Blows my mind, brother. Out of this world."

"It's all locally sourced, cage-free, free range stuff." Timmy said. "Chickens and pigs just wander around that garbage dump near the Tamaulipas incinerator eating a steady diet of rancid vegetables and dirty diapers, but what's a little mercury among friends?"

"You're kidding right?" Michael asked.

Timmy walked the rest of the way into the bar's dining room. He pulled out a chair and sat down at the table with Michael and Kermit.

"The answer to your question largely depends on whether you're going to pay me for that stuff."

Then Timmy grabbed a piece of bacon off of Kermit's plate and ate it.

###

After breakfast, Michael loaded his bike into the back bed of Kermit's El Camino and got into the passenger seat. He put his pack on the floor at his feet, and then leaned back, closing his eyes.

Kermit turned to him, with the key in the ignition. "Ready for takeoff?" His voice sounded concerned.

"Not quite." Michael kept his eyes closed. He had been working schemes and angles for so long, he didn't remember the last time he just enjoyed the moment. He got closest when he was with Andie, and there had been a few moments with Jane in Miami, but the danger was always there. It wouldn't let him rest.

Michael opened his eyes and turned to Kermit. "You think I'm doing the right thing?"

Kermit examined Michael, head bobbing. His graying dreadlocks danced around.

"What's the 'right thing'?" Kermit turned the key and the El Camino roared to life. "Everybody throws those terms around, but nobody ever defines them. What's right? You have to figure out what you mean by 'right' first and then you can answer your own questions." Kermit paused. "Or we could maybe go smoke some weed and eat some Sour Cream Pringles. Either one would be pretty right by me." Kermit laughed as he shifted the El Camino into drive and hit the gas.

"You're a horrible friend. You know that?" Michael shouted over the roaring engine. "You are truly horrible."

"What's horrible?" Kermit shouted back. "Everybody throws that term around, but nobody ever defines it."

Michael raised his hand in resignation. "Please stop. Wherever you're going with this, please stop now."

As they sped out of Punta Allen, Kermit checked the road for potholes and then turned to Michael.

"Two final words for you, mi amigo: quantum chromodynamics." Kermit beeped the El Camino's horn due to his sheer pleasure when saying those words, identifying an obscure branch of theoretical physics. "It's also known as QCD by those in the biz. That's what you need to accept in your life."

"Does QCD have anything to do with your new naked yoga obsession?"

Kermit dodged a pothole, jerking the car to the left side of the road and then back.

"Sort of, it's got more to do with my hair, yo, like Sampson in the Bible."

"I'll stay tuned for further information." Michael put on his sunglasses and leaned back in his seat.

"You got no choice, my man." Kermit smiled. "Information is forthcoming." He beeped the horn. "The ol' K-Dog is the only channel in town."

CHAPTER TEN

Andie was gone when Michael got back to Hut No. 7.

He stood in the doorway and examined his small living space. Everything appeared to be as he had left it. There was a pile of dirty clothes in the corner (to the extent that a round hut had a corner). His old battered briefcase was still collecting dust next to his dresser. And then, his black and white picture of the Irish revolutionary and his namesake, Michael Collins, stared down at the him from its place on the wall.

Michael, then, noticed a note on his pillow. He set his backpack on the floor and walked over to the bed. He picked up the note.

It was from Andie. She needed to talk with him.

Upon reading those words, Michael rolled his eyes. Of course she wanted to talk, he thought, she always wanted to talk.

But this time, Andie didn't want to talk about their relationship.

###

His mind flooded with a mixture of anger and grief. Michael ran outside, down the path toward the resort's bar and main office. It was the same path he had walked with Tad Garvin a little more than twenty-four hours ago.

He went in the back door, cut through the shabby lobby, and startled Andie when he burst into the office.

"What's going on with Father Stiles?" Michael moved toward her. She sat at the desk, her face drawn. She didn't say anything, and so Michael continued. "When?"

"This morning. I got the call this morning, but it happened a few days ago. The people at the church weren't sure how to reach you." Andie paused. She tried to find the right words.

Michael looked at her, and she stared back at him with tears in her eyes.

"Is he ..." Michael's voice trailed off.

He was unable to complete the question, but Andie understood. She nodded and got up. Andie walked out from behind the desk to Michael.

She held him, and she kissed his cheek. She whispered that she was sorry in his ear, and she did all the things that people do to comfort someone who had lost. They were the right things to do, but they were never enough.

Michael stepped back from her. He struggled to find the words. Father Stiles had been a mentor and a friend. He knew Michael's secrets, but never passed judgment. The priest had helped raise him after his mother died, and he had been the one constant in his life that he could always trust.

Michael shook his head. "I don't know what to think."

Andie didn't let him get too far away. She closed the space and took Michael's hand. "You don't have to think anything right now."

"I know, but I'm not sure ..." Michael's voice trailed off, again.

"They said it was cardiac arrest," Andie said. "There wasn't anything that anybody could have done." Michael looked away from her, thinking.

"We should just take it one step —" A loud crash interrupted Andie.

It came from the other side of the wall, wood splintering. Someone was in the bar. There was the sound of glass breaking, as liquor bottles smashed on the floor.

Michael wiped away a tear, his eyes narrowing.

He and Andie ran out of the office and into the lobby. Andie unlocked an interior door between the lobby and the bar.

They looked around. The bar's front door was broken and open and the floor was covered with shattered glass and a large puddle of alcohol. As they surveyed the empty space, Michael heard an engine start outside.

They went to the bar's open front doorway and stopped. Helpless, they stood and watched a forest green SUV bounce away.

Michael felt dizzy, confused. One second he had been thinking about going to jail, then Father Stiles, and now this. Michael turned to look at Andie, and, when he did, the breeze from the Caribbean changed directions. Air came through the bar toward the door, and Michael caught the smell of gasoline.

CHAPTER ELEVEN

The crowd was happy. It had been a long time since the crowd was happy, and it made him smile. He checked the rearview mirror as the fire grew and a thick line of smoke twisted up into the sky.

The crowd wanted to watch the show, but he didn't want to stop, yet. He needed to get further away.

"I know what happened," he shouted at them. "I don't need to watch." He giggled and pounded the steering wheel.

Some in the crowd disagreed, but he didn't listen.

"Don't you see? Don't you see what I can accomplish when you let me think.? You have to trust me sometimes." He shouted at them to be quiet. "Just let me get further away. Then I'll stop."

He turned onto the main highway, and he drove a half-mile further and then pulled over. He looked at the darkening sky. The fire continued to burn.

It had been a good morning.

After waiting for Michael Collins to return, the crowd had wanted to attack the lawyer in his hut. But he was too smart for that. The crowd was impatient, but he knew there'd be a better opportunity.

Collins didn't know he was there. Collins didn't know he was in danger.

The explosion was huge, bigger than the one he had watched on YouTube, better than the website promised.

He savored the moment, but felt a little sad that it was over so quickly. He had thought it would be more of a challenge, especially after the debacle with Father Stiles.

He yelled at the crowd again. "I want to hear some congratulations! I want to hear some praise from you."

He smiled.

Michael Collins and Andie Larone were dead.

He was sure of it.

CHAPTER TWELVE

It took ten minutes for the Sunset's bar to collapse upon itself. Flames shot up a hundred feet. The air had turned thick and gray. Unlike Cancun or even Playa del Carmen, there was nobody to call. Nobody was going to come and put out the fire.

Michael could only watch it burn.

Kermit was assigned the task of keeping the resort's guests from getting too close. Michael stayed away from all of them. He was worried that if he was forced to talk to the guests, there was a good chance he would kill the first person who requested a refund.

Instead, Michael limped through the rest of the resort with a fire extinguisher, inspecting the series of other huts and the resort's odd scramble of buildings. He looked for a stray ember, trying to prevent another one from catching on fire and figuring out what he should do.

When there was nothing left except a pile of charred wood and debris, Michael handed his fire extinguisher to Kermit.

"Keep an eye on things. I'm checking on Andie."

Kermit cocked his head to the side. "She gonna be fine?"

"Just a cut," Michael said. "Could've been worse. We happened to be in the doorway, and I smelled the gas. Managed to pull us out a few feet before it went up."

"Then go." Kermit puffed out his chest, trying to look tough. "I got it under control, muchacho."

The adrenaline had worn off and Michael started to feel the damage. His arms were red and raw from the sudden burst of heat, probably first-degree burns. His neck and lower back were sore from being snapped forward in the explosion, and his ankle was twisted and swollen from when he had turned and grabbed Andie.

The further he walked away, the more beaten he felt. The currents were pulling him under. People and the things that he loved were getting hurt again.

Michael found Andie sitting alone on 'The Point,' a rocky peninsula that curved off the Sunset Resort's shoreline and out into the water a hundred yards.

Andie sat on a beach towel, leaning back against a large boulder. Her face and clothes were dirty. She held a large white bandage with a little bit of dried blood in the middle. Occasionally, Andie touched her forehead with the bandage, using it to check to see if her cut was still closed or had started bleeding again.

"Need a beer?" Michael sat down beside her. He put his hand on her knee.

The edge of her lip curled slightly into a smile.

"You're trying to be cute now?" Andie looked up at the sky. "I'm not sure how I feel about that." She sniffed.

"About being cute?" Michael picked up a handful of rocks, letting the smaller stones and sand sift through his fingers while he retained the larger ones. They sat in silence for a few minutes, watching the waves. "Cuteness is one of my better qualities."

"Sometimes," Andie said. "Sometimes it's a better quality. Sometimes it isn't."

They sat without words for awhile longer.

"I know I'm somehow responsible for this," Michael nodded toward the smoldering pile across the water. "And I'm sorry."

"You don't have to apologize," Andie said. "I knew something would happen when I came back." She paused, before finishing. "I knew that it wasn't over."

Andie adjusted and turned, looking at Michael.

"You told me who you were. You told me what you did, and I came back anyway. Full disclosure." Andie looked at the bandage in her hand. "My fault."

Michael tossed a rock out into the water, and then set the other stones down on the ground by his side.

"They've frozen our accounts. I have to check, but I'm doubtful that they missed any."

"I know."

"There's probably an indictment and they're probably starting the extradition process to bring me back right now."

Andie nodded, again. "Figured."

"And then there's that." Michael looked back toward the shore; smoke rising from where the resort's bar and office was once located. "And this." Michael looked at the bandage in Andie's hand, and then he shrugged his shoulders.

"How many times can I get away?" Michael put his hand on Andie's knee. "How many people are going to get hurt in the process?"

Andie rolled her head back and around, letting the tension escape her neck.

"Depends on how bad you want to get away."

Michael nodded. "Or what it'll cost me."

"You had nothing to do with Father Stiles," she said. "It was a heart attack. You can't blame yourself for that."

"But I could have been there."

Andie nodded. "You could have." She shrugged. "But it wouldn't have made a difference."

"And what about you?" Michael looked at the cut on Andie's head, then back across the water to where the office and bar once were. "You could've gotten killed."

"But I didn't," she said.

Michael picked up another handful of rocks and started sifting them.

"While I was away, I thought about whether I could trust you. Can you believe that?"

Andie smiled. "Of course," she said. "I pop back into your life, and things go to hell."

"You said it, not me." Michael threw another rock into the water. "But if I don't trust you and Kermit, then I don't see what point there is in being here, in being anywhere."

Michael turned to her. "What if I turned myself in? What if I stopped hiding?"

Andie closed her eyes, sad.

"Are you wondering whether I'd wait for you? Whether I'd stick around for twenty years for you to be released?"

"The thought crossed my mind." Michael shuffled his foot in the sand, and then he threw the remainder of his rocks into the water. They plunked and popped in rapid succession. "Prison isn't exactly the best place for love to grow."

"Well, I do love you." Andie moved closer to Michael, taking his hand. "I'd try."

"About all that anybody could ask." Michael raised her hand to his cheek, rubbed it and then gave Andie's hand a soft kiss. "But I know the odds." He let her hand go. "It's asking you to give up a life."

"I said I'd try." Andie turned and kissed Michael. She playfully pushed him on his back and climbed on top of him, her legs straddling his torso. "But wouldn't you rather fight it and stay together? Go down shooting?"

Andie took Michael's wrists and raised them above his head, pinning him to the ground.

"I'm better at fighting, Michael." Her little grin spread into a wicked smile. It was the spirit that he fell in love with. "You have to have an idea."

"You want another Houdini act?"

Andie laughed and kissed Michael hard on the lips. It hurt his sore body, but in a good way.

"I always liked ropes," she said. Then Andie kissed him again.

CHAPTER THIRTEEN

The young agent walked across the FBI's bullpen of cubicles to the outer offices that were reserved for senior investigators. Agent Billy Armstrong knocked on the door.

"Busy," Vatch barked.

Armstrong knocked again, opening the door. He peeked his head inside, holding up a sheet of paper. "Thought you'd want to know about this."

"Doubtful." Vatch turned away from his computer screen and gestured for Armstrong to come inside. Vatch had been told that he was supposed to mentor Armstrong, which Vatch decided was permission to be even crueler to the young agent than he was to everybody else. "Must be another dress code memo."

Vatch reached out for the piece of paper, and Armstrong handed the memo to him. He adjusted the distance of the piece of paper from his face, trying to focus. Vatch had needed glasses for the past year, but he refused. They were too expensive and Vatch believed eye doctors were just hucksters selling overpriced plastic.

His beady eyes scanned the document, and Vatch's tongue flicked out his narrow mouth as he read the lines that Armstrong had highlighted. Then he nodded.

Agent Armstrong beamed, all optimism. "Looks like we're going to get him."

Vatch said nothing.

"Been checking the flight register every day since the priest died," Armstrong continued. "Figured he'd be coming back for the funeral."

"You're a regular Nancy Drew." Vatch put the paper down on his desk, and then he looked back at Armstrong. He had a strange, unfamiliar feeling. Vatch almost thanked Armstrong, but he was able to suppress the impulse. Vatch, instead, gave the young agent a nod, turned back to his computer and resumed typing.

"Shut the door on your way out, will you? Got plans to make."

###

The flight from Cancun was scheduled to arrive at LaGuardia in the late afternoon. Vatch reviewed the airline's flight manifest. Since the September 11 attacks, airlines had to submit lists of passengers to the government for all flights.

The CIA and the National Security Agency had always had access to the information, whether through legal or other mechanisms. But for the FBI, access to flight manifests was relatively new. It had been a significant help in tracking down people of interest, although none of the people of interest were terrorists.

According to the list, Michael Collins, Andie Larone, and the weird guy had booked their flight late the night before.

Vatch set the paper down on his desk and leaned back. He thought about how many agents he should call for backup or whether he should just rely on the immigration officers at the airport.

He wanted to do the arrest himself. He didn't want to share the glory, but he also didn't want to let Michael slip away again.

It seemed too easy, although Vatch doubted whether Michael Collins knew about the indictment. Grand jury proceedings were supposed to be confidential and he was thousands of miles away.

Vatch pulled up his email account, typed a summary of the situation, and then clicked the "send" button. Instantly, the message was directed to the bureau chief, his immediate supervisor, and United States Attorney Brenda Gadd. Go big or not at all, he thought.

It was a call for six to nine additional agents, but he made it clear that Michael Collins was only to be questioned by him.

Vatch looked up at the clock on his wall, and then checked the flight time again.

He had an hour and a half to get to the airport, which was just enough time to find a lowly federal prosecutor and get a warrant from a judge to detain Andie Larone and Kermit Guillardo as material witnesses.

Hopefully they'd lie or be uncooperative, Vatch thought, then he could charge them with obstructing a federal law enforcement investigation, maybe aiding and abetting after the fact.

That would be nice.

CHAPTER FOURTEEN

Kermit Guillardo leaned back in his seat, stretched his legs, and ordered another whiskey sour.

It felt good, not being packed in the back of the plane. He had conned his way into first class, despite Michael's refusal to buy him a first class ticket. That was the power of quantum chromodynamics.

Kermit looked at his hands, something that most ordinary people would view as a solid mass. Then he touched the armrest of his seat. His hand appeared to stop, but Kermit knew that was an illusion. Physical boundaries did not exist. It was all energy. He could feel the subatomic quarks pull apart, merge with the quarks that built the subatomic parts of the armrest, and then his foundation immediately regenerate to fill the void and stop his hand from going any further. Yet, energy was exchanged between his hand and the armrest and energy was created in preventing a merger between the two.

It was simple, Kermit thought. It was all rooted in the standard model of non-abelian gauge theory:

$$U(1)xSU(2)xSU(3)$$

The model was premised on the existence of twelve gauge bosons, some weak and some strong. This wasn't a particularly new area of physics and mathematics. It had been theorized for thirty years, but he was taking QCD to a whole different level of application.

Through QCD and yoga he changed the power within himself. Kermit built upon his foundational work with the concepts of numeric equilibrium as well as the practical application of general semantics to create a new understanding of the world and how to interact with it.

If only others could understand.

Kermit smiled. He touched one of his twelve dreadlocks, each representing a gauge boson. Kermit's fingers tingled as he felt the power and the chaos locked inside. Then he remembered the young, nubile ticket agent at the Cancun airport.

Kermit had simply freed the power in order to change the electrical energy of the space. The gravitational field had altered in his favor, and Kermit knew that he wouldn't even have to specifically ask for the upgrade. Instead, Kermit asked the agent how he could safely transport his new guitar to America.

The ticket agent looked at Kermit and then at the guitar case in his hand. "Are you a rock star?" Love was in her eyes.

"If you spend the night with me, sweetheart, you wouldn't have to ask that silly question." Kermit winked. He then wrote his number on a piece of scrap paper.

She took the number, giggled, and gave Kermit a first-class ticket in return. It wouldn't be the last time Kermit would call upon his ratty bosons for help.

A fake, high-pitched bell dinged three times and the pilot announced the plane's descent into New York. Kermit pressed the button for his seat to return to an upright position, and then gathered his various notepads and multi-colored note cards related to his QCD research. He put them in his knapsack and rebuckled his seatbelt.

"Ready, Mr. Guillardo?" The flight attendant touched Kermit's shoulder and gave it a slight squeeze. Word of his rock stardom had spread among the ladies.

"Steady, senorita, just keep the tin can steady."

"We'll try." The flight attendant winked, took her hand off his shoulder and continued walking down the aisle toward the other passengers in the back.

Kermit waited, making sure she was gone, and then dug through every compartment in his bag. He checked and rechecked every pocket.

They had a plan, and Kermit understood his role.

When he was arrested, it would be better if all illicit substances were absent from his pockets and luggage.

Vatch checked his gun, and then gave each of the agents a piece of paper. The paper had three pictures printed on it, photographs of Michael Collins, Andie Larone, and Kermit Guillardo.

"Arrest them and then keep them separate. I don't want them talking. I don't want them to know what's happening to the others."

Vatch could feel it. Everything was coming together. The airline confirmed that Collins and the others had printed boarding passes, checked bags, and boarded the plane. Kermit Guillardo had somehow gotten upgraded to first class, but nothing else was unexpected.

Collins was so arrogant, thought Vatch. Collins actually thought that he was just going to walk off the plane, as if he was untouchable. Vatch chuckled to himself, then he continued to lecture the other agents.

He pointed at the doors leading out of the airport's immigration center.

"I want two at each. Others need to be spread."

Vatch looked at the Immigration and Customs Enforcement agents working the "stamp desks."

"Their passports have been flagged and ICE has been directed to delay our friends during the review. The immigration desk boys will message their supervisor, and then they'll take them back to the holding area .... But watch for Collins to run."

Agent Vatch looked at the clock.

"The plane should land in a few minutes. I'll notify you all when the plane is at the gate and people start getting off. He's a runner, always has been."

Vatch waved. "Now get going." Then he spun his wheelchair around and started toward the gates.

"Where you off to?" Agent Armstrong asked.

Vatch stopped, turned back to his mentee, and flicked his tongue.

"Greeting Mr. Collins at the gate. Be sort of a one-man welcoming committee."

Armstrong didn't like that plan. He followed behind as Vatch tried to roll away.

"With all due respect," Armstrong kept following when Vatch didn't stop. "Wouldn't that give Collins a warning? Eliminate the surprise element? I don't know, seems like the situation could escalate."

Vatch didn't respond. He kept on going, ignoring Armstrong. There wasn't any point in arguing.

Vatch thought escalation was just fine. In fact, escalation would be great.

CHAPTER FIFTEEN

Vatch waited off to the side. He watched the first few passengers straggle up and out of the gate, into the waiting area, and then proceed towards customs and immigration.

Excitement spiked when Vatch saw the weird one amble out, a guitar case was strapped to his back. Vatch looked behind Kermit Guillardo, expecting to see Michael Collins or Andie Larone. Neither one of them, however, came out.

Vatch watched Kermit Guillardo walk into the waiting area, and then watched as Kermit stopped, looked back at the gate, and then sat down in an empty seat next to an old woman planning to board a departing plane.

Vatch remembered that Kermit Guillardo had been upgraded to first class. He figured Michael Collins and Andie Larone must be seated further back on the plane. He just needed to be patient.

Time passed, and Agent Vatch watched more and more passengers get off the plane. They stopped coming in a steady flow. Now they came in little clumps of one or two.

"Hey."

Vatch looked up at the person who had tapped his shoulder.

"Are you looking for me, dude?" Kermit Guillardo smiled. His gray dreadlocks bounced as his head bobbled. " Been sitting over there the whole time, like, totally waiting for you to arrest me."

Vatch was appalled. His eyes narrowed. "Did you just touch me?"

Kermit looked confused.

Vatch repeated himself. "Did you really just touch me?"

"Like sexually?" Kermit scrunched up his face. "No way, man. I don't like you like that. But I'm glad you're still looking." Kermit winked. "Never too old to find love, my man. There's somebody special out there for you, just gotta believe."

"Where's Collins?"

"Right now?" Kermit shrugged his shoulders. "Don't really know. Last I saw him, the man was in Mexico."

"He's supposed to be on this plane."

Kermit looked at the gate and watched as the flight crew emerged behind the final three passengers. Then Kermit nodded, deep in thought.

"Supposed to be, but not." Kermit picked up his guitar. "I'll let you wait it out further, if you don't believe me, muchacho. Just tell the other jack-boots to let me go to the bathroom before they take me into custody 'cuz I gotta disperse the liquid matter in the ol' bladder, you dig?"

CHAPTER SIXTEEN

In Mexico, Michael had mailed a package at the Cancun airport to the address for Brea Krane that Tad Garvin had provided. He paid a little extra for express mail service, and figured that the package would arrive about the same time that he would get to New York.

Michael and Andie then checked two bags full of dirty laundry, walked down to their gate, and then allowed a flight attendant to scan their boarding passes. Then, the two went halfway down the ramp to their plane with Kermit, and that was where they had stopped.

Michael and Andie wished Kermit luck, and then turned around. They weren't going to run from the FBI, but they weren't going to make it easy, either.

Kermit would be a great decoy with the bonus of likely embarrassing Agent Vatch once again.

Michael and Andie left the main terminal. They crossed the street and over to a smaller airstrip designated for private, charter planes.

Their pilot was drinking at the terminal's bar, which was never a good sign, but he had been cheap and available on short notice.

Michael handed him an envelope of cash, and after finishing his drink, the pilot led Michael and Andie outside to his small, twin-propeller plane.

They climbed up three steps and crawled into the cabin. The pilot waited for Michael and Andie while they settled in and buckled their seatbelts.

"One quick check, then go." The pilot pointed to the front of the plane, smiled, and closed the door.

He walked around to the front. He fiddled with a few of the levers attached to the plane's engine. After performing another series of pre-flight rituals, the pilot got inside, and closed the other door. He put on a pair of dark sunglasses, adjusted a knob, and then pressed a button.

The plane's rusted propellers popped and crackled to life. Within minutes, they were in the air.

The engine noise was too loud to have a conversation, and so Michael and Andie simply held hands as Andie rested her head on Michael's shoulder for the rest of the flight.

An hour later they landed in Chihuahua, Mexico. Because they hadn't crossed any borders, there were no passports or requests for identification.

They got out of the airplane, unloaded their packs, and walked to a hired van that was waiting to take them to a small town called Manuel Benavides and then to where the road dead-ended further north.

Michael and Andie were now about twenty miles from the U.S.-Mexico border, and Michael figured that they had about a fifteen percent chance of making it across.

###

The road from Manuel Benavides to Mexico's Santa Elana national park was narrow and dusty. Michael and Andie bounced along in the back of the van. They looked out the window at the desert landscape, cascading brown and tan hills streaked with red and specked with scrub brush and cactus.

Neither one of them saw another person or car the entire trip. That was normal. It was a part of the world where no human being was supposed to live. It was too hot.

Quick movement of any kind was rare, which Michael figured was both good and bad. It would make them easy to see, but it would also complicate matters for anybody following them to go unnoticed.

The van stopped. There were seven rusted metal barrels filled with concrete, each spaced a few feet from one another across the road. This was where it ended.

"Gracias." Michael paid the driver.

They gathered up their packs and got out of the van. They stood on the side of the road and watched the van turn around, and then they watched as it disappeared in a cloud a half-mile back down the road on its way back to Manuel Benavides.

With the van gone, Michael and Andie were now alone in the desert. It was quiet for the first time on their trip. The respite from constant engine noise was a relief.

Michael stretched. He looked up. It was late afternoon, but the sun was still high. The landscape baked in the heat and hummed with the sound of cicadas.

Michael shook out his arms and rolled his neck from side to side, and then he took a water bottle out of his pack.

He unscrewed the top of the Nalgene bottle, and then Michael handed it to Andie.

"Ready?"

Andie took a sip of water, and handed the bottle back to Michael.

"Ready as I'll ever be."

"Then let's do it."

Michael put the water bottle back in his pack, took out his GPS device, and then swung the pack over his shoulder. He'd used the GPS device more in the past few days than he had used it in the past year. Michael didn't really know what that meant about his current state of affairs. He figured it probably wasn't good, but he'd have plenty of time to think about it on the trail.

The two left the road and started hiking north. In the distance, they saw the red lunar peaks of the Chisos Mountains on the other side of the Rio Grande.

Andie and Michael were now just a half-dozen miles from the border.

CHAPTER SEVENTEEN

It was dusk when Michael and Andie got to the ridge. Below them, the free-flowing Rio Grande River cut deep into the rock. The river was the border, and on the other side of the river was the least-visited national park in the United States, Big Bend.

Michael and Andie sat down. He opened his pack and removed two granola bars and two apples. He handed one of each to Andie. Then Michael ate his granola bar faster than he had wanted to.

Michael was still hungry when he was done, but there wasn't more time. It was getting dark, and there was no way that they could safely climb down the steep canyon wall to the river at night, even with headlamps.

He checked his GPS, took a final sip of water, and then, after Andie finished her apple, they followed the ridge further east. They had another kilometer to go.

###

The drop was nearly straight down 1,500 feet on both sides of the river canyon, but there were a few narrow, jagged paths that led to sandy open areas. The paths, however, were difficult to find. A person needed the right coordinates.

Michael checked his GPS with increasing frequency until finally the device beeped. Michael and Andie stopped, looked at one another, and then walked toward the canyon's edge. They didn't see it until they were there — a five-foot drop, and then a trail just ten inches wide to the next drop.

Michael was relieved. They'd found what they had been looking for, just as the sun dipped out of view.

Half the sky had already turned black and within an hour there would be total darkness.   "We have to go," Michael said. "Don't want to get stuck."

When Andie didn't respond, Michael stopped just before climbing down. He turned and reached out his hand.

"You okay?"

Andie nodded, wiping sweat and dirt from her forehead, and then she took his hand.

"Just get me to the river." She let go of Michael's hand and rubbed the key that was on a necklace around her neck. She rubbed it for good luck, remembering her experience on Ayers Rock when she was a teenager. "Just get me to the river," she said, again, like a mantra.

Michael nodded, an attempt at confidence, and then they started.

They took small steps, trying to keep from sliding. Each step posed a risk of falling or turning an ankle, especially since they were both still recovering from the explosion a few days earlier.

It was one drop after another, a slow, twenty-foot descent.

Michael stopped. He looked down at another ten-foot ledge.

"I'll go first."

Andie didn't argue.

Michael wasn't worried about falling ten feet. He was more concerned about falling ten feet and being unable to stop himself from continuing to fall the rest of the way down the canyon.

There were dozens of boulders and sharp outcroppings that could easily crack open his head in an uncontrolled fall or snap a leg or an arm.

He put his hands down on the dirt. Michael lowered himself, searching for a foothold. He found one, put his foot in, and then descended the rest of the way.

After hesitation, Andie followed.

By the time they reached the small rocky beach, the sun was gone. The sky was pricked with thousands of tiny stars.

Michael and Andie limped toward the water. Their feet were blistered and sore. Their eyes stung with the salt from their sweat, and both were dehydrated and bruised. Michael and Andie had fallen straight on their backs a few times at the end of their descent. Their packs softened the impact with the ground, but most of their quad muscles ripped in the process. It was unlikely either one of them would be able to move particularly fast in the morning.

Luckily, they had some relief. The air temperature had dropped forty degrees and the high rock walls naturally kept the bottom of the canyon cool and in shadows.

Michael looked up at the night sky, put his hands on his hips, and closed his eyes, still trying to catch his breath. "Pretty nice down here."

Andie nodded. "It is."

"Pretty dark too." Michael's eyes opened. His voice rose with a hint of mischief.

Andie shook her head and laughed. "Are you actually trying to hit on me?"

"Dirty and sweaty women get me excited." Michael sat down. " What can I say?"

Andie shook her head. "You're gross."

Michael laughed. "I thought that this crisis in my life would be a good time to be more open about my various kinks."

"You sound like Kermit. You're hanging out with him way too much," Andie said. "He's a bad influence."

"Perhaps." Michael kicked off his hiking boots and pulled his sweaty socks away from his feet. Then Michael stripped and ran naked into the river.

He hit the water with a splash, and Michael emitted a high-pitched scream. "That's cold." He bobbed under the water and came up, again. "My heart stopped working for a minute."

"Good." Andie sat down on a large flat rock, unscrewed the top of her water bottle. She took a sip. "Stay in there for awhile. You need to cool off."

"Does that mean I'm not getting any lovin' tonight?"

Andie massaged her quad muscles. "Since I'm having difficulty moving my legs, I think that's a pretty fair assumption, young man."

Michael splashed some water toward her. "Why do you need to move your legs?"

###

After Andie drank all of her water, she set the empty bottle aside. She turned on a small flashlight and laid it down on the ground next to their packs so that they could find them again. Then she walked away from the light.

Andie got close to the edge of the river and stopped. Michael watched as she slowly took off her clothes. The shape of her body cast a dark silhouette.

Andie dipped a toe into the water, and then stepped in. She edged deeper into the river until the water met her thigh, and then she jumped toward Michael.

Swimming a few yards, her hands reached out and found him. Michael pulled Andie up, and they came together under the stars.

He pressed her close to him, caressed her back, and then kissed her neck. She returned the kiss, finding an intimacy that had been lost in the rush to leave the resort and the tension that had flared after the visit from Tad Garvin, the fire, and the passing of Father Stiles. All three events had happened so close together, it had overwhelmed them.

"Love you." Michael kissed her on the lips.

"I love —"

Bells and hooting filled the canyon. Spotlights blinded them from the United States side of the canyon. Then somebody yelled, "You kids want to be left alone, or can we all come in for a swim too."

Michael recognized the voice.

CHAPTER EIGHTTEEN

Chester "Cheeto" Strauss was always up for a good time. He had no interest in wearing a suit or following in his father, grandfather, or great-grandfather's footsteps. His family was filled with lawyers who had descended from lawyers who had descended from lawyers and so on, tracing back to a few barristers in Manchester, England.

He went to law school solely because it was a condition of gaining access to his sizable trust fund. Once he graduated, Cheeto took off. He started working as a river guide and had never looked back.

When he had decided Colorado was too cold, Cheeto moved south to a shack along the Rio Grande, which housed four other river rats. That's where he'd lived for the past three years, although now he was thinking about moving to somewhere in South America. He'd heard Chile had some nice big water.

"How's the boy wonder doing?" Cheeto grinned at Michael.

"Better if you'd have waited another fifteen minutes to arrive." Michael looked at Andie, sitting on the other side of the bonfire.

Cheeto howled, and then threw another log on the fire. "I bet." Cheeto looked at Andie. "You two make a real handsome couple. Although Mikey looks like he's gotten a little loose in the cage in his old age, if you know what I mean. Should've let him come visit me more often, get a real workout."

"I'll think about it," Andie said.

"Don't think too long, honey. Cheeto is always on the move." He walked over to the cooler and removed three large plastic bags of food and then found a few pots.

He walked back over to the bonfire where Michael and Andie were sitting. Cheeto spread out some coals, and then turned toward the group of adventure tourists he was guiding down the river. They were about thirty yards from the bonfire, sorting through their packs and trying to set-up camp in the dark.

"Our dinner shall be served in just a few minutes, my aco-lytes." Cheeto shouted at them. "Come on over when you've finished with your tents."

Cheeto, then, looked at Michael and Andie, and lowered his voice.

"Bet you guys are hungry for some chow?"

The dinner tasted amazing. Perhaps she was starving, but it was the best spaghetti Andie had tasted in a long time. She wanted another serving after the first two, but was too full.

She handed Cheeto her plate, and then walked up a slight hill to their tent.

Andie unzipped the front, climbed inside, and then slid into her sleeping bag. She was exhausted, and it felt good to lie down. She turned her head on the soft pillow and rolled over onto her side.

Michael had already settled in for the night.

"Not bad accommodations," he said.

Andie took in the small two-person backpacking tent, and then asked the question that had been on her mind the entire evening. "Are you really trusting a guy named 'Cheeto' to smuggle us across the border?"

"We've already made it across the border," Michael said, referring to their brief swim from the southern to the northern side of the Rio Grande.

"You know what I mean."

She was serious, and so Michael stopped joking.

"He just plays dumb." Michael leaned over and pecked Andie on her forehead, a little kiss. "Perfect LSAT score. Nearly perfect grades at Columbia. He didn't go by the name Cheeto back then. He was Chet, and he was right there with me, top of the class, but he refused to play the game. He rejected an opportunity to be on law review, refused clerkships, and never went to a job interview. He didn't want anything to do with being a real lawyer. He said the law made his dad miss his first six birthday parties because of various legal emergencies. His dad didn't exercise, ate rich foods, and died when Chet was in college. Chet decided early on that he was going down a different path. So now he's Cheeto, and apparently having a pretty good time."

"Does he know what's going on with you?"

Michael thought about the question, and then said, "We've talked."

"I've just never heard you mention him before."

Michael nodded. "He's a guy friend."

"Meaning what?"

"Meaning we can go years without talking, and we don't take it personally. It's just life." Michael shrugged. "We're friends and we help each other out when we need to."

"Okay." Andie repositioned her tiny backpacking pillow, then rolled over onto her side. "In Cheeto I trust." She was nervous

about the next day. There was certainly going to be an encoun-
ter with a park ranger or an immigration agent.

"In Cheeto we trust." Michael leaned over and pecked Andie
on the cheek. "Now let's get some sleep."

CHAPTER NINETEEN

Y ou gonna let me go?" Kermit leaned back in his chair, grinning at Agent Armstrong. "It's getting late, and I've been sitting in here for hours, going coo-coo for Cocoa Puffs, you know?"

"No, I don't know." Armstrong leaned across the table, and then he lowered his voice. "I need you to answer all my questions." A smirk.

"I think I have a right to freedom of speech, freedom of religion, freedom to love, freedom to hate, and the freedom to shut my trap from time to time." Kermit sighed and looked up at the fluorescent lights. "Seriously, dude, are we accomplishing any of the great tasks of mankind right now?"

"Why don't you just tell me where Michael Collins and Andie Larone are?"

"Mentally or physically? Because that's a pretty vague question. Even the physical location is difficult to identify given the chaotic dance of internal energy and the subatomic bopping of our little neutrinos and leptons. Have I ever mentioned my groundbreaking work involving quantum chromodynamics?"

Armstrong's eyes started to bug out, and he tried to control his temper.

"I think you have already shared with me your theories." He looked at his watch. "I think we spent about an hour on the subject, which is about an hour too long."

Kermit shook his head.

"You're just scared." Kermit looked away. "Not unusual for a simple man like you to be afraid of the unknown, afraid that what he sees with the naked eye is not an accurate depiction of the environment in which he resides."

"I need you to answer my questions," Armstrong said.

Kermit ignored him. "We must recognize that we only see representations of life, but not life itself," Kermit said. "We see and speak in generalities rather than specifics, approximations rather than measurements. Did you know that a cup of flour is never actually a cup of flour? Just a best-guess estimate using an imperfect tool in the midst of a myriad of factors like the fineness of the wheat's grind, the altitude, or the moisture in the air."

Agent Armstrong pushed back his chair and stood. Kermit's constant babbling, his odor, and the confined space had gotten to him.

"Physically," Armstrong put his hands on his hips. "Where approximately did they go when they left the airport, physically? And I'll accept an estimation."

"I don't know, it'd be less than an estimation. It'd be total speculation because I was cruising with the birds at the time. I saw nothing with my own peep-peeps."

"Why don't you speculate, then?"

"I don't like to speculate," Kermit looked up at the ceiling. "I dream." He smiled, and then added, "Do you know who also likes to dream?" Kermit didn't wait for an answer. "Lawyers. Lawyers dream a lot. Speaking of lawyers, I think it's about time for an attorney."

Armstrong didn't like that idea. He knew that an attorney would shut down all questioning, and so Armstrong held out his hands and softened his tone.

"What about this trip? What are you doing here?"

"You probably know about Father Stiles. I plan on going to his funeral. I'm also here to do a little business."

"Business?"

"I got a book idea that I'd like to pitch." Kermit cracked his knuckles. "It's like a children's book for adults, sort of a naughty introduction to my theories of QCD and hair."

"Why would an adult want to read a children's book about quantum physics?"

"Why do adults like to bounce on trampolines?" Kermit countered. "Because it's fun, muchacho. That's why we do it." Kermit slapped his hand on the table. "Do you ever play 'crack the egg' on a trampoline?"

Armstrong clenched his jaw. "No."

"Well, it's hilarious." Kermit laughed. "Anyway, this book is titled 'Why Too Much Hair Down There?'" Kermit paused and smiled, letting the revelation of his amazing idea linger for a moment in the U.S. Customs interrogation room. "Great title, huh?"

"Are you actually talking about —"

"Pubic hair." Kermit answered. "Through the use of humorous illustrations, this book charts our society's recently developed aversion to pubic hair and why this war is actually depleting our energy and ability to find inner happiness." Kermit touched one of his dreadlocks, believing that it would change the magnetic field of the room in his favor.

"Of course it all started with 'Sex and the City', season 3, episode 14." Kermit smiled. "You remember that one?"

Armstrong shook his head. "I'm not familiar with that one."

"I can tell you all about it." Kermit opened his mouth to describe a Brazilian wax, but stopped himself, sensing an opportunity. "Or you could just let me go."

Agent Armstrong stared at Kermit. The room was silent as the two evaluated their options. Finally Armstrong lowered his head in defeat. The possibility of an extended conversation with Kermit Guillardo about pubic hair was too much.

"We're done." Armstrong turned and opened the door. "Get out of here."

CHAPTER TWENTY

It was jacket weather. Although the rocks at the top of the canyon still radiated heat from the previous day, the bottom was cool. The early morning wind also added a chill at odds with the desert surroundings.

Cheeto crouched at the edge of the river. He finished washing the remaining breakfast dishes, while Andie and Michael laid their packs down in a pile of gear. Then they helped the others fill the large waterproof bags and load the rafts.

They pushed away a little after eight in the morning. The river's current pulled them out slow, and then they started to paddle. There were two rafts, each with eight people in a raft.

Andie and Michael rode with a newly married couple on their honeymoon, a middle-aged couple from Chicago, and a Japanese exchange student. Cheeto guided them all from the back.

The other raft was louder. It was filled with Tri-Delts from the University of Texas at Austin and a female guide from Boseman, Montana. The female guide was the opposite of the sorority girls in every conceivable way, but unlike high school, she was now being paid to tolerate the gaggle of queen bees.

The two rafts followed the gentle river for an hour, and then the guides steered them toward shore. When they got close to a rocky wash-out, Cheeto and the female guide steered the rafts to shore. They jumped off the back. Each splashed through the shallow water, grabbing the handles along the side and at the front of the raft and pulling hard until the rafts were beached.

Everybody got out, stretched their legs, and took the opportunity to jump around.

Although they couldn't see them, the group heard the churning waters of a series of rapids called "Rock Slide." Huge boulders had fallen a long time ago and created the most difficult water in this portion of the canyon. If crews didn't paddle hard enough through the middle, the raft would flip amidst the whitewater and whirlpools.

Cheeto finished talking privately with the other guide, and then he turned to the group, clapping his hands to get their attention.

"Okay," he said. "This is it. We make it through this, and then it's an easy drift to our final destination." Cheeto looked at the sorority girls. "The water's pretty low right now, so it's not as bad as it could be. But I'm going to take the sorority girls for this final run." He paused and looked at the queen bees, none of whom were giggling at the moment. "If you get sucked down in a whirlpool —remember — don't try and swim out of it. Tuck your knees into your chest and let the life jacket do the work to bring you up to the surface." Cheeto scanned the whole group of rafters, making eye contact with each one. He wanted them to know he was serious. "But the best idea is to not flip and not get sucked into the hole in the first place. Okay?"

The group nodded, and Cheeto gave them a thumbs-up. "Okay. Then let's paddle hard."

There was a collective gasp as they rounded the bend.

The churning water filled the canyon with deafening noise. Michael stole a glance at Andie, and then tried to figure out how the guide was going to safely steer them around the gigantic boulders and narrow passages.

He looked around to see if there was a place to escape and portage the raft, but the limestone rose straight up on both sides, revealing just a sliver of sky. The only way out was through. Then he heard their guide start screaming at them.

"Paddle, paddle, paddle."

Michael put his head down and started paddling harder than he had ever paddled in his life. He didn't look up. He didn't watch where they were going or how close they came to the boulders. He just paddled.

They were fighting the river. On the first dip, the raft tilted to one side. Michael thought for sure that they would flip, but the raft corrected itself.

"Keep going. Paddle. Paddle. Don't stop."

The current kept pushing them toward the rocks, but the guide somehow found the breaks in the current and steered them away at the last moment. Until, eventually the canyon widened and the river spat them out into calm waters.

It was a sudden change, going from violence to calm. Adrenaline switched to relief, and most couldn't stop themselves from laughing or giving a cheer. A couple sorority girls asked if they could go again.

The pull-out was a campsite run by the National Park Service. There were a half-dozen people waiting to greet them as the rafts glided to a rocky shore. Most of them worked at the tour company that had arranged the whitewater rafting trip, but there was also a park ranger and an immigration agent.

"I got this," Cheeto whispered to Michael as he walked past Michael toward the agent and the park ranger.

"Gentlemen," he said. "Another beautiful morning to be doing what we love."

The agent smiled, and he and Cheeto shook hands.

"Always a pleasure, Cheeto." The agent let go of Cheeto's hand. "Anything strange happen?"

Cheeto shook his head. "Just the same ol' death defying acts of stupidity for meager profits."

"I hear ya." The agent surveyed the group, lingering a bit on the sorority girls. "Looks like you had a surly crew this time."

"Not too bad." Cheeto shrugged. "Looking forward to a warm shower, however."

"You all going to Maria's tonight?"

"Only place in town." Cheeto handed the immigration agent a stack of papers. Then he caught the eye of one of the tour company employees, and gave them the approval to start loading the rafts and gear onto the truck.

"Okay," the agent said after giving the papers a cursory review. "Everything looks good here." He slapped Cheeto on the back. "See you tonight at Maria's."

Cheeto stood and watched the border agent walk over to his jeep and drive away. Then Cheeto turned and walked back to Michael and Andie.

"That's it?" Michael asked.

"That's it." Cheeto smiled. "They randomly stop cars on the road out of the park, but they don't have any computers or anything. They're mostly just looking to see the color of your skin and whether you've got some Mexicans in your trunk."

"Well then," Michael said. "God bless America."

"No," Cheeto said. "God bless Texas, 'cuz in Arizona they'd shoot you."

CHAPTER TWENTY ONE

Brea Krane stared at Agent Vatch and U.S. Attorney Brenda Gadd.

"I want to know why every time you all say you're going to arrest this man, you don't." She looked at her brother, then back. "We've cooperated fully with your investigation, given you thousands of documents. Now every time you say he's going to jail, he's actually quite free."

"We'll get Collins." Gadd leaned forward and tried to put her hand on Brea Krane's hand, a consoling act, but Brea pulled back.

"I don't believe you." She folded her arms across her chest. "I can barely sleep at night."

This statement was a lie. Brea Krane didn't really have any strong feelings about her father. By all accounts Joshua Krane had relatively little interaction with his two children. Brea Krane and her brother, Brent, were raised by a series of nannies until they were old enough for boarding schools.

Vatch grew tired of the performance.

"Listen if it's the money that you're worried about, we've now got it all frozen." Vatch's narrow mouth bent and his tongue flicked. He couldn't resist a poke at why Brea Krane and her brother were really interested in the case. "Of course there are creditors, which will have to be sorted out before any release of funds, but that's not of my concern right now."

Brea Krane ignored Vatch's slight. She was business. "How do you know you've got all the money frozen?"

Brea Krane was twenty-eight, tall, thin, and with striking features and an M.B.A. from Harvard. She was the product of Krane's first marriage. Clearly intelligent, she had no genetic relationship with her stepmother, who had quickly found another rich patron after her father's death and the pre-nuptial agreement with Brea's father held up in court. Her stepmother had no interest in Michael Collins, and the children hadn't seen her in years.

Brea continued. "We're talking about a half billion in assets or more. I'm not confident you've found it all."

Gadd nodded, and calmly replied.

"Forensic accountants have spent years tracking it —"

"That's not what I said or asked." Brea unfolded her arms. She sat up, staring down Gadd. "If you don't know the original total, then you can't say with any confidence that you've found it all. I mean, I'm sure you've frozen eighty percent, maybe ninety percent, but there could be millions more hidden. Collins doesn't need that much to live comfortably for the rest of his life."

"We're confident we have it all." Vatch looked at Gadd for support, but didn't receive any. They had been having the same arguments internally for the past six months.

"Let me rephrase my question then." Brea folded her hands in front of herself. "Are you as confident about the money as you were that Michael Collins was going to be on that airplane yesterday?"

Brent Krane laughed at his sister's question and ran his hand through his spiked and messy hair. The crowd thought the question was hilarious, especially since they'd seen Michael Collins burn. The government was evidently unaware of their prime suspect's demise.

Brea Krane waited for a response that never came. She let Vatch squirm in silence, before coming at him again. "I want to know the plan. Tell me the plan about how you are going to get Michael Collins."

Mention of a plan silenced the rowdy crowd in Brent's head. The crowd perked up, listening.

Vatch looked at Gadd, and then said, "Well, it's unusual for us to disclose such information. We can share some things as a courtesy, but —"

Gadd cut him off.

"We expect he'll be coming to New York in the next few days. When he does, we'll catch him."

"New York's a big place." Brea wasn't convinced.

"But we know where he's going." Gadd glanced up at the clock on wall. She was ready for the meeting to be over. "He'll be going to the funeral. I can't imagine he'd stay away."

"The funeral for the priest?" Brea asked.

"That's right." Gadd nodded her head. "Collins won't miss it. His friend, Mr. Guillardo, is already in town and we have a few agents following him, seeing where he goes."

Agent Vatch raised his eyebrows. There were no agents following Guillardo. They tried to follow him, but the weirdo lost them within an hour of getting out of the airport. Perhaps Gadd was lying or maybe she didn't know, either way Vatch decided that he wasn't going to correct her.

"But Michael Collins hasn't arrived?" Brent's voice cracked. His full participation took everybody by surprise, since neither Vatch nor Gadd could remember the last time Brent Krane had uttered a complete sentence.

"No," Vatch said. "But he's coming."

Brent wanted to ask a few more questions just to embarrass them. He liked feeling smart. "How do you know? I mean ..." His voice trailed off as the crowd warned him not to reveal too much. Brent stammered out a few more words and then shrugged away the rest of the question as Vatch filled the silence.

"He played a little game with us. Bought an airplane ticket, checked some bags, got his boarding pass, and then never got on the plane."

This was confusing. How could a dead man buy a plane ticket? The crowd didn't like this.

###

After the meeting, Brea called Tad Garvin. He picked up after the third ring. Brea walked a few steps away from her brother as they waited for the elevator.

"Anything?" she asked.

Tad Garvin told her that he checked the post office box that morning and nothing had arrived. There were also no emails sent to the account that he had established for her, and no phone calls to the cell phone that he had bought.

Of course the post office box, email, and phone were not created using Brea Krane's real identity. Garvin had created a series of limited liability corporations and subsidiaries to obscure the real owner. It was a simple service offered by the firm for its elite clients, and all for the bargain price of $700 an hour.

"Well, the bureaucrats say that Collins is coming to the funeral." Brea glanced over at her brother, and then at her watch. "I guess we'll just wait."

She tapped a button, ending the call, and wandered back to a small group gathered for the elevator to arrive.

"Talking to your lawyer again?" Brent Krane worked hard to convey a tone of snarky condescension.

"Yes," Brea nodded. "Just keeping him up-to-date."

Brent Krane rolled his eyes. "When's this elevator going to come. It's, like, taking forever."

"Why do you care, Brent? You have a job interview or something?"

"Ha ha, very funny." Brent put his hands in the pockets of his baggy, dirty jeans. "I got stuff to do."

"Like reaching level 45 in World of Warcraft?"

Brent shook his head. "I make good money at that."

"Collecting gold and storm jewels in a videogame and selling it to other losers over the internet so they can buy a virtual dragon mount is not a job."

The bell for the elevator rang, and its doors slid open.

"Whatever." Brent walked inside. "See you later, sis."

Brea watched him as the doors slid closed. She decided to wait for the next elevator.

CHAPTER TWENTY TWO

It was a solid three day drive from Texas to New York. While Michael and Andie drove Cheeto's Jeep across the south and up to New York, Kermit had a long list of tasks to complete.

He needed to find a place for them to sleep that wasn't a hotel. If the price was right, Michael preferred a furnished brownstone that also had plenty of ways for Michael to get in and out. Kermit was further instructed to purchase a half-dozen disposable pay-as-you-go cell phones, and set up a home office for them to work. The office needed desks, computers, pens, paper, an internet connection, and a scanner. Finally and most importantly, Kermit needed to find Michael a lawyer.

The People's Legal Center was located in a narrow, dilapidated, four-story brick house about a half-block off the intersection of Malcolm X and West 126th.

Built in 1880, the house had originally been the home of a prominent businessman who owned three garment factories on the lower East side. His wife died before him, and his only daughter inherited everything.

She promptly sold the factories, and turned the house into a meeting place for the local communist party. When she later died without heirs and the local communist party in hiding, her will decreed that all of her money "shall be used to provide free legal representation to the poor." The house became a law of-fice, although a very strange one, and the first legal aid office in the country.

Her financial endowment disappeared over time, the victim of poor investment choices. The house, however, continued to be a place where people could obtain a free lawyer. Operated on a shoestring budget, the People's Legal Center was now loosely affiliated with the New York Public Defender's Office.

Kermit got out of the cab and opened a black, wrought-iron gate in front of the house. He walked up the sidewalk to the en-trance. Kermit looked for a buzzer or a doorbell, but there wasn't one. So he just walked inside.

The house was chaos.

The front parlor, converted into a waiting area, overflowed with people of all shapes and colors and ages. Babies cried. Toddlers bounced on a torn, blue couch while their mothers pretended not to see. Others were talking on cell phones, a few were fighting imaginary devils, and some simply sat quietly with brown grocery bags filled with receipts and other papers that their attorneys needed to review. The veterans of the People's Legal Center — knowing it would be an all-day wait — had brought coolers filled with food and various malt liquor beverag-es.

Kermit grinned, digging the vibe. He strolled toward a young woman with a clipboard. She was in her early twenties. She wore black hipster glasses and a small nose ring.

"Hey pretty lady." Kermit entered her personal space. "You look like the boss."

She took a step back and looked Kermit over. She tried to figure out what legal box Kermit's problems would likely fit into: criminal, civil, domestic, landlord-tenant or all of the above.

"Have an appointment?" She looked down at her list of people who were scheduled for morning meetings.

Kermit shook his head.

"It's a personal matter," he paused, "for a friend."

She nodded. It wasn't the first time she'd heard that.

"Well, you're going to need to set up an appointment with intake and then they'll determine whether you qualify for our services."

"No." Kermit shook his head, undeterred. "I need to talk with Quentin Robinson about a mutual friend."

"Well, Mr. Robinson is already behind schedule, and he's got several people waiting."

Kermit took a few steps back, and he decided to turn on the K-Man charm. He closed his eyes, thinking about the twelve gauge bosons dangling from his head.

Kermit regrouped and came back at the young woman with a smile.

"What's your name?" He winked. Kermit allowed his graying dreadlocks to sway back and forth.

The question took the young woman a little off-guard, but she recovered. Her job was to be a gatekeeper. She couldn't just allow anybody back to see the attorneys or she'd be fired.

"Listen," she said. "I know you have a legal emergency." She pointed at the room. "But everybody's got a legal emergency. So, I need you to call intake and set up an appointment."

"That's not what I asked." Kermit put his hand on his heart and gave a little bow. "I am Mr. Kermit Guillardo, and I am introducing myself so that you may return the favor and elevate this perfunctory level of discourse to something more meaningful."

"Listen." She shook her head and put her hand on her hip. "I don't want to call security."

"Nor do I want you to take such a harsh action, senorita," said Kermit. "But I do want to call you something. At least give me that."

The young woman looked around, and then softly said, "Anna."

"Anna." Kermit closed his eyes and repeated her name. Then he opened them and continued with an offer. "Well Anna, I have a proposition for you. In my pocket is $100. All I ask you to do is to go to Quentin Robinson. Inquire of him. And, ask whether he will talk to me about his old friend, Michael Collins." Kermit paused. "Again, his friend's name is Michael Collins and Michael's in trouble. Ask him if he'll talk with me. If he says no, then I will leave. If he says yes, then I will proceed. Either way, my dear Anna, this is yours." Kermit stuck his hand in his jacket pocket. He removed a folded hundred-dollar bill and fastened it onto Anna's clipboard.

Anna looked down at the money, and then up at Kermit. She scanned the waiting room, thinking. Then she looked back down at the money, took it off the clipboard, and placed it discreetly into her pocket.

"You said your friend's name was Michael Collins?"

Kermit nodded.

"Yes, my love. Just ask if he'll see me, and then maybe later we could grab a bite to eat since I'm new in town."

She smiled. "I'll think about that. Give me a few minutes."

###

Quentin Robinson's office occupied one quarter of a third floor bedroom. Sometime in the 1960s, the legal center divided the bedroom into four individual offices, each one slightly larger than a cubicle. Since Robinson had been with the organization for ten years, he got the office with heat and a window. The other attorneys froze in the winter and baked in the summer.

Kermit sat down in a rickety wooden chair across from Quentin, and waited for Quentin to finish typing something on his computer.

Quentin pressed return on his keyboard, and then he swiveled around in his chair. He was a short, pudgy guy with a ponytail, beard, and round tortoiseshell glasses. He didn't look like a lawyer, but then, neither did Michael Collins.

Quentin brushed some cookie crumbs off of his 1998 Green Day concert T-shirt, and then he picked up his cup of coffee.

"Michael Collins." Quentin took a sip of coffee. "I hadn't heard that name for quite awhile."

"Well, he sent me here," Kermit said. "Told me you'd help."

Quentin rolled his eyes.

"Michael and I were in the same study group back in law school, but I can't say I ever expected him to ask me for help." Quentin took another sip of coffee and put the cup back down on his cluttered desk. "Michael was on the big-firm track from Day One." Quentin paused and looked around his humble office. "Me ..." he shrugged, "A little different track."

"Well," Kermit inched forward onto the edge of his seat. He tapped twice on Quentin's desk and then pointed at the puffy lawyer. "He wants to hire you."

Quentin shook his head.

"I'm not in private practice. Nobody gets to hire me."

"No?" Kermit smirked. "Maybe you don't understand." Kermit bent over and opened up his backpack. He removed a black leather case and put it on Quentin's desk. "He really needs to hire you."

Quentin looked down at the case that had been placed in front of him. Curious, Quentin took off the top and saw a roll of coins. "What the hell are these?"

"Gold coins, counselor." Kermit's head bobbled.

Quentin laughed. "Does Michael think I'm a pirate?" He pushed the coins away. "What am I supposed to do with gold coins?"

"I got a place in Chinatown that will gladly and discretely convert these coins into any currency you desire." Kermit touched one of his dreadlocks, spinning it around his finger. "So that problem is solved."

Quentin shook his head. "Sorry, but this isn't my thing. I work for poor people, and frankly Michael could hire somebody better suited for whatever he wants me to do."

Kermit nodded. "Collins thought you'd say that." He nodded toward the box. "There's probably a hundred thousand dollars worth of coins in there. Just take a leave of absence, pay off some student loans, and then come back to fight the good fight."

Quentin looked away. "I don't make career decisions based on money," he shrugged. "That's never been who I am."

"Fair," Kermit said. "But how about a career decision based on money *and* an old friendship. Philosophically, I think you'd agree, that presents a different scenario."

Quentin looked back at the roll of coins, then looked at his pathetic office, and sighed.

CHAPTER TWENTY THREE

The query rattled around in Michael's brain, and he couldn't quite kick it. Long drives always lent themselves to unanswerable questions. For him, the question was always, "Why? Why did he love Andie Larone?" Michael could never answer that question, and in the end, he wondered if he was just being a chump. Do people in love actually ask such a thing, thought Michael.

It was dark as they approached the city. Michael looked over at the passenger seat. Andie was asleep. She had rolled her jacket into a ball. Her head rested on it.

Michael drove, glanced over at her, drove some more, and then glanced again. The question circled. If he was objective, he never should have risked his own life to save her. If he was rational, he would have never let her back into his life after she ended their brief engagement. And if he was smart, he wouldn't trust her now.

But here he was, entering the city and preparing to end it all with Andie Larone as his partner. Why? Why was he so committed to her?

She was attractive, but there were a lot of attractive women. She was smart, but there were a lot of smart women. She was fun to be with, but fun is pretty easy to come by when you're living on the beach in Mexico.

Michael rubbed his eyes. He was exhausted after being on the road for more than thirty hours.

Michael turned on the blinker. He changed lanes, passing a tractor-trailer and a minivan. Then he returned to the far right lane, still thinking as they entered the Holland Tunnel.

Michael stole another glance, and then looked back at the road. Perhaps it was just a matter of timing, he thought.

There were moments when individuals were simply available to love and be loved, and maybe he had met Andie at just such a moment. She had managed to get through that secret door in his heart for the brief second that it had been open, and now she couldn't leave and Michael couldn't get her out. She offered him comfort when he had most needed it and a home when he was lost. Perhaps he was still repaying a debt.

Michael saw the sign for Varick Street and moved over to the left lane. The sound of the tires on the road deepened as they slowed and came to a stop. Andie started to stir, but she didn't wake up. Maybe that was for the best, Michael thought. He reached over and put his hand on her leg. Don't wake up until we're through this, Michael thought, because I can't let you break my heart again.

Kermit was proud. He and Michael stood on the sidewalk under a streetlight. They admired the brownstone that Kermit had found. The rental was located in the Carroll Gardens neighborhood of Brooklyn. It was marketed as a vacation rental for large families looking for an adventure away from Times Square: four furnished bedrooms, kitchen and an office.

Michael put his hand on Kermit's shoulder and gave it a squeeze.

"You did good, Kermit."

Kermit puffed out his chest. "Just a block to the subway, six blocks to the highway, and a half-mile to the warehouses and barges in the bay."

Michael nodded, already planning an escape if necessary.

"Perfect." He turned back to the truck. "In the morning, I'll need you to drive the truck to a long-term parking lot near the airport. I don't want Cheeto getting in trouble." Michael looked at Andie. She was still asleep in the front seat. "Let's unload, and once everything is out, I'll wake Andie. I'm looking forward to us sleeping in an actual bed."

"The upstairs queen is mine," Kermit said. "I already did a little jelly roll in it, if you know what I mean."

Michael shook his head.

"No, I don't know what you mean." He turned and started walking back toward the truck. "And please don't share."

CHAPTER TWENTY FOUR

Quentin Robinson was at the brownstone long before Michael and Andie woke up. He had claimed the office on the garden level, and he also appeared to have made peace with his decision to quit his job for a roll of gold coins.

Quentin's wife thought that he was going mad, but she reconsidered when Quentin told her that his student loans would be paid off and they could finally go on their long-delayed honeymoon to Hawaii when Michael's case was done. Then, the idea of representing an old law school friend didn't seem as crazy.

Quentin drank coffee and pecked away at the computer.

Based upon the information provided by Kermit, he researched cases similar to the allegations being made against Michael. He wanted to figure out what a likely sentence would be when Michael pleaded guilty.

Kermit hadn't said anything about Michael pleading guilty, but that wasn't unusual. Nobody wanted to plead guilty. Everybody wanted to take their case to trial. But quickly the offers from the prosecutor would start getting worse and the client would eventually change his or her mind.

Quentin called it, "growing into their guilt."

The case will settle, Quentin thought. Even the great Michael Collins will plead guilty. And then Quentin figured that life would return to normal. He would go back to practicing poverty law and living in poverty as is appropriate for any lawyer with a martyr complex.

He looked up from his computer screen when he heard somebody come into the kitchen and start rustling through the refrigerator drawers. Quentin saved his electronic research-trail on Westlaw and got up. Quentin walked around his desk, and then went down the hallway to see who it was.

"Mr. Robinson." Michael smiled when he looked up from his bowl of cereal and saw his former study partner. "You drive a hard bargain, I hear."

Quentin walked over to the kitchen island where Michael sat, and he pulled out the barstool next to Michael.

"I figure if I'm selling out, I've got to at least make it count." Quentin sat down, and then extended his hand. "It's been a long time."

Michael took Quentin's hand and they shook.

"Too long."

"Well, maybe not too long," Quentin laughed. "I could've waited to see you under different circumstances."

Michael looked around the brownstone, feigning insult.

"I don't know," he said. "This is a pretty awesome career opportunity that you've been presented with." Then Michael pointed down the hallway toward Quentin's new office. "And I bet you never dreamed of working in such a clean environment."

"It is clean." Quentin thought of his cramped quarter-room on the third floor of the People's Legal Center. "I'll admit that. It's the cleanest place I've ever worked."

###

Michael closed the office door, and he and Quentin started the interview. Within minutes, Michael knew that he had made the right decision. Despite the ponytail and the ill-fitting clothes, Quentin was going to be a fighter. More importantly, his friend was smart and cared about the outcome.

Quentin started the interview with Michael's basic personal background information: where he grew up, education, hobbies. Then he moved into Michael's time at Wabash, Kramer and Moore, and eventually to the incident. That's where he stopped. Quentin worked right up to the moment when Michael left the parking garage to drive Joshua Krane to Krane's bank to retrieve the account numbers and passwords. He didn't want to go any further.

Quentin knew not to ask Michael whether he stole the money or whether he was guilty.

When practicing criminal defense, ignorance was power. The truth about guilt or innocence limited options during trial and plea negotiations. Quentin merely needed to create a reasonable doubt, not prove innocence. Knowing the truth would only get in the way of that.

Quentin needed to be free to poke holes in the government's case. He needed to present alternate theories about what had actually happened to more than $500 million. Knowing the truth would ethically prohibit him from presenting alternate theories to the jury. In short, Quentin needed wiggle room.

After two hours, Quentin finished a note on his pad of paper and looked up.

"We're behind." Quentin made the declaration more to himself than to Michael. "The government has been working on this case for years. The amount of documents to review is going to be large." Quentin shook his head. "I'm going to need some help. They're going to have a team of lawyers and investigators."

"Wouldn't be the first time you've been outnumbered."

Quentin set his pen down on the desk, took off his round tortoiseshell glasses and rubbed his eyes. "I haven't even seen the indictment."

"Neither have I," Michael said. "But you know what it's going to say."

Quentin glanced out the window. He took a minute to watch a robin land on the sidewalk, peck at something on the ground, and then fly away. "I'm not seeing a lot of ways out, Michael. I say that as both a friend and now your attorney. They're going to have an electronic trail of money that leads right to you. That's why it's taken them so long to move forward. They needed to track the money."

Michael leaned forward in his chair. He lowered his voice, serious.

"Quentin, I've got faith in you." Michael waited until he knew Quentin was listening. Then Michael looked him in the eye. "When this is over, I'm going to walk away a free man."

Quentin's lips turned into a smirk. "You know something I don't know?"

"Maybe." Michael leaned back in his chair. "Or maybe I just have faith."

It was mid-afternoon when Quentin and Michael decided that they had talked enough for the day. Andie popped a bag of microwave popcorn and got some beers out of the refrigerator, and everyone gathered in the brownstone's living room.

They drank and ate junk food for an hour, and then the conversation lulled.

Michael took a breath and said, "I think it's time."

He stood and reached into his pocket and removed a disposable cell phone and Agent Armstrong's business card. It was the card that Armstrong had given Kermit as Kermit had left the Immigration and Custom Enforcement's interrogation room.

Michael walked over to Quentin. He handed Quentin the phone and the card.

Quentin hesitated.

"You sure you want me to do this?" He looked at Michael, and then at Andie and Kermit, who were sitting on the couch.

"It's as good a time as any." Michael turned and looked at Andie. "I'm not hiding anymore."

She nodded her head. They had already talked about it. Andie had questioned the plan, unsure of whether it would work, but in the end, she was supportive.

Michael turned back to Quentin.

"I'd rather I go in on my terms not theirs."

"But once I make this call, there's really no turning back." Quentin said. "And I'm not so sure I can get you what you want."

"He'll agree to it." Michael shrugged his shoulders. "It's Vatch and Gadd that will break the agreement. They want a big show. They're going to want a lot of cameras. They're going to want the perp walk — me walking to a squad car with my hands cuffed behind my back. They won't be able to resist, and that can be an out." Michael smiled. "That's also going to make this part a little fun."

"Okay." Quentin nodded. He began walking back to the office, so that he could make the phone call in private. After a few steps, Quentin paused and then turned back. "Shouldn't I be calling Agent Vatch, instead?"

Michael laughed. "Hell, no."

CHAPTER TWENTY FIVE

B rea Krane sat across from Tad Garvin in the firm's pent-house conference room. Typically Garvin would have an associate in the meeting with him, if for no other reason than to pad the client's bill with the added expense of another attorney. But this meeting was different. This meeting demanded discretion as well as deniability.

It was off-book. No record of the meeting would be kept. No bill would ever be sent. Garvin hadn't even reserved the conference room, out of precaution that those records could be discovered.

"So they think he'll be in town tomorrow for the funeral?" Garvin tapped his pen on his notepad. He had the pen and paper to look professional, but he didn't intend to write anything down.

"That's what Vatch told us," Brea shook her head, dismissively. "But they won't ever catch him, not unless he decides it's time. Collins has always been five steps ahead of Vatch, and I doubt anything has changed."

Garvin set his pen down. He rubbed his chin, thinking.

"Well, there are two other things that I needed to share," he said. "First, your brother seems to be spiraling, again."

Brea knew exactly what Garvin was talking about. "Off his meds."

"Likely," Garvin said. "Seems he made an unauthorized trip down south."

Brea tilted her head to the side. "Thought he looked tan for somebody who plays video games all day."

"Now you know why." Garvin bent over and opened his large briefcase, removing several photographs from a file folder. He slid the photographs across the table to Brea.

Brea looked down at the charred remains of the Sunset's bar.

"He always liked fire." She looked at the photographs one more time, then pushed the photographs back to Garvin. "I'll try and be nicer. See if I can manage him, maybe this might even work in our favor."

"You're not going to bring him in on this are you?" Garvin was concerned.

"Of course not." Brea shook her head, and then batted her eyelashes, trying to ease Garvin's nerves. "This is our deal, sweetie. Just you and me."

Garvin looked into the much younger woman's eyes. She was playing with him. Garvin knew it, but he didn't care. If Brea Krane asked him to leave his wife and spoiled kids, he'd do it in an instant.

"The second thing, which is more important, is what arrived in the mail today." Garvin then bent over and removed a bulky envelope from his briefcase. He set it on the table and pushed it over to Brea Krane. "Came this morning."

Brea picked up the envelope. She examined the postmark. "Mailed from the Cancun Airport," she said as she opened it. "I figured he'd reach out to me."

"He doesn't have many options," Garvin smiled. His fake-white teeth glowed. "The bigger question is whether he has any money. The feds think they've got it all."

"The feds are idiots. Years have passed." Brea reached her hand inside the envelope. There was a phone. She removed the phone and tried to find a note, but the rest of the envelope was empty.

Brea set the empty envelope aside and turned on the phone. It vibrated, found a signal, and then a notification appeared on the screen.

"Looks like I have a text message."

Brea pressed a button and a short text message appeared on the screen.

"It's a phone number." Smiling, she looked up from the phone to Garvin. "Collins wants me to call him."

"It's coming together." Garvin nodded. "Sure, you still want it. I mean, you don't exactly need the money."

Brea shook her head. She hadn't expected Tad Garvin to fully understand; very few people did.

"What's that supposed to mean?" she asked, setting him up.

Garvin shrugged.

"I don't know," he said. "There are risks."

Brea shook her head. "Do you think I'm rich?" Her tone and the question caught Garvin off-guard.

Garvin started to answer, but soon realized that there was no way that his answer could not offend. He stammered for a for a few seconds, and then Brea put him out of his misery with another question.

"How about this, instead: Are you rich?" Brea smiled at her lawyer. Tad Garvin billed clients like her more than $500 an hour. He made millions of dollars a year. Yet, she knew that Tad Garvin didn't consider himself rich. He was merely a high-paid servant. No matter how much money he made, his clients were always wealthier. He was the advisor to kings, but Tad Garvin knew that he would never be a king.

"I'll help you out," Brea Krane reached over and took Tad Garvin's hand. A little flirt to soothe his feelings. She still needed him. When the trial was over, he'd be gone. For now, however, she needed Tad Garvin on her side. "You and I are not rich. The masses," Brea gestured toward the view of the broader city from the conference room's large window. "The masses think we're rich. The liberals in Washington, D.C., think we're rich. But we know that we are not." She squeezed his hand.

"We are simply enablers. We have just enough power to enable the truly wealthy to continue to do whatever they want with the world. We're all the same, the middle managers, the junior executives, the vice presidents, the doctors and lawyers. We've been bribed by the system to keep the status quo. The truly rich let us own a nice house, drive a fancy car, maybe have a pool and a few vacations a year to some place warm, but we're not truly rich."

Brea Krane let go of Tad Garvin's hand. She stood up and walked over to the window, staring down at the life that circulated below. Then she turned back to Garvin.

"My father was rich," she said. "Truly rich. He and our family were on the Forbes list of wealthiest families in the world. His net worth when he died was $32 billion. Do you understand the difference between a millionaire and a billionaire? It's the difference between owning a diamond and owning a diamond mine."

Brea Krane looked out the window at the city. She put her hand on the glass.

"People like my dad could look at this city and buy anything or anyone that he wanted. He could buy that building and the building next to it. Cash. He could buy those ships. He could buy this law firm. He could walk into any store and buy the most expensive suit or piece of jewelry, and it wouldn't make a difference. He'd still be a multi-billionaire."

Brea turned away from the window. Her eyes were fire.

"When my dad died and the lawyers came in and seized our family's money, all I had left was a couple million dollars from a trust fund. My brother didn't get anything because his trust fund hadn't vested yet." Brea shook her head. "That's what the government and Michael Collins stole from me." Her face hardened. "So I'm getting every cent Michael Collins has left, whether it's $1 or a hundred million. I'm entitled to that money. It's the only way I can get back to where I belong."

CHAPTER TWENTY SIX

The conference room jumped with activity. The team of FBI agents, attorneys, forensic accountants, and support staff were giddy with the news: Michael John Collins was turning himself in.

"Don't trust him," Vatch tried to dampen their enthusiasm. "This guy has been running for years, and now all of a sudden he's got a change of heart? I don't think so," Vatch rolled his eyes at Armstrong's naiveté. "You're being suckered."

"He knows he's going to get caught sometime, and all he wants to do is go to the priest's funeral." Armstrong wasn't going to allow Vatch to belittle his accomplishment. Armstrong wanted the credit for getting Collins. "I think it's fair. His attorney said that he'll arrive in the front. I can meet his car and I will personally walk him inside for the service. When the service is done, Collins wants me to walk him out the back to a car to be processed."

"You're a fool." Vatch's tongue flicked. "Collins wants to make us look bad, again. He's wants to embarrass us."

"He doesn't want a show," Armstrong said. "That's what his attorney told me. Collins just wants me. No SWAT team. Nothing else. If anybody but me shows up, the attorney said that Collins isn't going to show."

131

Vatch shook his head and looked at Brenda Gadd at the head of the conference table.

"You believe this? You're actually going to go along with this?"

"Well, your tactics haven't exactly been successful." Gadd paused, and the room was silent. Nobody was going to say anything until United States Attorney Brenda Gadd had finished her thought. "Perhaps there might be a middle ground."

CHAPTER TWENTY SEVEN

The news had to be false. Brent Krane opened the bottle of prescription pain killers, got two pills, crushed them, and then put the crushed powder in a small glass of water. "Down the hatch." He picked up the glass and drank the clouded liquid in one gulp.

He'd seen Michael Collins and Andie Larone burn. He'd lit the fire himself.

A few drops of water rolled down the side of his mouth, but he didn't care. He'd gotten the hit he'd needed. Brent took a breath, trying to convince himself that it wasn't true. He told the crowd that Collins was dead, but they wouldn't stop yelling at him. They reminded him that they had wanted to go back, but he had kept driving away. He was a coward.

Brent Krane felt a wave of nausea, then a rush of pleasure that muted the crowd. The pills were twenty-four-hour time-release tablets, but crushing them meant that the full drug wouldn't slowly enter the system as designed. Instead, he got all the power at once.

Brent stood straighter in front of a full-length mirror in his bedroom.

"You'll see," he scolded the crowd and puffed out his chest. "The cripple cop is a liar." Brent Krane tried to make himself look bigger. I am getting bigger, he thought. He flexed his skinny bicep. I'm getting stronger, too.

Brent flexed, again. The crowd said nothing.

"That's what I thought. You're all the ones who are truly afraid." He flexed his muscles a final time. Brent took a moment to examine a new outbreak of acne on his neck, and then he went over to the closet and found a dress shirt.

The shirt was wrinkled, but unlike the other clothes in his studio apartment, it was clean. He put the shirt on, and then buttoned up.

He walked back over to the mirror and took a look. Brent didn't like what he saw. He looked like he was back at Saint Mark's Boarding School. All he had to do was add a blue and green striped tie and blue blazer.

Memories of boarding school flashed past him, uncontrolled. The drugs pulsed through his body and his head spun. Brent thought about his fall. It all came back to his fall.

He was never a popular kid, but he was feared. He was respected. Teachers coddled him. Why? Because of who he was, Joshua Krane's son — the wealthiest boy in a school filled with wealthy boys. Then along came Michael Collins.

Brent attacked the image in the mirror. He kicked it. He punched it. Glass cut into his feet and hands, but he didn't stop. He was numb to the pain and blood. Brent kept going, kicking and punching until he collapsed on the floor.

The voices returned, and he started to cry.

CHAPTER TWENTY EIGHT

Mourners began to arrive at Saint Thomas the Compassionate at four o'clock. Agent Armstrong stood in the balcony under the church's Rose Window, titled, "Formless Creation." It was comprised of various shards of mysterious blue glass, some big and some small, radiating from a cluster of five hundred diamonds at its core. The window cast the balcony and most of the church in a peaceful aqua light, but Armstrong was not at peace. He was furious.

Although Brenda Gadd had told him that she wasn't going to follow Vatch's advice, Armstrong had already spotted five FBI agents in the sanctuary and he saw two agents in a blue van outside on the street. And then there were two cops in an unmarked Dodge Charger. If Armstrong looked hard enough, he figured that he could spot a half-dozen more.

He took his phone out of his pocket. Armstrong checked the screen to see if Michael Collins or his attorney had called and he had missed it.

Armstrong pressed a button. There was nothing.

He shook his head. It's bad enough that he had to put up with Vatch, now Gadd was bringing in every goon with a badge that she could find.

Armstrong walked down the stone spiral staircase to the main level.

When he reached the bottom of the stairs, Armstrong stepped into the narthex. He turned his head to the right, looking for Collins. Instead of finding him, however, Armstrong bumped into a woman coming through the front door.

"Excuse me," Armstrong said, then he realized who it was.

"It's okay," Brea Krane smiled. "You're working."

Armstrong was stunned. He looked at Brea Krane, and then realized that her brother was also there. Brent Krane stood behind her.

Armstrong lowered his voice.

"What are you two doing here?"

"We were invited to see the show," Brea said. "Brenda Gadd told us that there might be some media here, and that they'll probably want to interview us."

Armstrong's fists clenched into tight balls.

"This is a man's funeral."

"A man who aided and abetted the murder of my father and the theft of our inheritance," Brea's perfect lips curled into a perfect smirk. Armstrong had no control over her.

"I've got work to do." Armstrong started to turn away, but then he noticed Brent Krane's waxy complexion and the white gauze bandages wrapped around his hands. "And you might want to keep your brother away from the cameras."

Armstrong put his hand on Brea's shoulder, and whispered, "The kid needs to sober up."

CHAPTER TWENTY NINE

The truth was that Father Stiles never wanted a funeral. As a priest, he understood the need for grieving and a human being's need for ritual. He didn't, however, like the idea of people staring at his dead body laying in an open coffin. He didn't like the idea of people being sad at his death.

"I'm a priest," Father Stiles had told Michael. "I've led a life of sacrifice. Death should be celebrated with a party, not a funeral. I'm going to meet Saint Peter and spend eternity in the presence of our Lord and dancing with the greatest musicians in the world. How cool is that?"

Michael thought about those late-night philosophical conversations with Father Stiles. They'd occur in Father Stiles' personal office and library, which filled the upper floor of the rectory. Michael wasn't as convinced about heaven and hell as Father Stiles. He certainly liked the idea of a better place. He liked the idea of a grand plan to provide boundaries and purpose for a chaotic world, but Michael had never heard a good explanation for the cruelty that existed around him, especially among the people who claimed to be acting on behalf of God.

"If there is a God," Michael would say, "then that God is ambivalent and spiteful. Why would I worship that? The absence of God makes more sense. We should do good for the sake of doing good, not because we think we'll get a big reward someday, not to curry favor with a deity that set a flawed people on a path toward destroying themselves for fun and profit."

At that (or something similar), Father Stiles would always smile. "Perfect," he'd pat Michael on the shoulder. "Doubt is the foundation of faith. Absolutism is the opposite of faith, and absolutism really has no place in religion."

Michael knelt down on a patch of grass on the edge of the open grave. He was still a doubter, but if anyone deserved to go to heaven, it was Father Stiles.

Michael stared down into the empty hole. It was where Father Stiles would be buried after the church's formal mass. A vault had already been placed in the grave in which a pine casket would be lowered. For a tombstone, Father Stiles had requested a simple white wooden cross.

It was a beautiful site on a small rolling hill deep within the grounds of New York's Woodlawn Cemetery.

The large garden cemetery was over one hundred and fifty years old. It had served the urban community as a spiritual oasis as well as a natural refuge for plants and wildlife. It wasn't uncommon to see a fox, turkey, or deer roaming the grounds in the early evening, despite the cemetery's location in the heart of the Bronx.

Kermit and Andie knelt beside Michael, one on each side. They all stared into the hole in silence, and then finally Michael spoke. He had promised Father Stiles a private ceremony, and Michael was going to keep his promise.

"Father Stiles." Michael began, looking up at the sky. "I don't know if you're watching me. I don't know if you're looking out for me, but I remembered my promise made long ago." Michael paused as a tear rolled down his face. He wiped it away.

"Sorry," Michael said. "You told me no tears, but you know me — always have to break the rules." Michael laughed, and then wiped another tear away. "You wanted me to do a dance and celebrate, but I don't think I can. I know you weren't afraid of death. I know you didn't want to be a burden on anyone, but you need to be thanked."

Michael looked at Andie. He held her hand and squeezed. Then he started again. "And Father, I want you to know that I love you, and that Saint Thomas is full of people right now who are suffering through a boring mass on a beautiful sunny afternoon because they also love you. ..." Michael lost his train of thought. He closed his eyes, and then recovered. He went back to the list. He went back to Father Stiles' instructions. He circled back to the beginning.

"I remember what you wanted me to do," Michael nodded. "That's what I'm trying to say."

He looked at Kermit, signaling that it was time and Kermit got up. Kermit walked over to his backpack, and then he brought his backpack to Michael.

Michael unzipped it. He found a plastic grocery bag. "I got the stuff you wanted." He removed the plastic bag from the backpack, smiling and crying at the same time. "One box of frozen pizza rolls. Your favorite."

Michael took the box of pizza rolls out of the plastic grocery bag and opened the box. "You should know that it'll take years to get the pizza roll smell out of your office. That smell is going to haunt whatever priest replaces you at St. Thomas." Michael, poured the individual miracles of modern processed food onto the ground. Then he looked at the gravesite. There was about a four inch opening between the vault and the edge of the hole.

"On television there isn't a concrete vault, so I'm just going to slip these suckers in between here." Michael knelt down and pushed the pizza rolls into the crack. "That way our friends at the cemetery don't mistake them for garbage, which in a sense they are, and clean them out before they put you in there."

Michael handed the empty box to Kermit, and then he took a CD out of the bag.

"I know you wanted the original 45 record from your collection, but I didn't have access to your things at the moment." Michael looked down at the Elvis Presley's Greatest Hits album that he had bought on the way to the cemetery. "So this is going to have to do. You and the King, buried together." Michael slipped the CD into the same crack where he had put the pizza rolls.

Michael opened a carton of eggs. He took one out of the carton and held it up in the sunlight. "And finally, a perfect egg, just like you." Michael smiled, and allowed a few tears to fall. "You wanted me to do this, to remind me of Easter, to remind me of forgiveness and resurrection."

Michael looked at the egg in his hand, and then slipped it through the crack.

"Always trying to convince me, even in your death. Although this time, you aren't even that subtle."

Michael, Andie, and Kermit met Quentin at the car. Quentin had been watching the private funeral service from afar, as his cell phone repeatedly vibrated with incoming calls from Agent Armstrong. Quentin had no obligation to answer his phone, and he perversely enjoyed witnessing the mighty FBI panic and squirm.

"You ready?" Quentin opened the back door of his rusted Toyota Camry.

"Ready." Michael shook Quentin's hand, and then climbed inside.

Andie followed Michael. She got in the back, while Kermit got into the front.

"Shotgun, baby." Kermit clapped his hands and closed the door. "Me and the Q, a new dynamic duo sprung upon the scene. Up front, loud and proud."

Kermit tapped on the dashboard, and Quentin pulled away.

CHAPTER THIRTY

Agent Armstrong got the phone call toward the end of the funeral mass.

"Where are you?"

He spoke softly, and then walked out the back of the church. Outside, he wouldn't have to whisper.

"That wasn't what you told me," Armstrong's eyes widened. His face turned red, and a bead of sweat rolled down the back of his neck. "You said you would meet me here and Collins and I would walk out the back together when the funeral service was over. That's what you said. You told me —"

Agent Armstrong was about to lose his temper, but he calmed himself. He couldn't lose sight of the ultimate goal. For now, Collins and his attorney held the cards. He had to salvage his reputation.

###

Quentin ended the call and placed the cell phone in his pocket.

"That was just about the greatest moment as a lawyer that I think I've ever had."

Michael smiled. "I knew you'd like this job." Michael looked around. "I mean, if I'm going to go down, I might as well do it with style."

Michael leaned back in his chair, smiling and stretching out his legs.

Quentin had told Agent Armstrong that they had been waiting for half an hour, and that they were wondering where he was. When Armstrong said the same thing, Quentin had denied ever saying that they would meet him at Father Stiles' funeral. Then, Quentin revealed the twist: He and Michael were waiting patiently for Armstrong and Vatch in the lobby at the FBI's downtown headquarters.

"What's a guy gotta do to get arrested in this town?" Michael folded his hands together over his stomach and closed his eyes as various FBI agents and investigators scurried past him, oblivious to the most wanted man in New York.

###

It took a moment for Agent Armstrong's heart to slow down after the phone call ended. This was his first major assignment. He was supposed to be the hero when this was done, and now he looked like an idiot.

Armstrong watched the agents discreetly positioned on the street and in nearby cars, and he figured Gadd and Vatch couldn't be too far away. Vatch, Armstrong thought, he'd never let me hear the end of it.

Then Armstrong decided he needed to create a plan of his own. He wasn't going to take the fall.

###

Armstrong worked himself up. He took quick breaths. In and out, he purposely hyperventilated. If he was going to do this, he needed to sell it.

Once his heart rate had spiked, Armstrong called Gadd.

She answered, and immediately started questioning him about the blown operation.

Armstrong cut her off.

"Collins knew. His attorney called me and said he knew about the agents. He knew about the media. He knew that Brea and Brent Krane were here to give a statement to the media. He knew everything."

Armstrong didn't stop. If anybody was going to take the blame, it was going to be Gadd and Vatch, not him. It didn't matter that what he was saying wasn't true. It could be true, and that was all that mattered.

"I told you he wouldn't show," Armstrong continued. "I told you he clearly said that it could only be me. He wanted to turn himself into me after the funeral, but you didn't listen. You didn't trust me. So now he decided that he wasn't going to show up."

Armstrong stopped, and waited. Gadd was silent, as his full verbal assault sunk in. Gadd was clearly running a series of mental calculations in her own head, figuring out how to deflect the blame. That was what a politician did.

"I trusted the advice of Agent Vatch." Gadd decided on her own defense. "He was more familiar with the case."

The response from Gadd delighted Armstrong. A small victory in the bureaucratic war. He waited another moment so that all blame was placed on Vatch, and then it was time for the victory lap.

"I might, however, be able to negotiate an alternative resolution." Armstrong paused. He held Gadd in suspense. "They won't like it, but I believe that it'll get the job done."

"And what is that?"

"Well," Armstrong said. "Collins and his attorney will meet us at headquarters, but no cameras and no big show. Somebody just gets them and escorts Collins and his attorney back into one of our conference rooms. Then we go from there."

"Fine," Gadd said. "Makes sense."

The phone call ended and Armstrong put the phone back in his pocket, smiling. The rookie agent came to play.

CHAPTER THIRTY ONE

A receptionist tapped Michael's shoulder. "Mr. Collins?" Michael opened his eyes and saw a young woman and a bulky man standing behind her. She was smiling, as trained, but the man was wound tight. He was ready to jump on Collins with the slightest provocation.

Collins smiled at them both, cool. "I wondered when you'd all be ready."

The bulky man didn't laugh. He stared at Collins, and then he looked at Quentin. "You two can follow me."

Michael Collins and Quentin stood up and followed the two back toward the front reception desk. There was a steel door. The man swiped a magnetic card through a slit in a black box that was fastened to the wall. A small green light flashed. The door's lock clicked open.

The receptionist returned to her desk, and the bulky man waved Quentin and Michael through and to the right. He led them down a hall to a large conference room.

"Make yourselves at home," he grimaced. "The others will be here soon."

Michael and Quentin walked over to the long wooden table and sat down as the bulky man closed the conference room door. Although he wasn't sure, Michael was confident that the

147

man did not return to his office. His bulky host was likely standing guard in the hallway, his gun ready, just in case.

Michael looked around.

It was a standard-issue government office, complete with an American flag and two gigantic, framed pictures of the President of the United States and the Attorney General of the United States. The two men stared down at him. The last time he had seen a conference room like this was with Jane Nance in Miami. They were there under different circumstances, but his feeling of uneasiness was the same.

Quentin saw what Michael was looking at and pointed.

"You like the artwork?" Quentin asked. "Not very creative, but certainly in the same spirit as the portraitist Chuck Close. Or maybe Chairman Mao, circa 1962?" Quentin's expression and tone softened when he saw that Michael wasn't playing along. "You doing okay?"

"Not sure," Michael shrugged.

They sat in silence for a few more minutes, and then Michael turned to Quentin.

"You think I'm doing the right thing?"

Quentin thought about prison. It was a place he never wanted to go, and a place where he was pretty sure Michael was headed.

"You're doing the brave thing."

"That's not what I asked," Michael said. "But it was a good dodge."

Agent Armstrong and United States Attorney Brenda Gadd arrived about thirty minutes later. Michael noticed that Agent Vatch wasn't with them, which made him as happy as he could be under the circumstances. But he knew that Vatch was somewhere nearby.

There wasn't any small talk or introductions. Neither Armstrong nor Gadd sat down.

It was obvious to Michael what was coming, although he had, up until that moment, held out some delusional hope that he would ultimately walk away.

Armstrong placed a black digital recorder on the table and pressed the button on its side. Numbers appeared on the recorder's small gray screen, counting the seconds.

"Michael Collins, I am now serving you with an indictment and placing you under arrest," Armstrong handed a small stack of papers to Michael.

Michael closed his eyes.

He let the words wash over him as he pictured himself back at Hut No. 7, a paperback in one hand and a Corona in the other.

"You have the right to remain silent," Armstrong continued with the speech. He knew that Michael knew his rights and did not need the recitation, but it was required. It was part of the dance. "Anything you say can and will be used against you in a court of law. You also have the right to an attorney. If you cannot afford an attorney, one will be appointed to you."

Agent Armstrong paused. "Mr. Collins, do you understand these rights?"

Michael opened his eyes and nodded his head. "I do."

"Would you like to waive your right to be silent and speak to us today?"

Michael looked at Quentin, and then looked back at Agent Armstrong. "No, I do not." Michael attempted to muster a brave voice.

"As you know, I have an attorney and invoke my right to silence and to an attorney."

Agent Armstrong nodded.

"Very well." He looked at Brenda Gadd. It was as they both had expected.

Agent Armstrong then picked the digital recorder off of the conference room table and turned it off. The numbers that had been counting the length of the recording stopped, frozen.

Armstrong put the device in his pocket and asked Michael to stand up.

After Michael pushed his chair away from the table and stood, Armstrong put his hand on Michael's shoulder. Armstrong gently turned Michael around.

"Please place your hands behind your back."

A cold chill ran up Michael's spine. A sickness settled over him as he complied with the request.

"Are the handcuffs really necessary?" Quentin asked, but his question was ignored.

Agent Armstrong tightened the cuffs. He led Michael out of the conference room and down the hallway. In the distance, Michael saw a freight elevator next to an emergency exit. That was where they were headed.

Quentin started to follow behind, but Gadd told him that he couldn't.

"You can meet Mr. Collins at the federal courthouse where he'll make his first appearance," she said.

Gadd pointed in the direction of the reception desk.

"I'll see you out to the front door. It's sort of a maze in here."

Silently, Michael and Armstrong continued by themselves. They walked down the hallway until they reached the elevator. They stopped and Agent Armstrong pressed the button. Behind the heavy elevator doors, its mechanicals hummed.

"This is a beautiful sight."

Michael didn't turn around. He knew who it was, and he wasn't going to take the bait.

"Come on," Vatch said. "Cat got your tongue? I wanted to take a moment to reminisce about all the good times we —"

Agent Armstrong interrupted. "I think Ms. Gadd was clear that I'm handling the transport."

"Hear that, Mr. Collins?" Vatch hissed. "Looks like you might've made a friend."

"I think that's enough." Armstrong pressed the elevator button, again, hoping that it would arrive a little faster. A second passed that seemed like an eternity, and then the elevator bell rang.

"I'd watch your back, Armstrong," Vatch said as the elevator door opened. "You're playing out of your league, here."

Armstrong and Collins went inside the elevator. Armstrong pressed the button for the basement, and the doors started to close. Michael thought that would be the end, but Vatch couldn't resist one more shot.

"And Collins," Vatch's voice rose. "I correct myself. Armstrong's not your friend. You haven't got any friends anymore." His tongue flicked. "Remember that while you sit in jail. I give your girlfriend two days before she flips."

CHAPTER THIRTY TWO

Michael sat in the basement holding cell of the federal courthouse, imagining a different life. He could have continued at Wabash, Kramer and Moore. He could have made partner. He could have married a woman that was content to live in a big house, take care of a few kids, and spend his money while he was working seventy or eighty hours a week. In other words, he could have been just like the thousands of other depressed, unhealthy, workaholic lawyers who populate the outer-ring suburbs of every major metropolitan area in the country.

That could have been his life, Michael thought, could have been.

For the first time, Michael actually wanted to be a schlub. It sounded nice, driving into the office at five in the morning to avoid traffic and avoid any interaction with the family and their problems. It seemed to be a far better alternative to his current surroundings.

Michael looked around the dark room. It was gray cinderblock. Metal benches were bolted to the floor around the perimeter. Large fluorescent lights hung down from the ceiling, but still too high to reach.

There were about twenty people waiting to be processed. Michael stood off to the side. Nobody in the room talked. They just stared at a large, flat-screen monitor bolted on the wall. The screen had the time, date, and a list of three names. It dictated who needed to be transported up to the courtroom and in what order.

Michael watched as three names disappeared, replaced by three new names. A half-hour passed, and the names changed again. This time, he was on the bottom of the list. It was his turn.

He walked to a white line painted on the floor underneath the monitor. Since he was the last name on the list, Michael lined up behind two other men in custody. The elevator doors opened, and the man at the front of the line was led inside. The doors slid shut, and he disappeared.

Five minutes later, the elevator returned. The second man was led inside and disappeared up the shaft.

Eventually it was Michael's turn.

The elevator doors opened. Michael stepped inside the polished metal box, and the U.S. Marshal instructed Michael to stand with his back against the wall. Then the U.S. Marshal turned a key and pressed a button.

The doors closed.

As the elevator moved upward, Michael saw his reflection in the stainless steel. He almost didn't recognize himself. Wearing an orange jumpsuit and his hands cuffed behind his back, Michael stared at the image. He was different now. He looked like a criminal.

###

A door opened. Michael was escorted out of the small, back holding room on the tenth floor and into the courtroom. The benches in the back were full. Michael scanned the room for Andie's face. She had to be here, thought Michael, starting to panic when he didn't see her.

He walked toward Quentin and stopped, still scanning the crowd.

"Mr. Collins," The judge coughed. "The important stuff is happening up here."

Quentin put his hand on Michael's shoulder.

"You have to look at the judge, Michael."

Michael nodded, and, as he turned, Michael saw Andie and Kermit in the far back corner of the room. The sight of them made Michael feel better, although he didn't know why.

"May we now note our appearances for the record?" The magistrate judge leaned forward, writing down the names of the various attorneys as they introduced themselves. Writing down the names was simply a habit. It served no discernible purpose. All of the appearances would be recorded by the court reporter, and they were also simultaneously entered into the court's computer system by a court clerk. But it made the judge feel like he was in control, so writing the names down was just something that he did.

The magistrate judge wasn't going to handle Michael's case. The trial would be assigned to a Federal District Court Judge. The magistrate, one step lower in the judicial hierarchy, was simply processing the initial appearances and hearing preliminary arguments.

"Have you received a copy of the complaint and indictment?" The judge peered at Quentin over a pair of thick glasses that rested on the tip of his nose. The glasses looked like they were purchased in 1978. They were so out of style that they were now back in style.

"We have, Your Honor." Quentin handed Michael a packet of paper. "Let the record reflect that I've handed my client another copy of the complaint and the indictment, and we waive a formal reading of the complaint and charges."

The judge nodded. Nobody ever asked the court to read the complaint in its entirety and on the record. In fact, if a defense attorney did, their client would pay dearly for wasting the judge's time.

"Very well." The magistrate judge turned to the prosecutor. "As for release pending trial?"

"Yes, Your Honor." United States Attorney Brenda Gadd stood. Usually these preliminary hearings were handled by a fairly low-level Assistant United States Attorney, but Michael Collins was a priority. Brenda Gadd wanted the judge to know that this was not an ordinary case, and so she came to the hearing herself.

"We believe that Mr. Collins is a flight risk." Brenda Gadd looked over at Michael Collins. Her eyes narrowed, making it clear that she had no empathy for him, and then she looked back at the judge.

Once upon a time, she was considering a run for the United States Senate. Her arrest and prosecution of Michael Collins nearly five years ago was going to show how tough she was on white-collar criminals, especially lawyers (who very few voters held in high esteem). But Michael Collins had evaded arrest and prosecution. Her nascent dreams of being Senator Brenda Gadd faded away. She'd never forgiven him, and perhaps she was also looking for a political comeback.

"He has no permanent residence in New York. He has no family that we are aware of, and he has been living abroad for

NO TIME TO HIDE | 157

several years. Therefore, we're asking that this hearing be continued for three days to allow for the defendant to be interviewed by pre-trial services and evaluated."

The magistrate judge laughed, leaning back in his seat.

"Evaluated? You've been investigating this case for years,
what's left to evaluate?"

Gadd was used to the give and take, and the judge's sarcasm didn't rattle her.

"I think it's appropriate." Gadd paused and looked down, as if
carefully considering the judge's concern. "Of course, we have
a lot of information regarding Defendant Collins, but the ordinary procedure is to go through a pre-trial services interview."

A pre-trial services interview would also give her a little free
discovery, an opportunity to probe into Michael's life.

The judge turned to Quentin. "Mr. Robinson?"

Quentin looked at Michael, not quite sure how to read the
magistrate judge's mood. He then looked at the judge. He said,
"I'd also like a little more time to prepare for the argument as
well, Your Honor. Mr. Collins does have a house that he is rent-
ing in New York and he turned himself in. That shows stability
and a willingness to appear at all court hearings, which will be
verified and assuage any concerns that the court may have
about my client."

"Very well." The judge turned to the clerk. "Set a hearing for
three days. The defendant shall cooperate with the PTI."

The judge wrote the information down on his notepad. The
hearing was over within minutes. Paper shuffled.

Brenda Gadd gathered her things and left. Michael stood still
as Quentin put his hand on Michael's shoulder. Quentin whispered something in Michael's ear, but Michael was in a fog.

His first court appearance was over. There was no drama. There were no surprises. He was just another widget being processed through the law factory.

Michael bowed his head, and started walking back to the transport elevator.

Reality came.

He wasn't going home this time, Michael thought, he was going to spend his first night in jail.

CHAPTER THIRTY THREE

It was a shock to see him. The crowd raged when Michael Collins had emerged from the side door of the courtroom. It took everything for Brent Krane to sit still. He wanted to scream out. He wanted to run down the aisle. He wanted to attack.

When the hearing finally ended and Michael Collins was led back into custody, Brent remained seated. He sat motionless, staring at the ground.

When Michael Collins had not shown up at the funeral, Brent Krane rode high. Collins' absence was confirmation that he was dead. He chided the crowd for its lack of faith.

Now the new information swirled, kicking the crowd into a frenzy.

"Let's go." Tad Garvin tapped Brent Krane on the shoulder. "I want to catch Brenda Gadd before she leaves."

Brent Krane looked up. Garvin and his sister stood above him. Brea gave him a look of pity, and then they both turned and walked toward the exit.

Brent Krane waited a second, then followed.

In the hallway, Garvin gestured at the U.S. Attorney.

"Ms. Gadd, a moment?" Garvin's voice was authoritative. He took a half-dozen quick steps to close the distance.

The United States Attorney lowered her shoulders at the sound of Garvin's voice. It was bad enough that she had been forced to handle an initial criminal hearing, now she had to help an overpriced attorney pad his legal bill.

"Yes," Gadd turned, forcing a smile. "How are you?"

"Fine," Garvin extended his soft, manicured hand. The two shook, and then Garvin gestured to his clients. "As you know, this is Brea Krane and back there is her brother Brent. The victim's children."

"Yes," Gadd nodded. She had a difficult time considering Joshua Krane a victim. Krane was a thief that was killed and then robbed by another thief. Cops often called such situations a "two-fer," as in getting two crooks for the price of one.

"Thank you for coming to the hearing today," Gadd checked her watch, suggesting that she was late for a meeting. "It will be especially important for you to be at the trial," she said to Brea Krane. "The judge and the jury need to see you and know you."

"About that," Garvin interrupted. "I was a little surprised that you didn't ask for Michael Collins to be held today without further evaluation. I have to admit that I agreed with the judge. You've had plenty of time. In private practice, a client would be furious about the delays." Arrogance oozed from Garvin. "I didn't see any reason for a pre-trial investigation. It's obvious that he should be held. And we're just wasting resources by having him submit to some questionnaire —"

Gadd held out her hand. She had to be polite, but she didn't need to be second-guessed by a rich lawyer who had never gone to trial in his life.

"It's standard procedure."

"I know," Garvin said, even though he knew very little about criminal law. His expertise focused more on wealthy people buying and selling things from other wealthy people, and then suing when things went bad. "But it seems like this case is not very standard. It's a very important case to me and my client."

Gadd didn't raise her voice, but she was the United States Attorney for New York and she was done. The conversation was over.

"I agree that this case is important, which is why I handled this hearing myself instead of sending a deputy or an assistant to court." Gadd paused, but it was clear that she did not want anybody to respond. "The pre-trial assessment will give me some free discovery about Michael Collins, box him into a narrative early in the case, and eliminate issues for appeal. A pre-trial investigation will illustrate to any appellate court that this magistrate judge's decision to hold Collins was not arbitrary and capricious, which, as you know, Mr. Garvin, is the standard of review."

The dig sent Garvin a message and he backed down.

"Very well. We'll see you at the next —"

Brent Krane interrupted. "Where's he staying?"

Brea shot her brother a look of concern. She stepped forward, between her brother and Brenda Gadd.

"Thank you," Brea extended her hand to Gadd, ending the hallway conversation and preventing her brother from saying anything further.

"No," Brent said. "We're not done." He tried to move around his sister. The crowd encouraged him to keep pushing. "Is that true? He's rented a house in New York. Did you know that? Nobody had said anything about a house. Where is it? Where is he staying? I'm supposed to be kept informed. That's what you promised us."

Gadd, somewhat startled by the new interrogation, took Brea's hand and shook it, and decided to simply ignore Brea's brother.

"It was a pleasure seeing you again. All of the information about Mr. Collins should be available in the PTI report. I'll make sure Mr. Garvin receives a copy."

Gadd turned and walked away.

Brent started to protest, but Brea pulled him aside.

"You need to shut up."

"Get your hands off me," Brent pushed away from her.

"I told you to cool it," Brea looked back down the hallway.

"I just want to know."

"Why?" Brea lowered her voice and continued in a whisper. "So you can light it on fire?"

CHAPTER THIRTY FOUR

The chubby prison bureaucrat placed a small white card in front of Michael.

"This is your number." She pointed at the number printed on the card. "It will be your number for as long as you are in the custody of the Federal Bureau of Prisons. It's critical that your attorney, family and friends have this number and include this number on all correspondence to you."

Michael adjusted himself, trying to find a comfortable position.

The chair, however, was not built for comfort. The chair was manufactured to be indestructible.

Michael tried a different position, and noticed that the table as well as all of the other furniture in the Metropolitan Detention Center's intake room appeared to be designed by Soviet utilitarians.

After two other failed attempts, Michael gave up. He sat as upright as he could without his legs going numb, and continued listening to the orientation speech.

The Metropolitan Detention Center was called the MDC. If somebody called it the Metropolitan Detention Center, that person would receive nothing but blank stares. The government was addicted to acronyms. It was the language of the machine, and being indecipherable to the common man or woman vested the operators of the machine with power, which the chubby bureaucrat with rosy cheeks clearly enjoyed.

He was informed that the MDC held men and women awaiting trial in the federal court system in New York. Therefore, theoretically, everybody who resided at the MDC was "innocent until proven guilty." She stressed the words, "in theory."

For Michael's safety, however, she informed him that the MDC was operated as if all detainees were guilty.

"For your safety," she smiled to emphasize the point. "Everything is done for your safety and to ensure you get to your court appearances in a timely manner." She winked, and Michael half expected a bell to ring and one of her teeth to sparkle like a toothpaste commercial.

"You should further note that all newspapers, magazines and books must come directly from the publisher, a book store, or a book club. You can have no more than five books or ten magazines at one time."

Michael nodded his head, hoping the orientation would soon end.

"All incoming mail is opened and inspected for contraband. Contraband includes items that are deemed a nuisance by the Federal Bureau of Prisons including: postage stamps, unsigned greeting cards, musical greeting cards, nude personal photographs, and plastic novelty items of a sexual nature." The woman blushed at the mention of the last item. "You wouldn't believe some of the things that we've confiscated."

"I understand." Michael nodded, thinking that Kermit had about an eighty percent chance of sending him something that violated the plastic novelty rule.

"Visiting hours are from 8:00 a.m. to 4:45 p.m., and you are allowed one brief hug and kiss at the beginning of the visit and one at the end. By brief, I mean very brief. The guards do not allow make-out sessions in here, and, if you violate that rule, the visit will be ended and you may lose visitation privileges. Further, all phone calls are monitored and recorded except phone calls to and from your attorney. If you wish to speak to your attorney, you must make those arrangements with the MDC administration." She paused. "Do you understand that?"

"I do," Michael closed his eyes. A weight pressed down on him. Michael felt himself falling into a depression that he figured would only get worse.

"Now, as for personal information," The bureaucrat removed a piece of paper from a folder. "I'll just fill out this section on race and gender." She checked the boxes for Caucasian and male, and then looked back up at Michael. "Now, how about your age?"

Michael told her his age, and then told her his birth date and place of birth.

"Last level of education completed? High school diploma, GED ..."

"Juris Doctorate from Columbia School of Law."

The woman started to write, but then paused before continuing. "Seriously?"

"With highest honors," Michael said. "Seriously."

The guard walked a few steps behind Michael down a hallway. The hallway was gray polished concrete. One side of the hallway was solid cinderblock with no windows. The other side of the hallway had four doors, spaced thirty yards apart. There was one door for each "pod."

When Michael was halfway down the hall, the guard told him that they were getting close.

"Pod 3. It'll be the next door. When we get there, press the button and look up at the camera. Then, when the buzzer sounds, you can proceed inside."

Michael followed the instructions. He pressed the intercom button, and after a moment, the large magnetic locks within the door buzzed and released.

Michael opened the door. He had expected to walk into another hallway or a large room. Instead, he walked into a small space. It was six feet by six feet.

One wall had a door marked with a large "3". The other wall was half cinderblock and half bulletproof glass. A guard sat at a desk on the other side of the glass. He was surrounded by security monitors, watching as the screens flashed from one camera view to another. The monitors showed what was happening in the hallway, various parts of the pod, including the individual cells, and, the monitors also showed a picture of Michael standing in the small room looking at the monitors. Everything was being recorded.

"This is the on-duty guard for Pod 3." Michael was told by his escort. "There are another two inside. This pod holds approximately twenty men. The door to the pod will not open until the door to the hallway is closed and secure or vice versa. Nobody, including the guards within Pod 3, have the ability to open these doors. Only the on-duty guard in the control room has that authority."

The guard stopped and thought for a moment.

"I'm telling you this, because I tell everybody this. In a few hours you'll start thinking about escaping from here, and I figure it's better if you have the facts and don't try anything stupid."

Michael nodded, although he believed that the guard's estimate as to when an individual starts thinking about escape was wrong. Michael had started thinking about escaping the moment he stepped foot in the MDC.

The guard continued. "If, however, the control room for Pod 3 is breached, which has never happened, there is a master control room located elsewhere. From the master control room, everything can be shut down."

With that final piece of information and the hallway door locked, the on-duty guard in the bulletproof room pressed a button. The Pod 3 door clicked and buzzed.

His escort pulled it open and they walked inside.

Pod 3 was a "U" shape. In the middle, there was an open area with metal tables and built-in benches bolted to the rubber floor.

"This is where you eat. This is where you play." The guard pointed at the tables. Men were sitting at the tables dealing cards and reading.

"Every time we move people, it's a risk for fights, escape or misbehavior. So there is no cafeteria in the MDC. The food is made and brought to the pod, and then everything is taken away. Once a day, smaller groups are allowed to go outside for recreation, but it is through that door to the yard." The guard pointed at a single metal door on the other side of the room.

Then he led Michael to a desk where one of the two internal guards sat. Michael presumed the other internal guard was up and patrolling the pod.

"We've got a new one."

The man at the desk looked Michael over, nodded, and then handed Michael a stack of bedding.

"This is for you. You're in 9-A. Welcome to the fish bowl."

Michael put the bedding under his arm, and he was led over to his cell. As he walked, Michael felt the eyes on him. Everybody was evaluating him. Was he weak or strong? They needed to know whether he was smart or dumb, scared or cocky, sane or insane.

It was a closed environment. Although there was calm, it was false. They were twenty men in a locked room. If a fight or riot broke out, people needed to know where they were in the pecking order. They needed to pick their friends wisely.

Michael thought about this, and then he decided that he should start figuring out the same thing.

CHAPTER THIRTY FIVE

The three of them sat on a bench in Saint Mary's Park. It was a dark, linear park. Sunlight only lit the playground in the early morning. The rest of the day, the park was covered in shadow from the large concrete train bridge directly above it. The bridge gave the park a disorienting feel, as though somebody put the basketball courts and playground equipment there without permission.

"You order the torpedo?" Kermit examined a sandwich wrapped in waxed paper.

Quentin nodded, and took the sandwich from Kermit.

"This beauty looks like mine, so this must be yours." Kermit handed the turkey and Swiss to Andie.

They ate in silence as the trains rumbled above them.

When Kermit finished, he crumpled the paper and dirty napkin. Then he got up and tossed his garbage into a nearby trash can.

"Nobody likes a litter bug, yo." Kermit came back toward the bench, but he didn't sit down. "Got a bad vibration from that hearing this morning, Q." Kermit started swinging his arms, doing some ballistic stretches as if he were a swimmer about to enter the pool. "What's the next step? How you gonna free the bird?"

Quentin took the final bite of his sandwich, chewed and swallowed, figuring out how to answer.

"Listen, guys. I have to be straight with you." Quentin looked around, ensuring that nobody else was nearby.

"Michael is in a terrible place. I know he has a history of getting out of tough jams, but ..." Quentin shook his head. "You have to understand that I don't have a magic bullet. I'm going to fight for him, don't get me wrong. It's just ..." Quentin paused, trying to phrase it delicately. "It's just that Michael may be better taking a plea deal. That's my honest analysis. I just don't understand how we're going to win at trial."

"Michael's got a plan," Andie said, thinking about Brea Krane. "Just trust him."

"Well, he hasn't told me the plan." Quentin had an edge to his voice, a bit of annoyance. "I've been reviewing the government's file. The evidence is overwhelming."

Andie shook her head.

"Just take it to trial." She got up off of the bench. "Let's get back to work."

The three walked down Nelson Street and cut over toward the rental via Clinton. Quentin scrolled through an email on his iPhone, and his shoulders slumped a little as he saw ten emails from Brenda Gadd. The subject line stated that there were more discovery disclosures. The email attachments were huge.

"Looks like I need somebody to help review and organize documents." Quentin sounded defeated. "The U.S. Attorney's Office sent me a bunch of zip files. I'm afraid they're so big that they're going to crash my computer."

"I can do it," Andie said as they turned the corner. "Got nothing else to do." Then she saw him. He was about a block away. "You expecting anybody?"

Brent Krane stood in front of the brownstone with a brick paver in his hand, trembling. He had taken it out of the neighbor's tiny, front garden to quiet the crowd. He didn't want to do anything extreme. After checking the Court's public computer terminal, he just wanted to see the place where Michael Collin's attorney was working. When the attorney entered a certificate of representation, this was the address listed. When Brent had arrived, he realized this was also the place where all of them were living.

Now he didn't know what to do.

Of course the voices wanted to light it on fire, but he convinced them that was foolish. Then they wanted him to hide and wait, but he wasn't prepared for a fight. He didn't have a knife, and he was still working on the gun.

Then he had seen the pavers. Brent held one in his hand. Perhaps the sound of shattered glass would quiet the crowd. He was tired of fighting them. He needed sleep, but they wouldn't allow it. He needed peace, but they kept on.

Brent cocked his arm back, getting ready to throw the paver through the brownstone's front window.

That's when Brent saw them. They were about a half block away, and it looked like the weird guy with dreadlocks was running toward him.

Brent hesitated, conflicted. It would only take a second to throw, but he didn't have a second.

###

Kermit was in a full sprint. "Hey!" was all he could get out.

The skinny white dude dropped the brick, turned, ran toward the car, opened the door, and jumped inside.

Kermit got to the vehicle just as it pulled away. All he could do was slap the back window, and shout.

He watched it speed down the street. Kermit read the license plate, repeating the letters and numbers over and over.

Soon Andie and Quentin caught up.

"You get the license plate number?" Andie asked.

Kermit nodded his head, continuing to repeat the letters and numbers.

"Good." Quentin nodded. "I got the whole thing recorded." He smiled and held up his iPhone. "Technology is pretty cool."

CHAPTER THIRTY SIX

B rea Krane watched the whole scene play out from the safety of her white SUV parked around the corner. After meeting with Tad Garvin, she figured that she needed to keep a better eye on her brother. She figured that he would do something stupid. It was a safe assumption.

She picked up her cell phone once her brother had sped away. Brea pressed a button.

Tad Garvin's number appeared on the screen and the phone started to dial. A few rings, and Tad answered.

"My brother is a psychopath," Brea said as she shifted her SUV into gear and started driving back to her condominium.

Garvin laughed. "What did he do now?"

"Almost threw a brick through the window of where Collins was staying."

"Anybody see him?"

"Me."

"Anybody else?"

"The lawyer and the other two. The hippie almost caught him, but Brent got away." Brea stopped at a light, waited, and then continued.

"But Brent didn't actually throw the brick."

"That's right."

173

"Then it shouldn't be too big a problem. No actual damage to property, and it's not a crime to think about naughty stuff." Garvin paused. "Speaking of naughty stuff ..."

Brea rolled her eyes

"Are you getting frisky with me, old man?" Brea grimaced, pretending she was actually interested.

"What are you doing later?"

"I've got some stuff for work, but maybe we could meet." Brea turned. Traffic wasn't too bad for mid-afternoon. "What are you thinking?"

Garvin was thinking about a lot of things, most of which could not be spoken over the phone. "Let me see if I can blow off the wife with an excuse, and I'll let you know."

"Sounds good." Brea stopped the car in front of her building. The valet opened her door, and Brea got out. She walked to the condo's front door and a doorman opened it for her.

She walked through the marble lobby, underneath an ornate glass chandelier, and toward the elevator. Once inside, she swiped her card and the light for the twenty-third floor lit up.

Brea got out on her floor and walked down the hallway to her condo, swiped her magnetic card, again, at her door and waited for a green light. The black cell phone on the kitchen counter was already ringing. It wasn't a surprise.

Brea walked through the entryway into the main living area.

The cell phone stopped ringing for a few seconds, and then started again.

She tossed her purse on the couch and walked into the kitchen as the cheap disposable cell phone continued to rattle.

Brea picked up the phone and pressed a button.

"Hello." She smiled when she heard the voice of Andie Larone. "I thought you'd be calling."

CHAPTER THIRTY SEVEN

The beat cop wasn't a mover and shaker in the department. In fact, it was highly unlikely that he'd ever get promoted to sergeant, but he was okay with that. As long as he had enough seniority to avoid working the holidays, Officer Barts was fine with his position in life.

He liked people, especially if they bought him a cup of coffee or something from time to time, and respected the badge.

Vatch pushed a plate of hot, crispy, fresh-cut French fries toward Barts.

"Like I said before," Barts picked up three fries, dunked them in ketchup, and shoved them in his mouth. "We don't have anything to charge him with at the moment, but Anthony's name is coming up in more and more conversations."

"Conversations?"

Officer Barts nodded.

"You know." Barts shrugged. "Just talking. I ask who was at the party or who were you playing ball with and stuff like that, and Anthony's name is coming up more and more as trouble." Officer Barts took a sip of soda. "But he doesn't go by Anthony any more. His street name is Cards."

"Cards?" Vatch shook his head. The idea that the little boy who used to crawl through his window had a street name repulsed him. "So is he in?"

"In what?"

Vatch's eyes narrowed. He hated conversing with anybody, especially a law enforcement officer with minimal intelligence. Play nice, Vatch thought, you need him to be on your side.

"A gang," Vatch responded. "Is Anthony in a gang?"

Barts smiled. "It isn't like that anymore. Used to be we had the Bloods and Crips, maybe the Gangster Disciples or Vice Lords, and those were real criminal enterprises, like the mafia. They were all set up to sell crack, and there was a hierarchy with rules and order."

Barts waved at the waitress and lifted up his empty water glass.

"Now it isn't like that. We were too successful."

Vatch's slit of a mouth bent into a frown. "Too successful?"

Barts nodded, waiting as the waitress refilled his water from a large plastic pitcher and then went on to the next table.

"Exactly," he continued. "The police were too successful breaking up those gangs, and so now we got a mess. Instead of two or three big gangs, we got hundreds of them. Take any four kids, put 'em together, and they're now a gang. They come up with some stupid name for themselves, and that's it. No initiation. No leader. No rules. Just four thugs who like to smoke weed and steal stuff, sell the stuff to buy more weed, and then repeat." Barts ate a few more French fries. "Maybe they do something more violent, but living the lifestyle is more the goal than actually being a gangster."

Vatch raised his eyebrows. "So Anthony is in with this Spider person."

Barts laughed, again. "You don't get it." Barts dunked a fry in the ketchup. "There are no rules anymore." He ate the fry. "Not only are there hundreds of gangs, but kids are in three or four of them at the same time. Just depends on who's hanging out, who's partying, and whether somebody wants to shoot."

"You mean shoot other people?"

"Maybe. Doesn't matter." Barts shook his head. "It's all random. It's chaos out there. You're lucky you're in an office, man. Stuff makes sense in an office. On the streets, here in the hood, it's just wild."

CHAPTER THIRTY EIGHT

Michael didn't trust the phones. The government claimed that it didn't monitor or record the phones reserved for attorney-client communications, but he doubted it. "Safety" was an exception to every government policy related to privacy. It just took one civil servant to decide that somebody's safety was at risk, and the confidentiality was gone. In his case, Michael knew that civil servant's name was Agent Frank Vatch.

Michael wanted only in-person conversations. Those were the safest, even though it made the MDC a lonelier place that got lonelier every minute.

He'd been on self-imposed solitary confinement since his arrival. Although the individual cell doors didn't close until after the evening head-count, Michael wasn't in the mood to make friends. He didn't wander around Pod 3. He didn't play board games or explore the MDC's small library. He didn't go outside to the yard. Michael only came out of his cell for meals.

One of the MDC's psychologists stopped by to see if he was depressed or whether she should place him on a suicide watch, but Michael declined her services.

He didn't think he was depressed, which was likely what a depressed person would think, and Michael had told the psychologist that he'd be more social after the hearing. He was just waiting it out.

Michael had one more day. The custody hearing was scheduled for 9:00 am, and Michael hoped that the judge would release him.

The court could make Michael surrender his passports. Michael could be placed under house arrest with an ankle bracelet. Hell, Michael thought, he'd agree to the judge implanting a microchip in his shoulder, if it'd get him out.

In the meantime, Michael sat in the cell for hours.

He thought about the money being spent to keep him caged. Then, he thought about all the money wasted on the people around him.

The United States had the highest incarceration rate of any country in the civilized world. Yet it was still one of the most violent. The money spent on prisons and jails could be spent on schools and roads, but America was a land of immediacy. Investing in schools and roads provided little immediate pleasure, Michael thought, locking up a crook was more fun.

He took a deep breath and closed his eyes.

Then he felt shame and guilt. Who was he kidding? He deserved to be locked up.

When he was still the highest-billing associate at Wabash, Kramer, and Moore, Michael remembered reading a law review article about white-collar criminals like him. Two psychiatrists interviewed three hundred white-collar criminals residing in various federal prisons throughout the United States. The psychiatrists created a personality profile, listing the most common traits.

Michael thought about the list and the three most common traits.

The first one was that white-collar prisoners believed that they were the focus of government harassment and that his or her prosecution had been politically motivated or a personal vendetta. The second trait was that none of the white-collar criminals believed that they had actually committed a real crime or that they were real criminals, like a murderer. The third trait was that they were narcissists. Deep down, they all believed that they were the smartest people in the room. They believed they were smarter than their attorney, smarter than the investigators, smarter than the judge. They had it all figured out. They believed that they had found a loophole to avoid any consequences for their actions. They believed that they deserved the money that had been stolen. They were entitled to it.

Check. Check. Check.

How could he be so self-righteous about education and incarceration rates when he had rolls of gold coins in a dry box, fake passports, a history of evading investigators, and had just snuck across the United States border from Mexico in the past week?

Michael sighed.

Maybe I am depressed, he thought. Maybe I should be on a suicide watch.

A guard knocked on Michael's door. "Visitor."

The word lifted Michael's spirits. He opened his eyes. Michael sat up and got out of his cot, and then followed the guard out of his cell. They walked through the common area, and through the series of secure doors leading out of Pod 3.

As they walked down the hallway to a door, Michael studied everything. He tried to remember the route. He noted the cameras and the location of the guards. Michael realized that most of the doors that they had walked by were unmarked, probably to make escape more difficult and the MDC's layout more confusing.

Escape would be hard, thought Michael, probably impossible.

They stopped.

The guard that had escorted him from Pod 3 pressed an intercom button. They both looked up at a small camera above the door. They waited, and were buzzed inside another small room a few seconds later.

A second guard sat behind a glass window surrounded by security monitors. The second guard waited for the door to the hallway to close and lock, and then he buzzed Michael inside the visitation room through a second door. As stated during his orientation, neither door could be open at the same time, another obstacle for escape.

Michael walked into the visitation room. It was an open area with four tables spaced evenly apart. It was brightly lit, but sterile. There were no pictures on the wall. There were no lamps or wall sconces. There were no magazines or pencils. In short, there was nothing that could easily become a weapon.

The guard led Michael across the room to a door with a small window near the top. It was a private room for attorney-client conferences. The various detainees that were visiting in the public area looked at Michael with jealousy. They wanted a private room too, but for other reasons.

The guard opened the door and pointed inside. "Have a seat."

Quentin arrived a few minutes later. "How you holding up?"

Michael shrugged. "How are you holding up?"

Quentin shook his head. "It's been interesting." Then he told Michael about the person with a brick in front of their rental and the offer from United States Attorney Brenda Gadd.

CHAPTER THIRTY NINE

United States Attorney Brenda Gadd had offered Michael twenty years if he pled guilty to three counts of wire fraud. With good time, Michael would be released shortly before his sixtieth birthday. He'd come back into the world as an old man.

"That doesn't sound like much of a deal."

Quentin bowed his head, because he knew Michael was right. "Well, they're confident. They've already put the work into the case, so a plea doesn't really save them many resources or time at this point," Quentin said. "Plus they're pissed at you. You've made them look like idiots for a long time."

"Any upside?"

"It's not fifty years, so you'll be able to walk out of prison." When Michael didn't laugh, Quentin added. "And they're guaranteeing you a spot at Sherrod Pines." Sherrod Pines was a white-collar country club comprised of six dorms and a lodge near Mount Mansfield in Vermont. There was no fence, a two mile walking-hiking path, and recently updated work-out facilities. The population were all convicted of non-violent crimes, like drugs or theft, or they were over the age of sixty.

"They usually don't negotiate placement." Quentin shrugged. "But I think this is a high enough priority that Gadd got personally involved with the Bureau of Prisons." When Michael didn't respond, Quentin filled the silence with another bad joke. "Are you worried about the cold winters in Maine or something?"

Michael smiled, allowing a little levity. "My blood has thinned considerably over the years." He knew Quentin was in a tough spot. He was the deliverer of bad news.

Quentin didn't push Michael on the plea deal any further. Instead, he talked about the massive document dump that the government had just performed on him. Then they talked about the custody review hearing and Quentin prepared Michael for the pre-trial services interview.

"Anything else?" Michael asked.

"Just that nut in front of the rental."

"A nut?"

Quentin laughed. "A nut with a rock. No worries though, Kermit was there to chase him off."

"Weird."

"What's weird, Kermit or the guy with the rock?"

"Both," Michael said, "but I was referring mostly to the visitor."

"I got it on video. Kermit got the license plate number. I was going to call the cops after talking with you about it. Figure out who it was."

"What does Andie think?"

"She said she didn't want us to make any calls until I talked to you."

Michael nodded, thinking. He thought about Brea Krane and her brother.

"Just call the non-emergency number and report the suspicious activity. Don't tell them about the license plate and video."

"Why?"

Michael thought about her brother and the fire at the Sunset.

"Just so that there's documentation, but not too much documentation."

Quentin seemed puzzled, but he wasn't going to argue. Then he checked his watch. Michael knew that Quentin needed to leave, but Michael didn't want him to go. Quentin sensed that, so they just sat together for a few more minutes. Then Michael stood up.

"You should head out." Michael held out his hand. "Thanks for doing this."

Quentin stood and shook Michael's hand. "You're getting pretty formal on me now."

"You took a big risk taking the case."

Quentin shook off the compliment. "The People's Legal Center will always be there." He picked up his notepad and put the notepad and various other papers back into his briefcase. "And if they don't take me back, there are always more poor people needing legal advice than lawyers, so I've got a natural client-base of people who can't afford to pay me anything."

Michael nodded. "It's a great business model."

As Quentin started to leave, Michael blurted a question. He felt uncomfortable the moment that it had been asked. "Is Andie coming tomorrow?"

"She is, and Kermit wants to say hello. He's got some new theories to offer you, something about neutrinos and sub-particles. He's going to come by during visiting hours to share." Quentin turned back toward the door, and then stopped, returning back to their initial conversation. "What should I tell them about the offer?"

Michael felt a wave of nausea run up from his stomach. He swallowed it back down. "I know you want me to take it."

Quentin shook his head. "I didn't say that."

"You didn't have to." Michael put his hands on his hips and looked up at the ceiling. He took a deep breath, and then looked back at Quentin. "It's good advice." Michael nodded. "If I were you, I'd advise me to take the deal, but ... I can't and I won't."

"You've got a secret plan?"

Michael took a deep breath. "Maybe."

CHAPTER FORTY

The days passed, and Michael returned to the group holding room in the basement of the federal courthouse. There were ten of them waiting to be processed this time, and it seemed to be a livelier group.

Four of the men stood off in the corner. They told stories, each trying to top the other with a tale of who had "partied the hardest" before their most recent arrests.

Michael sat on a metal bench that ran the length of the wall. He sat alone, watching the monitor for his name to appear on the list.

His interview with pre-trial services had gone well. Quentin had warned him about some of the questions, and so Michael had avoided any answers that may theoretically be used at trial to corroborate the prosecution's case against him. Now it was up to Quentin and the judge.

###

The elevator doors slid open. Michael walked through a smaller holding area, and then into the courtroom. The room was filled to capacity again, but Andie and Kermit were easy to spot this time. They sat in the front row.

Michael forced a smile while his stomach churned. Andie blew Michael a kiss.

He took his place next to Quentin, and the magistrate judge called the case and noted the appearances.

"Where we last left off," The judge peered down at Michael over his thick glasses. "We had a discussion regarding the status of Mr. Collins pending trial. The prosecution requested time to prepare as well as the defense, and so ..." The judge opened his hands, palms up, and extended them toward Quentin. "Let's hear your thoughts."

"Yes, Your Honor." Quentin looked at Michael, and then back at the judge. "My client poses no safety threat to the public. He is accused of theft, that is all. And, he obviously will make all court appearances because my client turned himself in." Quentin paused for emphasis, but he was careful not to pause too long. He didn't want to invite questions from the judge.

"He has rented a brownstone here in the city, and so everybody knows where he is staying. It seems like a good use of resources to allow him to be discharged from the MDC and be under house arrest pending the trial. We'd agree to electronic bracelet, independent monitoring, whatever the Court needs to feel confident in my client's continued participation in these proceedings."

The judge rolled his eyes. "It took you three days to come up with that?" He shook his head. "That's all information that we knew at the initial hearing. You're wasting my time." The judge stopped talking and pouted-out his bottom lip. He stared at Quentin, daring him to speak. When Quentin did not say another word, the magistrate judge continued.

"Your non-violent client also happened to have led law enforcement on a wild chase through the streets of New York City a few years ago. He struck an FBI agent in the face, breaking his nose. Why he was not charged, I haven't the faintest idea, and now — with his back against the wall — he turns himself in and expects to be released." The magistrate judge shook his head. "No, counselor. Your request for release pending trial is denied."

Realizing that the prosecution hadn't even made an argument, the magistrate judge looked at Brenda Gadd. "I assume you don't disagree with my decision."

Gadd stood. Her round, Mother Hubbard face was frozen, serious. She shook her head slowly, and decided to forego the speech that she had prepared. "No, I don't disagree with you, Your Honor." Gadd sat back down.

"Good." The magistrate judge nodded. "We'll place this on Judge Husk's trial calendar." The judge turned to the court clerk. "Call the next case."

Within seconds, Michael was back in the elevator. He was shocked by the swiftness of the proceeding. The total hearing lasted less than five minutes.

It was over.

Michael was going back to the MDC. He'd be there until trial.

Michael chided himself for thinking he actually had a chance at release. It was apparent that the whole thing was an unrealistic fantasy. Did Quentin know that it was all a show or did Quentin actually believe he had a chance? What was worse?

Michael had always found a way to escape, and now he was stuck. As the elevator doors slid shut, he saw his reflection again. He was nothing but a man standing in an orange jumpsuit.

His grand plan now didn't seem as clever as it once did. He had wrongly assumed he'd be free pending trial. He assumed he'd have time to check all of his accounts and find money that hadn't been frozen. He wrongly thought that he could personally negotiate with Brea Krane and orchestrate an ending. It was a stupid thought.

As the elevator sunk to the basement of the courthouse, Michael realized that this might be his life for the next twenty years. Kermit's plan of plastic surgery and a new resort in Brazil now didn't sound quite so bad, but it was too late.

He could only hope that Andie could handle it. He had no options. He had to trust her for the first time in his life.

PART TWO: PLANS

"Everybody's got plans … until they get hit."

---Mike Tyson

CHAPTER FORTY ONE

The West Side Line was an elevated railroad spur built in 1929. It was built because people and trains didn't mix too well in the early days of New York City. After numerous deaths, commuter trains were sunk into the ground, creating the city's subway system. Freight trains were raised above ground. The West Side Line was part of the original elevated freight train system, which was eventually abandoned about fifty years later.

The structure fell into disrepair. Connections to the spur had been dismantled. The empty platform stretched over the neighborhood for a little over a mile, then stopped. Train tracks to nowhere.

It was slated to be torn down, but the West Side Line escaped demolition due to a couple of neighborhood dreamers. It became New York's High Line Park. Its tracks were turned into walking trails. The garbage was removed. Trees were planted and sculptures were installed. Now Andie Larone wondered if Michael could make a similar escape and transformation.

She had almost sold him out, once. It was a desperate attempt to get herself out of jail, but despite her betrayal, Michael had kept fighting for her. He had saved her. Then she had the audacity to run after Michael had told her the truth about his past.

Andie never let go of her guilt. Maybe that's why she was here. Andie wanted them to be even. If their plan worked, she wouldn't owe Michael Collins anymore. Then perhaps they could just love one another again.

Andie checked her cell phone. She looked at the time, waiting.

She watched the joggers and the walkers. She watched a young woman sketch a planting of grasses, Liatris, and coneflowers. She waited some more, and eventually Brea Krane arrived.

Brea wore a pair of running shoes, yoga pants, and a sweatshirt. Her eyes were hidden behind a pair of large sunglasses. She sat down next to Andie, but didn't look at her. She fiddled with the volume of her iPhone and removed the buds from her ears. "Wait long?"

"Not too long." Andie looked at her, but Brea looked straight ahead. "How do I know you're not recording this?"

Brea shrugged. "About to ask you the same thing."

The question hung between them. Neither answered, and so Andie continued. "With Michael in jail until the trial, you're going to have to deal with me now."

Brea nodded. "Figured. How much do you know?"

"Some," Andie lied. She wanted to see if Brea had changed her offer. It was test.

"Well, it's pretty simple," Brea stood up and started stretching. She did it in a way that nobody who had a camera with a zoom could read her lips.

She was smart. Andie conceded that.

"I want money," Brea said. "The more money you give me, the more I help."

"Like what?" Andie played dumb.

"Like, I'm the victim's daughter. I'm consulted on any plea offers that Brenda Gadd makes to your boyfriend. I can influence them up or down, because the prosecutor — if there is a plea — has to tell the judge whether the victim's family is in agreement." Brea stood and started rolling her head side to side. "That little service is for the bargain basement price of $1 million."

"$1 million." Andie narrowed her eyes. "For that?"

"Could mean five or ten years less in prison, or maybe just one. How much is that worth? How much is a year of Michael's life worth to him and you?"

"I don't know." Andie shook her head. "I don't know if we have that sort of money."

"Well, you'd better find it." Brea was running out of patience. "I know he's got it. He has to." Then she leaned in closer. "For $50 million I become your witness."

"$50 million?" Andie looked away. "What can you say that would be worth $50 million?"

"That's the great thing about this offer," Brea said. "I will say whatever you want me to say. For example, I could swear under oath that it was all a set-up. That my father and Lowell Moore had your boyfriend framed. I can say that Agent Vatch is crazy and made it all up. I can say that my brother did it. I don't care."

Brea sat back down next to Andie Larone. She put her arm around Andie, then she whispered. "I don't care what I say. You tell me. Long as I get my money."

"I understand." Andie nodded. "In the meantime, it'd be nice if we got rid of your brother."

Brea nodded. "That's taken care of. Free of charge."

CHAPTER FORTY TWO

Brent Krane had made a realization. It was early in the morning. He had been up all night. Drugs and the crowd hadn't permitted the sleep to come, and so he had been forced to cut. He made a half-dozen cuts to the back of his leg, releasing the pressure inside himself. It mollified the crowd.

The silence was pure. Then the realization had come.

He sat on the couch in his little apartment, surrounded by filth. There was no future here. Beyond revenge, there was nothing he needed to accomplish. This reality had been there for a long time, but Brent hadn't put the pieces together. He hadn't drawn the necessary conclusion. But now it was so obvious.

The epiphany absolved him of worry.

The opinions of the crowd seemed less important.

He was simply going to do whatever he needed to do, and he knew that the crowd would understand. They would probably like it. They liked action.

Brent Krane decided that he was finish getting a gun. He'd fill out the forms. He'd wait as long as it took. And then, if they denied him, he'd try to buy it some other way or he'd steal it. He didn't care.

That was the realization. That was the epiphany: He didn't care. Brent Krane just wanted it all to end.

His sister told him that he needed to get out of the city. Brea said that Michael Collins and his friends knew about his trip to Mexico. She claimed that they got access to his passport file. He wasn't sure he believed it, but Brent didn't care anymore.

He wasn't going to fight her.

Brent decided he'd go to the beach rental in Montauk. If his sister was going pay for it, he'd humor her and get out of the filth for a few months. Then when the trial was going to start, he'd come back.

It wouldn't be hard, and the time away would give him a chance to plan for the end.

CHAPTER FORTY THREE

A gent Frank Vatch knew that the visit was coming. The government's dysfunction was well known and reported. The dysfunction started with the elected officials and then trickled down and through the bureaucracy.

Every federal agency had been squeezed, including law enforcement. They were looking to save money. Vatch had seen the boss work his way down the hall. He had visited each of the senior cogs in the bureaucratic machine and made them an offer that most couldn't refuse.

Now it was Vatch's turn.

The knock on the door was perfunctory.

Martin Nix was the Special Agent In Charge of the New York Field office. Vatch had been supervised by seven different special agents over the course of his career, and Vatch had discerned that there were only two types: gunners and caretakers. The gunners were young and ambitious. They came in from outside the New York Office with big ideas and a burning desire to be promoted to something better in Washington, D.C. The caretakers came in after the gunners. They cleaned up the mess, soothed the troops' ruffled feathers, and then retired a few years later.

Nix was a caretaker.

He came into Vatch's office. Nix sat down in the chair across from Vatch. Nix looked at Vatch, apologies in his eyes. "You know why I'm here."

Vatch nodded.

"Gotta do it." He looked up at the ceiling, as if the head of the FBI was watching him. "Orders."

"Well you're wasting your time." Vatch was short with him, but Vatch wasn't as rude to Nix as he was to his other colleagues. The fact that Nix was his boss didn't matter. Vatch didn't care much about his place on the organizational chart. Vatch simply appreciated Nix's management style, which was to leave him alone.

"Gotta do it." Nix repeated, and then put his hands on his knees. "Because of the cuts, every field office has a target that we have to meet. Rather than lay people off, I got the authorization to offer buy-outs to the old-timers."

"Get rid of the experienced investigators and leave everything to the rookies." Vatch shook his head. "Sounds like a plan that the politicians would love"

"Hey." Nix raised his hands. "Not here for a debate." Nix wasn't interested in a fight. He just needed to make his pitch and move on to the next office. "The offer is $30,000 in cash, and then full retirement benefits if you've got enough years of service. People with less years get the cash and maybe a little less benefits, but you have enough credit. You qualify for the full boat."

"A bribe?"

"We prefer to call the $30,000 an 'incentive.'"

"Well, I don't want it."

Nix stood. "Figured." He walked toward the door. "But you got some time to think." Nix shrugged his shoulders. "I'm taking the money. Then I'm taking my wife on a cruise, getting the hell out of New Jersey and kissing that damn commute good-bye." Nix paused at the door. He turned back. "Frank, you're an ass-hole, but give it a little more thought." Nix's eyes took in Frank Vatch's spartan office. "There's real life out there in the real world. Might be time to hang it up after bringing down Michael Collins."

Vatch shook his head. "Collins isn't down yet."

CHAPTER FORTY FOUR

Andie sat across from Michael at a small table in the corner of the visiting room. They held hands, and Michael told her about the boredom and routine of life in the MDC. Then Andie talked about their mutual friend.

"You know my cousin Nicole was in town."

"Yeah." Michael knew that Andie didn't have a cousin, Nicole. Andie didn't have any family. She grew up in foster care until she was old enough to run away. "How's she doing?"

"The same," Andie said. "She's always looking to get paid, but nobody's got any money."

"I thought you had that list of people that were looking for nannies or cooks or whatever."

"Maybe." Andie shrugged her shoulders. "Couldn't find it in my bag."

Michael shook his head. "I think it may have been put in my bag, because there wasn't much room in yours." He thought of the dry-box and the list of account numbers. "Go down the list with her. See if anybody's willing to hire her. Might get lucky."

"Really?"

"Might be a little something to keep her interested." Michael squeezed her hand. "Keep her busy." Then Michael stood up. Andie stood, too.

He wanted to touch her, caress her, but the rules didn't allow it. So he leaned in. He kissed her quick on the lips, and then whispered in her ear. "Don't trust Brea Krane. Play along. Give her a little money, if there is any. But stick with our other plan."

Andie pulled away. "Sounds good." She nodded.

CHAPTER FORTY FIVE

Michael lay flat on his back with his eyes open. The thin mattress was coated in thick plastic. The intent was to easily repel blood and other bodily fluids. The plastic crackled underneath him as he stared at the picture.

It was a black and white photograph of his namesake. The Irish revolutionary stared back down at him. It was out of the frame. Glass and wood weren't allowed. But the picture didn't violate any of the MDC's rules, so he was allowed to have it.

Michael thought about the days back in his mom's apartment in Boston, staring up at the picture of the Irish revolutionary, Michael John Collins. It had hung on the wall above the kitchen table. It was next to the pictures of John F. Kennedy and the Pope.

Michael loved the fight and the honor that the photograph represented. When life in the MDC became dark, the photograph provided him a little light. He just needed patience.

Michael Collins had a Constitutional right to a "speedy trial." It was a right derived from the Magna Carta; written in 1215, developed over time by English judges, and eventually enshrined in the Sixth Amendment to the United States Constitution. Various state courts interpreted the word "speedy" differently, but, in federal court, the definition of "speedy" was clear. The government had seventy days.

Seventy days, in the abstract, may have sounded fast, but the trial could not start quickly enough. Every day in Pod 3, Michael felt his spirit die a little bit.

He was being institutionalized. His routine never varied, and he wondered how he could survive if he was convicted. He'd be sentenced to at least twenty years.

The only thing that kept him going was the picture of the Irish revolutionary and the little, growing stack of paper near his bed.

PART THREE: TRIALS

"To survive it is often necessary to fight
and to fight you have to dirty yourself."
---George Orwell

CHAPTER FORTY SIX

It was remarkable how fast the city changed with the season. The pavement no longer sizzled. The air became easier to breathe. People became a little more relaxed. The collective sought to enjoy the final days in a park or a long lunch at a sidewalk cafe before winter came and the mood changed again.

Michael, however, could only experience it in the abstract. He only knew the seasons were changing by the calendar on his wall. Michael kept socializing to a minimum. The nature of the MDC meant that there was a constant shuffle of people. Accused men rotated through the MDC by the hundreds: intake, transfer, release, repeat.

Michael had watched the faces change every day for over two months, feeling more and more like a lifer each time a new face appeared or a familiar person disappeared.

Time passed slowly. Life fell into a routine. Every day Michael got up, ate breakfast, and then he spent the rest of the morning at one of the six computers in the MDC's library.

He'd then eat lunch, go to the small yard and run around the loop, regardless of whether it was raining or cold. Then he'd either go back to the library or meet with Andie, Kermit, or Quentin in the visitors room. After dinner, he printed.

There were no exceptions, especially with regard to the last activity of the day. He always printed after dinner. He needed to build the stack of paper in his cell.

There was usually an hour and a half between dinner and lights out. Michael used that time to print all of the Securities and Exchange Commission documents that he had found that day related to Joshua Krane and his various engineering and manufacturing companies. These were dense legal documents and mind-numbing financial disclosures, exactly what Michael was looking for.

There were thousands of them posted on the Securities and Exchange website. Michael knew that he wasn't going to get every document. But he was going to try.

In the beginning, library staff had found it amusing. After a week, however, they were concerned.

Michael used an inordinate amount of paper. The laser printer's toner cartridge had to be replaced, and Michael was blowing through the library's tiny budget for supplies.

During the second week, library staff had told Michael that he could not print any more documents. Michael politely complied, knowing that Quentin would intervene.

The next day Quentin informed the staff and the Director of the MDC that Michael had a constitutional right to participate in his own legal defense. Michael was a lawyer, and he was researching the charges against him as well as the man that he was accused of stealing from. The MDC wasn't persuaded.

Then Quentin offered a compromise that no government agency would ever turn down: Quentin offered to pay.

With an agreement that the MDC would send Quentin a bill every week for Michael's expenses, there was nothing more that they could do. No more interference.

Michael knew that the MDC guards and library staff wanted to see what he was printing. Michael knew that they were curious. But because it was for his legal defense, the documents were privileged. He had a right to confidentiality, and so the jail staff watched helplessly as Michael brought a new stack of papers from the library to his cell at the end of every day.

In the corner, by his bed, Michael put each new stack on top of the old. When the stack on the floor became ten to twelve inches high, Michael brought the paper to a meeting with Quentin.

Quentin then took them back to the rental, and Michael started a new stack.

It was tedious and repetitive, but it was Michael's only chance.

Although Michael used the Sixth Amendment to get the earliest possible trial date, his future actually depended on the Fifth Amendment.

The Fifth Amendment to the Constitution prohibited any criminal defendant from being put on trial twice for the same offense. It meant that if Michael and Quentin could get the jury to say two words — not guilty — he would never stand trial again.

Agent Vatch could do nothing. The government couldn't continue to prosecute him. There would be no second chances for Brenda Gadd. It was the rule that prohibited double jeopardy. The government cannot prosecute an individual twice for the same crimes or any crime alleged to have arisen from the same conduct.

The Founding Fathers, of whom Michael had grown quite fond during his time at the MDC, had been concerned about a tyrannical government. The only exception to the rule was when the jury could not agree on a verdict and a mistrial was declared.

Michael wasn't interested in a mistrial or a "hung jury." He wanted a unanimous "not guilty." Either his plan was going to work or it wasn't. He was betting everything.

He had made his choice. It was done. Michael pushed the doubts aside. He'd do whatever it took to get out. Whatever it took to be free. He wasn't going to play fair. The truth didn't matter. The truth was the government's problem, not his.

CHAPTER FORTY SEVEN

Michael looked at the clock on the far wall of the MDC's library. It was early afternoon. Quentin was scheduled to arrive in an hour and a half.

Michael glanced over at the librarians at the desk, and then at his computer screen. It was time to vary the routine, slightly.

He placed his notepad on the desk next to the keyboard. On the notepad, he had fifteen pages of handwritten notes. It was a legal document he had been thinking about for months.

Hundreds of times, he had written and re-written the document in his head. Michael had always resisting the urge to write it down. He feared that it would be discovered.

Then, finally, last night he had to put pen to paper.

He worked through the night. The language had to be exact. It needed to be worthy of the bright young associate attorney at Wabash, Kramer and Moore, which Michael John Collins once was.

Michael took a deep breath, and then clicked over to the computer's word processing program.

Although what he did in the library was supposed to be confidential, Michael didn't trust anybody. He wasn't going to save any drafts. He was just going to type, review, print, and delete, hoping that nobody would ever go to the trouble or expense of finding the clicks and keyboard strokes buried deep within the computer's hard-drive.

His freedom depended on this.

###

Michael read the document, looking for typos. He quietly read it aloud, making sure it flowed. He revised and then read the document again. It needed to be perfect. Michael looked up at the clock, and then back at the computer screen. He decided that it was time.

Michael pressed print.

The light on the laser printer flashed to yellow, and then to green as its little internal fan spun to life. The librarian looked over. She had gotten used to Michael's routine, and this was different. He didn't usually print during the day. Usually Michael only printed in the evening.

Michael met the librarian's eye and smiled. "Found a really good case today."

"Great," the librarian said. "We'll add it to your bill."

Michael watched as the printed sheets of paper rolled out of the printer. He gathered them, and read them one last time, looking for errors.

Satisfied, Michael closed the document and the word processing program on the computer without saving. He picked up the printed document and turned to the back page.

There was signature line at the bottom with his name and attorney license number as well as all of the old contact information for his former law firm.

Michael picked a blue pen out of a cup near the computer. He thought for a moment about the line that he was about to cross, and then he crossed it.

Michael signed his name and dated it. The date of his signature was five years earlier, before the incident and before he had ever set foot on the beautiful beach at the Sunset Resort and Hostel.

CHAPTER FORTY EIGHT

Quentin was already in the small conference room when Michael arrived. Michael put the new stack of paper down on the table. "Last batch." Michael tapped the pile, and then sat down. "Any word?"

Quentin shook his head. "No offers, Michael. I'm sorry."

Michael shrugged his shoulders. He hadn't expected any miracles. Brenda Gadd had been clear. When Quentin and Michael had rejected twenty years at the minimum security facility in Maine, they were told it was over. Gadd, in that sense, was a woman of her word.

"Are you ready?" Michael asked.

Quentin removed his glasses. He rubbed his eyes and nodded. "I've reviewed everything. The witness list is long. Kermit and Andie are on the list, but I'm not sure they're going to be called. I personally wouldn't call them."

"Why's that?"

"They're unknowns." Quentin folded his arms over his chubby belly. "Gadd can't be sure what they're going to say on the witness stand. Plus she's got all that paper to testify for her."

Michael looked at the stack of documents on the table. I've got paper, too, thought Michael, but he didn't say it.

219

Quentin paused. He lowered his voice as if he was sharing a secret.

"The exhibits are overwhelming, Michael. The documentation is thorough and the forensic accounting is clear." Quentin started to go further, but stopped himself. "They just don't need Andie and Kermit. They could probably get the conviction with five witnesses, maybe seven."

"But this is the government," Michael said. "They don't know when to stop." Michael looked Quentin in the eye. "And that's going to be where they'll go wrong."

"You seem pretty confident." Quentin stared at Michael. He examined his client. "Please don't embarrass me."

Michael shook his head. "I'm not going to embarrass you." Michael glanced at the stack of paper on the table and then back at Quentin. "Just keep demanding that Gadd produce all relevant documents in her possession, everything."

"I have been," Quentin said.

Michael nodded. "Good. Keep doing it, and memorialize each request with a letter."

Quentin lowered his shoulders and sighed. "As you wish."

The meeting continued for another hour. Quentin and Michael talked about jury selection, witness order, and gossiped about the judge. "He's old."

"Like how old?" Michael responded, as if it were a vaudeville joke. He's old. How old? He's so old that when God said 'let there be light' the judge hit the switch.

"He was appointed by President Ford fifty years ago."

"So a hundred-year-old judge is going to be deciding my future?"

"He's not one hundred." Quentin stood. "Only ninety-one." Quentin laughed a dark laugh and then he picked up the stack of paper on the table. "What do you want me to do with this stuff?"

"Did you look at any of it?" Michael wasn't expecting that Quentin would have reviewed it closely, but figured that he would have been curious.

"I've scanned it," Quentin said. "Looks like financials. A lot of it's the same as what the government has already produced."

Michael nodded, suppressing a smile. "I figured that."

"You had asked me to just put it in a box, and so I have been," Quentin said. "It's sitting in the corner of my office. Anything else you want me to do with it?"

Michael nodded. He looked at the stack of new documents in Quentin's hand.

"Just put the new stuff in the box with the rest of it," Michael paused. "Then tell Andie it's time to get rid of it."

"Like throw it away?" Quentin looked confused.

"No," Michael said. "Just tell her to get rid of it. Andie will understand."

CHAPTER FORTY NINE

It was getting dark. Vatch had already had a long day, but the rumors about Anthony had become more serious. He watched, from a distance, as Anthony left their apartment building, and then Vatch followed.

Anthony, Spider and three other boys met in front of a pizza shop. They messed around for a few minutes, and then they walked together to the park around the corner.

Vatch continued to watch them from a safe distance, unnoticed. Anthony wasn't on the periphery any longer. He wasn't an outsider. Anthony was one of them. He sat on the park bench next to Spider and another kid, while the others stood around. They shared a joint, laughed about nothing, and harassed anybody that dared to walk by.

After fifteen minutes, Vatch turned and started home. There wasn't any reason for him to stay. He had seen enough. Vatch rolled home and wondered if he was too late, whether Anthony was already lost.

CHAPTER FIFTY

On the morning of trial, Kermit lingered in the bathroom. He looked scared. His eyes narrowed to prevent a tear. They widened and then narrowed, again, as he stared at his reflection. Kermit's body was still wet from his morning shower.

He stood in front of the bathroom mirror. A small towel wrapped around his waist. An electric razor was in his hand.

Andie knocked on the door. "You okay?

Kermit didn't respond.

Andie knocked, again. "Kermit?" She carefully opened the door and peeked inside. "Did you do it?"

Kermit looked at the razor, and then turned his sad eyes toward her.

"Sure I gotta do this?"

Andie understood that she had asked him to sacrifice a core piece of his identity. She had endured hours of discussions about bosons and quantum physics. She had to affirm Kermit's beliefs in numeric equilibrium, then general semantics, and now sub-atomic chaos and magnetic fields. Then Andie had to posit counter-arguments and justifications for what Kermit had to do. "I'm sorry."

"I mean ..." Kermit shook his head. "My dreads, man." He touched a strand of tangled hair. "It ain't right. Just seems like there's a million disguises to which the K-Man can fit the profile without doing such a drastic deed."

Kermit thought for a moment. "Like pizza guy. I already look like a pizza guy. Just give me a box and one of those insulated bags they got. No need to fix the follicles for that action." He paused. "Homeless dude. That's another one. People always think I'm a homeless dude for some reason. How about we change the plan to incorporate a ninja transient? You know, somebody who fights the powers with a series of improvisational kung-fu grips and wicked metaphors related to unsustainable wealth disparities and inequitable resource distribution?"

"I didn't know you were a socialist."

Kermit shook his head. "Don't matter what I am." He cocked his head to the side. "It's all part of the back-story created for the character needed to bust Michael out of jail, yo."

"Well," Andie looked at the electric razor. "Unfortunately the character we need can't have the—" Andie stopped herself, trying to be sensitive. She rephrased. "Unfortunately the character we need for this master plan — which is pretty set at this point —needs to look very different from how you currently look."

"You mean that I need to be a dork."

"Yes." Andie nodded her head. "A dork with a lot less rhythm."

Kermit shook his head. "No can do." He set the razor down on the bathroom counter. "Not today."

"Then I'll need to talk to Michael and tell him there may be a delay."

"Tell him whatever you want." Kermit shrugged. "I need more time to think about this." Kermit turned and took a step toward the door. "On second thought, don't tell Michael that there's a problem. Brother's got enough on his mind. Just give me some time."

CHAPTER FIFTY ONE

The guards woke Michael up earlier than usual. He ate breakfast alone at a table in Pod 3. It consisted of stale Cheerios, a banana, and milk. Then he was escorted out of Pod 3, through the security doors, and down to a garage underneath the detention center.

There were six men scheduled for court. Others would be transported later in the morning, and even more would be transported in the afternoon.

A white, unmarked fifteen-passenger van served as the shuttle. It had no windows in the back. The van looked like a delivery truck, which, in a way, it was.

Michael and the other five turned and faced the wall, as instructed. They put their hands behind their backs and spread their legs a little wider than normal. The guard cuffed their hands with a plastic tie.

The narrow band was pulled tight. It cut into Michael's wrists. Then Michael and the others were instructed to sit on the ground and wait.

Everything was routine. They followed refined procedures created for institutionalizing and controlling people, and it worked.

Michael cooperated. With each command, Michael obeyed. Logic dictated that he obey. Obedience made life easier in an institution. There was no point in fighting it.

"Stand." A guard slid open the door to the van as the driver started the engine.

Michael and the others stood and shuffled inside.

In the beginning, there weren't prisons, Michael thought as he sat down. Early criminals were just maimed or killed. They weren't always warehoused under the guise of education and reformation.

Progress?

As the van pulled away, Michael tried to figure out which system was worse.

CHAPTER FIFTY TWO

The procedure at the courthouse was a little different this time. Michael wasn't arriving for an arraignment or pre-trial hearing. Michael was there for trial.

The deputies separated him from the other men.

They led Michael down a different hallway. They walked through the bowels of the courthouse, and then to a room with ten brown lockers.

"Your attorney sent these over." The federal marshal pointed to the first locker on the end. "I assume they'll fit." He then cut the plastic ties off of Michael's wrists, and he told Michael that he had about two minutes to change clothes.

"Judge Husk is always ready to begin on time. Hates it when people are late." The guard walked away from Michael. "That judge is going to live forever."

###

Michael stared at his reflection in the elevator doors. It was clear that Andie had picked out the suit and tie. Michael never liked trendy suits or elaborate, patterned ties. He liked dark blue suits, maybe a subtle pinstripe, and a conservative striped tie. That was the costume.

Andie had complied with his fashion requests, although she deviated slightly. Rather than a striped tie with two diagonal lines (either dark blue and maroon or forest green and yellow), Andie's tie had something beyond the requisite diagonal lines. From a distance, it simply looked like an extra narrow yellow line, but up-close it was actually a series of very small yellow suns all in a row. It satisfied Michael's fashion requirements, but Andie wanted to remind him why he couldn't give up the fight. Sunny Mexico, Michael thought, message received.

He stared at the reflection of himself in the metal elevator doors. It was odd seeing himself as a man again, and not as a prisoner. It had been almost three months since he had worn anything but an orange jumpsuit.

The polished metal doors slid open. He was led down another hallway, then into a secure courtroom on the twentieth floor.

The federal marshal then guided Michael toward counsel table. Quentin was waiting.

Michael stayed focused on his attorney, ignoring the other people packed in the rows of seats in the gallery.

He sat down. Quentin slid Michael a notepad and a pen, so that they could communicate with one another during jury selection, and then there was a knock.

The clerk of court rapped the gavel three times. "All rise, the federal district court for the State of New York is now in session, the Honorable Harold G. Husk presiding."

Everyone in the courtroom stood.

A door behind the bench opened, and then Judge Husk emerged.

His skin was thin and paper white. His face was gaunt. His back hunched, seemingly pressed down by the weight of his robe.

Judge Husk's law clerk held his arm and walked him up to the bench. They took tiny, deliberate steps.

The clerk lowered the judge down into a large, black leather chair, which enveloped Judge Husk. He looked like a child in his father's easy chair. The judge now seemed even smaller and more frail than when he had first come through the door into the courtroom.

The law clerk placed several pieces of paper down in front of Judge Husk on the bench, and then held out a pen. Judge Husk's hand slowly lifted, shaking, and eventually took hold of the pen.

There was a long pause as Judge Husk remembered the words that he should say, processed them, and then mustered the strength to instruct the people in the courtroom to be seated.

Relief.

Another pause, as Judge Husk caught his breath and reclaimed his next thought. "Good morning." Husk was still breathing heavily from the walk from his chambers to the bench. He looked down at the pieces of paper in front of him, and then back up. "We are here in the matter of the United States versus Michael John Collins." Another pause. "Please introduce yourself for the record."

Michael sat and watched as United States Attorney Brenda Gadd noted her appearance. The judge struggled to keep his head up and his eyes open during the brief introduction.

Michael leaned over. "You said he was old." Michael whispered in Quentin's ear. "You didn't say he was half dead."

Before calling up the jury pool and beginning voir dire, which was a fancy lawyer word for jury selection, Brenda Gadd requested a moment of the court's time to discuss, "preliminary matters."

Judge Husk rolled his cloudy eyes and looked at his law clerk. The law clerk, seated at a computer workstation to his right, nodded her head. This gesture prompted the judge, who then permitted Gadd to proceed.

"Thank you, Your Honor." Gadd stood up. "We have noticed that there are several people in the courtroom that are potential witnesses in this case," she said. "We would like them to be excluded at this time until their testimony has been obtained and there is no chance that they would be called as a rebuttal witness."

Judge Husk labored a few breaths, and then turned to Quentin. He didn't verbally tell Quentin to respond. It was obvious that the judge needed to preserve every ounce of energy to keep his own heart beating and other vital organs functioning. So Quentin stood.

"Thank you, Your Honor." Quentin turned to Gadd. "I guess I don't understand. U.S. Attorney Gadd hasn't said who she specifically wants excluded and how this is going to be prejudicial to the government's case. And even if they needed to be excluded during witness testimony, it doesn't make sense to exclude them during jury selection or opening arguments."

Gadd didn't hesitate. She didn't wait for permission.

"I'm concerned about witnesses colluding with one another to reshape their testimony. I want an order that says that nobody can speak about the testimony or the facts of this case with one another or be present during the testimony of others." Gadd looked back at Andie Larone and Kermit Guillardo. "I don't want to encourage perjury or risk a mistrial."

"Your Honor, it appears as though Ms. Gadd is already disparaging and impeaching witnesses that haven't even testified.

These are my witnesses, but they are also on her own witness list. And I think my client deserves to have his friends in the courtroom. This is a public trial. The public should be able to attend."

Judge Husk's eyelids fluttered and then closed. His chin dropped. His head bowed. It appeared as though he had fallen asleep thinking about the motion.

The courtroom was silent as everyone waited. Only a few seconds passed, although it seemed longer, and then Judge Husk opened his eyes. He turned and looked at his law clerk, who nodded at the judge to verbalize his thought.

"All witnesses. ..." Judge Husk took a deep, unsteady breath. "All witnesses..." He faded again. "All witnesses for both the defense and government shall be excluded from the courtroom until their testimony is complete."

Judge Husk looked at Gadd. "That applies to your witnesses as well." A sparkle brightened his eyes. "You might say, 'what's good for the goose is good for the gander.'" The corners of the judge's mouth curled into a devilish smile, and for the first time in months, Michael felt like he might be okay. It just depended on whether the law clerk made the decisions or Judge Husk.

CHAPTER FIFTY THREE

He would have preferred the Hampton Luxury Liner or even the Hampton Ambassador, but Brent Krane didn't have enough money and the crowd needed to get out of the damn rental. So, he packed his bag and paid $24 for a seat on the Hampton Jitney. It was still an upgrade over a city bus, but he had to settle for goldfish crackers and water rather than the wine and cheese offered on the Hampton Luxury Liner or the Ambassador.

It was hard having good taste and being poor at the same time, thought Brent, which the crowd found amusing.

Their laughter was a break from the screams and taunts he had endured over the past few weeks. As the trial approached, the crowd had become more abusive. They promised him that there would be no sleep until he returned to New York and confronted Michael Collins. They wanted their revenge for ruining his life. They didn't like taking orders from his sister. They didn't like being caged. The rental in Montauk reminded the crowd too much of the fancy treatment facilities Brent's parents had been sending him to since he hit puberty.

The rage built. Brent Krane felt himself rising.

He glanced around, checking to make sure nobody was looking. Then he carefully lifted up his sleeve. His forearm was covered with cuts, each at different stages of healing.

There wasn't any more room on his flesh to release the pressure that way. His actions would be his opportunity for release. His actions would be his salvation.

Brent Krane unzipped the top of his duffle bag. He stuck his hand inside, groping through the dirty clothes. Then he felt it. His fingers pulled at the T-shirt, and, without taking it out of the bag, Brent unwrapped the gun. He put his hand on the grip and his finger on the trigger. It felt good. It felt better than that stupid knife. He held it tightly, allowing the gun to help him focus on the end.

Brent Krane leaned back in his seat and closed his eyes. His right hand still held the gun, concealed by the duffle bag. He thought about how he felt after starting the fire at the Sunset. He thought about how he felt when he saw the explosion, and then he tried to recapture the calm. Maybe he didn't need to cut.

CHAPTER FIFTY FOUR

Andie and Kermit walked into the rental feeling like kids who didn't get asked to the big dance.

"Well that was quick." Andie took off her jacket and put it on the couch. "I don't like leaving Michael there alone." She clapped her hands together and rubbed. "But we've got some work to do."

Kermit had already fetched himself a bottle of beer, opened it, and had consumed about half on his way back to the living room.

"I know what you're saying, yo. Michael don't belong in a courtroom. Courtrooms are, like, too quiet." Kermit plopped down on the couch. "The judge needs to put on some music during those down times. Let the people dance or something. Zumba would be good. People need to Zumba more in court."

He took another sip of beer, and then glanced down the hall toward Quentin's office. "So you want me to get the box?"

Andie nodded. "It's either that or going back upstairs and getting out the razor."

"Making me pick the poison." Kermit shook his head in disgust. "Not nice." He chugged the remainder of his beer, and then pulled himself up from the couch. "Guess it's the box, yo."

###

Kermit picked up the white cardboard document box in Quentin's office. He hauled it down the hallway. Thousands of such ubiquitous boxes filled storage rooms in law firms and government agencies throughout the United States. They were the perfect size: large enough to hold a significant amount of paper, but small enough to never become too heavy for one person, even an overweight and out-of-shape attorney, to carry.

Kermit put the box down on the kitchen table.

Andie stood next to him as Kermit took off the lid, and then they stared at the stacks of paper inside.

"Ready?" Andie asked.

"Ready Freddy." Kermit started to unload the paper. The box was filled with the various Securities and Exchange Commission filings and audits that Michael had printed every day for the past two months and given to Quentin during their daily attorney-client conferences.

Andie and Kermit weren't exactly sure what they were looking for, but, after three hours, Andie was sure that she had found it.

"Check this out." Andie handed the papers to Kermit. "This has got to be it."

The document was a ten-page legal agreement signed by Michael.

Kermit read it a few times. "What the hell does this mean?"

Andie shook her head.

"Don't really know." She leaned over and pointed to the space next to Michael's signature. "But we need to get this other signature."

Kermit rubbed his chin, looking at the blank signature block. "Isn't that dude dead?"

Andie nodded. "Yep."

Kermit cocked his head to the side, thinking. "Shouldn't be a problem."

CHAPTER FIFTY FIVE

With all of the potential witnesses excluded, the courtroom was less crowded. Michael was disappointed to see Andie and Kermit leave and equally disappointed to see Brea Krane's attorney, Tad Garvin remain. But he took particular delight when Agent Vatch was forced to roll away. He knew that Vatch wanted to savor every moment of the trial.

After the exodus, the courtroom settled back into the mechanics of a trial.

A message was sent down to the jury room by Judge Husk's law clerk. Thirty potential jurors were commanded to put away their paperback novels, magazines, and iPads. They were required to throw away their unfinished sodas and coffee. Then they were ordered to meander toward a bank of elevators and come up to a courtroom somewhere in the building where their services may be needed.

Some were happy to be moving, excited about the possibility of seeing a real trial like on television. Others were thinking up subtly racist comments or biases that would result in them being struck from the jury and sent home.

In sum, the jurors were largely comprised of morally ambivalent schemers. A jury of his peers, Michael thought.

###

"Please rise." The people rose as the potential jurors filed in-to the courtroom. A clerk read a list of names, and these people were directed to the open seats in the jury box. The remainder of the jury pool were directed toward two open benches off to the side of the box.

"Jurors, please remain standing." Judge Husk then turned away from the jurors to the attorneys and others in the court-room. He raised his shaking hand. "You all may have a seat." He gestured for them to sit, lowering his hand.

"I am Judge Harold G. Husk." The judge paused and rubbed his chin. "I'm going to now swear you all in."

As Judge Husk continued talking to the jurors about the rules and expectations, Michael watched as life came back into the old man. He was still frail and spoke softly, but the jurors were riveted. There was an immediate bond. They listened as if Judge Husk sat at the head of a Thanksgiving table, telling sto-ries about the days before electronic screens, large and tiny, dominated every aspect of daily life.

When the judge had first emerged from the back and took the bench, Michael had wondered how Judge Husk could pos-sibly manage a trial and keep attorneys in line. Now he knew: the jury.

None of the attorneys were going to want to upset the jurors by being rude to Judge Husk, and as Michael listened to Judge Husk, it was as if Moses was reading the Ten Commandments. Rather than weak, his voice took on a mystical tone.

"Now, we're about to begin voir dire. The process of select-ing a juror. If you are not selected, it does not mean that you are bad or unfair. It just means that you may not be right for this jury. Obviously all of you cannot sit on this panel." Judge Husk picked up a tissue and rubbed his nose. "This is a criminal trial."

Judge Husk shifted. He looked at the prosecutor's table. "The United States Government is represented by Ms. Brenda Gadd. Could you please stand?"

Brenda Gadd stood. She offered the jury her best smile, but she was careful not to smile too much. She couldn't be perceived as too soft.

"The defendant is represented by Mr. Quentin Robinson." Judge Husk looked toward the defense table as Quentin stood. "And the Defendant is Mr. Michael John Collins."

Michael stood, briefly, and then both he and Quentin sat back down.

"My clerk is going to distribute a written jury questionnaire. You all are instructed to fill out this questionnaire and you are under oath. You are to answer the questions truthfully and honestly." Judge Husk took a deep breath, closed his eyes, and collected his final thoughts.

"When you are done," Judge Husk opened his eyes. "Give the questionnaire back to my clerk, and then you are free to go for the day. You are to return tomorrow morning at 8:00 am so that I may ask you more questions. Do not discuss this matter amongst yourselves. Do not conduct any independent research about any of the attorneys or the defendant. Do not conduct any legal research, nor should you discuss this case with family members or friends. If they ask what you are doing, simply respond by saying that you are a potential juror in a criminal case and that is all."

Judge Husk paused again. It was obvious that he was getting tired. "Now, finally, you are all likely wondering how long this will last." Judge Husk shook his head. "The honest answer is that I do not know." Judge Husk scanned the jurors, ensuring that they followed every word that he spoke. "But I assure you all that the trial will be completed as quickly as possible. I start on time, and often work late. I do not tolerate duplication and redundancy." Judge Husk smiled. "And, at my age, frankly, I don't have a lot of time left to waste."

CHAPTER FIFTY SIX

The taxi dropped Kermit Guillardo off in front of a Chinese bake shop near the corner of Mott and Pell. Andie rolled down the back window and leaned her head out. "Meet you at Jay's Diner in an hour."

Kermit nodded. "Sure thing, senorita." He winked, pointed at the large envelope in his hand, and gave a thumbs up. "This mission is in capable hands." Then he turned, and walked down the crowded street.

Andie watched him. Easily a foot taller than most of the other people in Chinatown, Kermit wasn't difficult to follow.

When Kermit disappeared around a corner, Andie instructed the cab driver to go.

"Where to?" The cabbie shifted the car into gear and he pulled away from the curb.

"Columbus Park."

"Easy enough." The street was too narrow to turn around. So the cab driver followed it down to Worth and then over to Mulberry.

Traffic was tight, because traffic was always tight. But, at least the line of cars and trucks moved forward. That was all anybody hoped for.

It took ten minutes to go less than a mile. Andie thought about just getting out of the cab and walking, but they arrived at the park just as her patience neared the end.

The cab driver pressed a button on the meter box, Andie paid, and then she got out. She wasn't quite sure where she was going, and so Andie decided to just pick a path.

For years, Columbus Park had been a forgotten plot of land. The park system had allowed it to deteriorate. There weren't many people engaging in legal activities at the park, and there had been nothing to do except run around on a large, cracked concrete slab.

Now, as Andie walked through the park over to some benches and a kids' play area, Columbus Park was a true extension of Chinatown. There was still a healthy percentage of crazy, but the park had been restored. It was filled with families enjoying a little space and solitude. Musicians and singers entertained on the edges, and a contingent of older men, who all took checkers extremely seriously, dominated the center.

Andie sat down. As one of the few white faces in the park, Andie questioned whether this was really a good place to meet.

She checked her watch, and decided that there wasn't enough time to find another location. So, Andie removed the cell phone from her purse. She scrolled down the numbers that Michael had pre-programmed into the contact directory, and then Andie found the one she wanted.

She pressed a button. The connection was made, and, after two rings, there was an answer.

"Hey." Andie looked around, checking to make sure there wasn't anybody listening. "I'm past the pavilion near the children's playground."

Then Andie hung up.

Brea Krane was coming. She'd be there in thirty minutes.

###

Hoa Bahns was no longer located in a back alley. It's discovery years ago by Agent Vatch never resulted in criminal charges, but it did force the owner to rethink his business model. Many of the services provided by the original Hoa Bahns were still provided, but the delivery was more discreet.

Kermit found it squeezed between the Ginseng Company and a shoe store that prominently displayed counterfeit Nikes at a very affordable price.

Hoa Bahns' storefront was a polished maroon stone. In the window, there were various bottles of lotions, shampoos, and gels. One of the oldest unregulated banks in Chinatown was now a nondescript pharmacy.

Kermit Guillardo walked inside. There was nobody in the store, which seemed to be the goal. Every item in the store was priced five times higher than what the product should cost, and Kermit wondered whether the bored cashier would even know how to operate the cash register if Kermit decided to buy some deodorant, not that he believed in deodorant or wasted money on such substances.

Kermit walked to the very back of the store. There was a sign, "Prescriptions Filled Here." A man in a white doctor's jacket stood behind the window. He looked like a regular pharmacist, except for a long scar that ran from the corner of his eye, down his cheek, and over to his chin.

"I need this filled." Kermit put his large manila envelope down on the counter.

"You have an account here?" The pharmacist's eyes narrowed as he evaluated Kermit. "Only people with account can have prescriptions filled."

Kermit nodded. "It's not for me," he said. "My friend has an account."

"Friend?"

"Michael Collins."

The pharmacist didn't say a word. He just shook his head and made a clucking sound. "Don't think so."

"It's important," Kermit said. "All the paperwork is here." Kermit slid the envelope through the small opening at the bottom of the glass window. "And of course I'm willing to pay."

The pharmacist's eyebrows rose. "I take it and see."

"That's all I ask," Kermit said, then he turned and walked away.

###

Brea Krane sat down next to Andie. "Glad you finally came to your senses."

"It just makes me nervous." Andie's eyes scanned the people in the park as well as the vehicles parked along the street, wondering whether Agent Vatch or some other investigator was watching.

"But it's necessary," Brea said. "Do you have it?"

"I do." Andie took a folded sheet of paper out of her pocket. "These are the accounts and one of the passwords. They're in the Cook Islands. Seems like that's the only place left that doesn't really care what a court order in the United States says."

Brea took the paper and put it into her purse. "Is any of the money accessible?"

Andie nodded. "The first account is available to you now. Michael calls it a down payment." Andie took a breath. "We'll give you the other two passwords and you can transfer it when you've fulfilled your end of the deal."

"How much?"

Andie shook her head. "About fifteen million. These are the only accounts the government hasn't frozen, and there's still a risk. I mean, just because the government can't get at it, doesn't mean they aren't watching it. There's a risk to you."

Brea laughed. "There's no risk. As soon as I've got it all transferred, I'm gone. I'll be perfectly content to never step foot on American soil again. Your boyfriend should've had the same attitude."

"So what's next?" Andie tried to hurry the meeting along.

"My brother is still holed up in Montauk. I've been feeding him a steady stream of pot and free food, so that should keep him under control until the trial is done."

"Good." Andie nodded.

The meeting was ending, and Brea stood.

"But I want it all upfront." She looked at Andie. "Before I testify. I want it all."

"That wasn't the deal."

Brea shook her head. "You either give me the money upfront or the deal is off."

CHAPTER FIFTY SEVEN

It took another two days before the jury was selected. Michael's heart pounded through his chest as he watched the jurors stand, raise their right hands, and take another oath to follow the court's instructions and deliberate fairly.

These were the people who would decide his fate.

Judge Husk coughed into a handkerchief and concluded. "Do you promise to faithfully execute the duties and responsibilities of a juror for the Federal District Court of the State of New York and administer those duties to the best of your abilities?"

In unison, the jurors agreed, lowered their hands, and sat down.

"Very well." Judge Husk nodded his head. "Then I see no reason to delay." He looked at the prosecutor's table. "Ready?"

United States Attorney Brenda Gadd stood. "I am, Your Honor."

"Then proceed."

Gadd walked up to a podium in the center of the courtroom, but it wasn't an ordinary podium. This was federal court. A mere wooden stand for an attorney to put his or her notes was inadequate. This podium was outfitted with its own computer, projector, and touch screen. The thousands of documents that had

251

been dumped on Quentin when the case had first begun were now pre-loaded into the podium's computer. Each document image was one-click away, if Gadd needed any of the documents at any point during the trial.

"As you may remember from our brief introductions at the beginning of jury selection," Gadd paused and smiled, making eye contact with each of the individual jurors. "I am Brenda Gadd, and I'm the United States Attorney for the State of New York."

Gadd took a step away from the podium. She walked toward the jurors. "We're here because the government must prove beyond a reasonable doubt that Michael Collins is guilty of multiple counts of wire fraud. Michael Collins is an attorney, and we will prove that he stole his client's money and ran away to a beach in Mexico. Some people might say that this is a complicated case." Gadd shook her head. "I don't think so. There's no such thing as an easy case---otherwise you wouldn't be here---but the documents do not lie. The documents speak for themselves. The wire transfers tell a clear story of theft."

She turned and looked at Michael, and then dismissed him with a shake of her head. "Here, Michael Collins had an opportunity to get rich by taking a client's money. He took it, and then he ran. That's it. That's theft. That's wire fraud, because he transferred the money multiple times across state and international boundaries via telephone and electronic wires. If you find that this money didn't belong to him, which obviously it did not, then that constitutes fraud."

Gadd stepped back to the podium, allowing the silence to emphasize her last word: fraud. Then she began a new thought.

"Sure there are a ton of documents, spreadsheets, and reports issued by forensic accountants. I'll try not to overwhelm you with numbers." Gadd smiled and a few jurors smiled and nodded back at her. Everybody hated numbers.

Gadd was attempting to establish trust and familiarity with the jurors. Michael and Quentin saw that it was working.

"But all the stuff is mostly about Michael Collins' elaborate scheme to cover-up his crime," she said. "The spreadsheets and numbers merely document the lengths that Michael Collins went to cover-up his crime and escape prosecution for wire fraud. By electronically transferring money from one foreign bank account to another, Michael Collins tried to stay one step ahead of investigators."

Gadd paused as she allowed the jurors and opportunity to think about what she had just told them. Gadd's message was unmistakable: anybody who used foreign bank accounts must be guilty of something.

"But in the end, Michael Collins got caught and here we are. By the end of this trial you'll know---beyond a reasonable doubt---that Michael Collins saw the opportunity, took the money, and ran." Gadd lowered her head, a subtle bow. "Thank you."

As Michael watched Brenda Gadd return to the prosecutor's table a cold bead of sweat ran down his neck. It was a confident opening statement. Gadd kept it vague and simple. She was careful not to over-promise. Michael couldn't think of any opportunity that she had given Quentin to claim that Gadd didn't deliver. And, unfortunately, Michael thought, everything that Gadd said was true.

He had seen the opportunity, took the money, and ran.

Wouldn't anybody?

CHAPTER FIFTY EIGHT

Quentin Robinson was the opposite of Brenda Gadd. He approached with a stack of notes and papers, most of which were unnecessary. His hand shook, slightly, as he put the papers down on the high-tech podium.

When the papers on the top of his stack started to slide, Quentin caught them, but when he did, Quentin pressed a button. An overhead projector came on and a screen behind the empty witness stand lit up in a bright, white light.

"Sorry." Quentin pushed the papers to the side, trying to locate the button that he had accidently pressed. He found it. The light went off, and he tried to begin, again.

But the papers were still a problem. The top sheets started their downward slide. In mid-sentence, Quentin stopped. "Why don't I put these back at my table."

Michael watched in horror as the jurors raised their eyebrows and exchanged concerned looks. One woman suppressed a giggle, as Quentin gathered up his papers and walked back to the defense table.

Judge Husk leaned back in his gigantic black leather chair, amused.

"Okay." Quentin set the papers down near Michael, and then returned to the podium. "Let's try this, again." He took a deep

255

breath. "And I promise not to touch any more of these buttons." He put his hands behind his back. Standing like a child who had just been caught stealing a cookie, Quentin continued.

"Listening to the prosecutor, sounds like they have a pretty good case." Quentin looked back at Brenda Gadd as a few of the jurors shifted uncomfortably in their seats. "But remember what the Judge said when he was giving you your instructions. He said, 'wait.' And you all swore an oath to follow his instructions."

Quentin's voice trembled. He was used to the dirty, crowded, and noisy city courts. He was used to the hustle and bustle of poverty law. They were cases that were won more by bluster than the rules of evidence. He could get a good deal by being a pain in the ass, rather than using an actual legal defense. The federal courtroom, however, was a different world, Quentin was an invader. He didn't belong, but he pushed his self-doubt aside and barreled forward.

"The judge told you to wait before all the evidence is in before deciding whether my client is guilty or not guilty. That means you will listen to the prosecutor, and then, you will also wait...and listen to me. The defense gets an opportunity to call witnesses and offer evidence too. The defense gets an opportunity to tell its version of what really happened and make a closing argument. So, wait until everything is done before reaching your decision. This proof that Ms. Gadd speaks so highly about," Quentin tilted his head to the side, "may not be all it's cracked up to be."

Quentin wiped the sweat off of his forehead. He looked at Michael, and then back at the jury. He needed to repeat his theme one more time. Quentin needed to be sure that the jurors understood.

"It will be only natural to think that my client appears guilty when you see some of the documents that the prosecution offers and listen to the testimony of their witnesses. It will sound, just as Brenda Gadd said, like a simple case of a guy who takes a bunch of money and runs. But, I ask you and, more importantly, this Court has instructed you, to withhold judgment. Wait until the end." Quentin's confidence had now returned after his disastrous beginning. "I assure you that things are not always as they appear." He held out his hand. "Just wait."

Quentin turned and walked back to the defense table. He sat down next to Michael, and then Judge Husk adjourned for the day.

"We'll return tomorrow for the start of testimony. You are not to discuss this matter with anyone or conduct any independent investigation." The judge nodded. "Very well."

A gavel sounded. A bailiff shouted. "That concludes the day's calendar. Court is adjourned." The gavel banged a final time.

People in the courtroom rose as the jurors walked out a side door in a line, and then Judge Husk was assisted out of his chair and led out of the courtroom with the aid of his law clerk.

Michael could hardly control himself. "What the hell was up with the stack of paper and the projector?"

Quentin whispered back. "Michael, I'm sorry," he said. "It happens sometimes. I was just off at the beginning. Don't worry. We'll get it back."

CHAPTER FIFTY NINE

His apartment was depressing. Brent Krane had been gone for so long that he had forgotten, for a moment, that he was actually poor. Unlike his sister, he had no trust fund and his mother had forgotten him as she started her new life with a new man.

Brent turned on the kitchen light. He walked over to the refrigerator and opened the door. There was nothing in the refrigerator except a bottle of spoiled milk and a block of moldy cheese.

He shut the refrigerator door and walked back to his bedroom. Although he wasn't happy, leaving the rental house in Montauk had made the crowd happy. They were quiet for the moment, and Brent decided to get some sleep.

Tomorrow he had to figure out a plan, and find out what his sister was scheming.

CHAPTER SIXTY

There weren't any other bank accounts or boxes of gold coins. The accounts in the Cook Islands were it. All other foreign banks had cooperated with the government's requests, and either the government didn't know about the Cook Island accounts or they weren't telling.

It had taken Andie about three weeks to test all of the accounts that Michael had identified. She didn't do it all at once. She spaced the inquiries, waiting and seeing if there would be any reaction.

Eventually she discovered that the relatively small amount of money in the Cook Island accounts were still active and apparently unfrozen. This made some sense to Michael, since he hadn't funded them directly through a wire transfer. Rather, the accounts were built indirectly through a series of skims.

It was a combination of processing fees, which he charged himself every time the money was moved from one account to another, to innocent looking fees written into his purchase agreement of the Sunset Resort & Hostel. The purchase agreement, like all closing documents, had line items for property taxes, property insurance, appraisals, second mortgage pay-off, a standard 10% real estate agent commission, and a finder's fee. Some of these line item charges were inflated and

261

others were bogus. None of the individual amounts, however, were large enough to raise suspicion. But, all together, the skims added up.

Andie stood and leaned into Michael. "We're going forward." She whispered into Michael's ear, knowing that the government was listening.

Michael nodded. "Good." He looked around at the people sitting at the various tables in the MDC's visitation room, wondering who was actually an FBI agent.

"Everything else okay?" Andie pulled away.

Michael closed his eyes. "It's okay." He tried to be strong. "It'll be better when it's all over."

Andie turned, but Michael stopped her.

"Just don't trust her," he said.

"I'm not." Andie smiled.

CHAPTER SIXTY ONE

It was early in the morning, but Vatch was already awake when there was an unexpected knock on his door. "Coming." Vatch closed a notebook filled with five years of notes about the Michael Collins investigation, and then rolled away from the small desk in his bedroom.

Today was the day he was scheduled to testify. Agent Frank Vatch was preparing to be the prosecution's first witness, and he was annoyed at the interruption.

He crossed the living room, stopping in front of the door. "I said I was coming." Vatch looked through the peep-hole, and then turned the deadbolt and removed the chain. "It's open." He rolled back.

Anthony's mother came inside.

"He ain't home." She looked at Vatch. Then she looked around the apartment, hoping to see her son. "Thought he might be here."

Vatch shook his head as he closed the door. "Haven't seen him." Vatch shrugged. "Not as popular as I used to be."

"I'm worried." She sat down on Vatch's couch. "He comes and goes whenever he wants. Got a call from the school. They're thinking about dropping him." She started to cry. "Don't know what to do."

263

Vatch looked at his watch. It was a quarter past six in the morning. "Where have you been all night?"

"Working." She answered too quickly, defensive.

"Well, like I said, he's been avoiding me. Hanging out with me isn't cool."

"You've got to talk with him."

"I'm not his dad." Vatch looked past her at the clock on the wall. He didn't want to talk about it. Vatch told himself that he was just a guy who lived in the same building, and Anthony was just another kid from the neighborhood. Vatch didn't want to believe that somebody like Anthony could hurt him. A kid shouldn't make him feel sad or lost. Vatch tried to tell himself those things, but he knew that none of it was true.

"You're as close to a father as he got." Anthony's mom stood up. "You've got to help him. I don't want to lose Anthony. I don't want to lose him."

She walked toward the door with a little stumble and left.

Long after she had gone, the room still smelled like alcohol.

CHAPTER SIXTY TWO

The gavel tapped three times. The people stood, and Michael watched as Judge Husk was slowly led up to the bench for the second day of trial and the first day of testimony. Judge Husk's law clerk lowered the old man into his gigantic chair, careful not to break him. Then the judge was given a pen and a clean, new notepad.

Judge Husk took a moment before raising his hand. With a small gesture, the people in the courtroom sat back down. Court was called to order.

"We're here in the case of the United States versus Michael John Collins." Judge Husk looked at Michael, and Michael saw, for the first time, a weight in the judge's eyes. There was a touch of sadness, pity. How many defendants had Judge Husk sent to prison over the past forty years? Michael would just be another notch in his belt. Interesting for the moment, and forgotten the second the trial was over.

The attorneys noted their appearances for the record, and then Judge Husk asked if there were any preliminary matters. Both Brenda Gadd and Quentin Robinson told the court that they had none.

Judge Husk nodded.

"Very well. We'll bring out the jury and the government may call their first witness in a few moments."

Gadd rose out of her seat.

"Thank you, Your Honor. We'll be calling Agent Frank Vatch."

"And how long do you expect him to testify?"

"He's the lead investigator. Most of our evidence will come in through Agent Vatch."

Judge Husk took a deep breath. His face lowered. "That's not what I asked."

"Two days, Your Honor," Gadd said. "At least two days."

Judge Husk rolled his eyes. "That's a long time."

"It's a complex case, Your Honor."

The sadness in Judge Husk's eyes disappeared. It was replaced with a spark. The fighter was back. Judge Husk leaned forward in his large chair. He peered down at Brenda Gadd.

"That's not what you told the jury in your opening statement yesterday."

Jurors were always excited on the first day of testimony. As they were led into the courtroom, Michael saw that they were doing their best to look solemn and thoughtful. Underneath, however, adrenaline pumped.

As much as people complained about jury duty and how much they didn't want to do it, deep down, nearly everybody wanted to be on a jury. It was the ultimate reality television show. A juror had the power to decide another person's fate. Compared to a boring office job or carting kids to and from soccer practice, it was real power.

His jury was comprised of all shapes, sizes, and colors. Michael considered himself to be good at evaluating and selecting jurors, but he had difficulty understanding this one. He was too close. Unlike the trials at Wabash, Kramer and Moore, he couldn't figure out the people who would now pass judgment upon him. It was easier for him when they were deciding some- one else's fate.

On the chairs in the jury box, there was one pen and one pad of paper for each juror. The jurors picked them up and sat down. Once they were settled, Judge Husk asked Brenda Gadd to call her first witness.

"The United States calls ..." Gadd spoke louder than she needed and paused to add some drama. "Senior FBI Agent Frank Vatch."

Vatch rolled down the center aisle. He wore a dark suit and tie. He did not turn or look at Michael as he passed. It must have been difficult for him. Michael had endured countless taunts and sneers over the past several years. He had figured Vatch would not be able to control himself. He had hoped that the jury would see how personal the investigation had gotten and how Vatch was not an impartial investigator. But there were no comments or nasty looks. Vatch was on his best behavior.

He rolled up a small ramp to the witness stand, was sworn in, and then Brenda Gadd began.

Normally, a prosecutor begins with foundational questions for the witness. They are background questions about where the witness lives, where they went to school, professional li- censes and awards, and then a brief description regarding job duties.

But Brenda Gadd was not a normal prosecutor. Gadd was one of the best government attorneys in the country, and she wasn't going to waste the moment. She knew that the juror's minds would begin to wander within ten seconds. Jurors got bored. She needed to strike.

"Thank you." Gadd nodded toward Judge Husk, and then looked down at a piece of paper in front of her. "I'll offer exhibits and solicit a lot more background information in a moment, but I'd like to get to the point."

Gadd glanced over at Michael Collins, and then turned her attention back to Vatch.

"Is there any doubt in your mind that the Defendant, Michael Collins, stole over $500 million from Joshua Krane and his companies?"

"No." The initial question had likely been rehearsed a hundred times. "There is no doubt in my mind that Michael Collins is a thief."

"Objection, Your Honor," Quentin was on his feet. "Lack of foundation, speculation, argumentative, calls for a legal conclusion."

Judge Husk raised his shaky hand in the air, silencing Michael's attorney.

"No speaking objections," he said, softly. "I've been doing this awhile." A spark fired again, in Judge Husk's tired eyes. "I know the rules. Just object and I'll tell you whether it is sustained or overruled."

Judge Husk took a breath through his nose and exhaled through his mouth. There was a moment in the process of inhaling and exhaling that Michael thought Judge Husk had stopped breathing entirely.

"In this situation, the objection is overruled. In fact, I rather like attorneys who get to the point."

The first battle with Brenda Gadd had been lost.

Agent Vatch's testimony soon gave way to tedium. Dozens of documents were flashed on the overhead projector's screen as one exhibit after another was analyzed and described. They were mostly bank account records.

Gadd meticulously followed the money trail. It started with Joshua Krane's accounts, and Michael knew where it would end.

After a brief lunch break, the "Agent Frank Vatch Show" continued. Hours passed. More documents were projected onto the screen.

Michael noticed that Judge Husk's head tilted downward. His eyes closed, and the judge appeared to be asleep for most of the afternoon testimony. Quentin didn't object, because there was nothing to object to, and so the testimony continued without interruption.

The jurors did a better job than Judge Husk. They kept their eyes open, but they were also struggling to remain engaged. The early excitement was gone.

Mercifully, Judge Husk interrupted Gadd at three o'clock.

"I think we're done for the day. We'll excuse the jury a little early so I can talk with the attorneys."

The jurors were visibly relieved. At the words granting them freedom, the juror's faces lit up. Judge Husk was their hero.

The courtroom stood as the jurors lined up and were led out the side door.

Michael watched. A few of the jurors looked at him, briefly, and then looked away. After being pounded with documents for more than six hours, it seemed like they had already found him guilty.

When the jurors were gone, Judge Husk directed everyone to sit.

"Ms. Gadd, I don't mean for you to take any offense at this, but I think you're killing me."

Brenda Gadd stood, a little confused.

"I'm sorry, Your Honor. I guess I don't understand."

Judge Husk leaned his small frail body forward and raised his voice.

"I said, 'you ... are ... killing ... me.' " He paused between each word for emphasis. "It's getting cumulative and redundant."

"Your Honor, we have the burden to prove this case beyond a reasonable doubt. I'm merely trying to —"

Judge Husk raised his hand.

"I've been a judge for nearly a half-century, Ms. Gadd. I know the legal standard and the burden of proof expected of the government in a criminal case. What I am saying now, is that you do not need to describe every document. The documents are admitted into evidence. They speak for themselves."

Judge Husk looked at Quentin.

"I assume you agree."

Quentin Robinson stood. He knew better than to disagree with a judge, especially when a judge was irritated with opposing counsel.

"That is correct, Your Honor." Quentin sat down.

"Good." Judge Husk turned back to Brenda Gadd. "We'll start again tomorrow. In the meantime, rethink how you present your case. All of these thousands of documents are in evidence, and have been graciously stipulated to by Mr. Robinson. So, please do not torture me." Judge Husk's ancient lips curled into a smile. "As the young people say these days, 'life is short.'"

CHAPTER SIXTY THREE

Across town, Kermit Guillardo returned to Hoa Bahns. He walked past the cashier who was flipping through a celebrity gossip magazine while sipping on a bubble tea and snacking on a coconut croissant from the nearby bake shop.

He went past the shelves of overpriced toilet paper, Band-Aids, and cosmetics to the back, where he stopped at the pharmacy counter.

Kermit looked through the glass and didn't see anybody, then Kermit noticed the bell. He hit the button, and a few seconds later the man with the scar appeared. He wore a white pharmacist's coat, just as he had before.

"Here for a pick-up." Kermit's head bobbled. Kermit let the magnetic energy from his dreadlocks fill the space. "Hoping it's done." He took an envelope filled with cash out of his pocket and slid it through the small opening at the bottom of the glass window.

The pharmacist didn't say anything. He just picked up the envelope and examined its contents while making a soft clucking sound.

"It's for Michael Collins," Kermit added. "I think that should be sufficient."

The pharmacist turned and disappeared into the back. Kermit heard shuffling from behind a shelf of bottles and plastic containers filled with various powders. A minute later he came back holding the same envelope that Kermit had dropped off a few days earlier.

The pharmacist slid it under the window, and then walked away. He didn't say anything. There was nothing to say.

Kermit took the envelope, which wasn't sealed. He opened the top flap and removed the document inside. Kermit turned to the last page.

When he had dropped it off, there was only Michael's signature. Now there were two.

CHAPTER SIXTY FOUR

Michael ate a dinner of institutional meatloaf and gravy. He had been too nervous to be hungry, but he forced himself to eat something. Then Michael went back to his cell and waited. The phone call was supposed to come after dinner, but he wasn't sure when.

He flipped through a few magazines, trying not to think about the mountain of evidence that Brenda Gadd and Agent Vatch had submitted to the court. It was only the first day, Michael thought. Tomorrow will be worse.

Michael looked at the photograph of his namesake taped to the wall. Then he closed his eyes. He imagined that the noise of the MDC's air exchange were waves crashing on the beach. He imagined that he was back in Hut No. 7.

Michael tried to prevent darkness from taking over. If he had a bottle of whiskey, he'd have drank it all. But there wasn't anything like that in his little cell.

Instead, he focused on the beach, imagining every detail. He had to remain hopeful, although nothing was in his control.

###

A guard knocked on Michael's door. The sound startled him. Michael had fallen asleep, and he wondered how long he'd been out.

"Phone call from your attorney."

The guard knocked, again. He wanted Michael to move faster.

"Thanks."

Michael sat up and got out of his bed. He followed the guard out of the pod, through a series of locked doors and hallways, to a small room with a telephone.

The room was designated to be used exclusively for phone calls between attorneys and their clients. Unlike the other telephones in the MDC, nobody was supposed to monitor these conversations. They were theoretically private, but Michael didn't believe any of that, so he was careful.

"Hello." Michael put the receiver to his ear.

"Is this Michael Collins?" It wasn't Quentin. It was a female voice. It was Andie.

"Yes, this is Michael Collins." His mood brightened.

"I just wanted to tell you that the documents you've provided to us are ready." There was a pause. "Would you like me to proceed?"

Michael felt a smile involuntarily break across his face.

"Yes." Michael nodded. "Absolutely."

"Very well." Andie was curt and professional. She didn't break character. "Anything else?"

Michael wanted to tell Andie how much he loved her. He wanted to say how much he wanted to see her. He wanted to hold her and fall asleep with her next to him, all the things that he usually kept bottled up inside.

NO TIME TO HIDE | 275

But, Michael pushed those thoughts away. It wasn't the time. He couldn't take the chance.

"No," Michael said. "There's nothing else. ... Except ..." He thought for a second. Michael tried to focus. He ran through different scenarios. "Just make sure you keep a copy for our records."

"Makes sense," said Andie. "And before I hang up, your friends wanted me to pass on a message."

"What's that?" Michael asked.

"That they love you very much."

"Thanks for letting me know." Michael melted. "I love them more than anything."

"Of course," Andie said, still professional. "They all know that."

CHAPTER SIXTY FIVE

Brew was the name of the latest gastro-pub to open in what was one of the most cursed corners of Park Slope. New restaurants cycled through the space about every year, sometimes a restaurant would hang on for two years, but never more than that.

They were usually owned by well-intentioned but naive men who were running away from dead-end, white-collar jobs. In the midst of their mid-life crisis, opening a restaurant was perceived to be easier than either going back to school or getting a divorce. Although the divorce inevitably came shortly after the restaurant tanked and the couple's life savings evaporated.

Brew was still in its initial honeymoon period. It was a novelty, and the neighborhood do-gooders were interested in "helping it succeed" for fear of a national chain or a Starbucks taking over the corner. That dedication would fade in a few more months, but at the moment, the bar was filled.

Pierced and tattooed young people sat on stools next to new moms who had babies strapped to their chests.

The new, hipster moms were trying to live their pre-birth vow that the "baby won't change me." It was an admirable goal and entirely plausible right up to the point when the infant refused to be strapped to the mother's chest like an enormous fleshy brooch.

Andie Larone walked to the back of the restaurant. There was a booth in the corner. She sat down, picked up a menu, and waited.

###

Brea Krane arrived twenty minutes late, but Andie didn't say anything. Brea kept her coat on, and sat down across from her.

"Do you have it?" Brea got to the point.

"Yes."

"Then let's see it."

Andie opened her purse. She took out the envelope and handed it to Brea.

Brea Krane took the envelope. She opened it and removed the sheet of paper with the passwords for the other two Cook Island accounts.

"Good." She nodded.

"Now what are you going to say to get Michael out?" Andie asked, but Brea immediately held up her hand.

"Not now and not here." Brea looked around. "I testify in two days. I'm going to make sure these accounts and passwords work." Brea removed a new disposable cell phone from her purse. "Call me on this tomorrow. My new number is the only one programmed in the contacts."

Andie nodded.

"Fine." Andie took the phone. "So that's it?"

"That's it." Brea Krane got up from the table and walked out the door.

Andie watched her. She doubted that Brea Krane had any intention of making good on her promises.

###

Brent Krane followed his sister down 8th Street. The crowd could not believe that she was with Michael Collins' girlfriend. They went mad when they had greeted each other like old friends. His sister was a traitor. She was a liar. He now understood why he had been sent away. He had been tricked.

Brent felt the gun in his pocket. He thought about killing her right then. Why not? Brent picked up his pace. Within a few seconds, Brent had closed the gap to twenty feet. He slid his finger onto the trigger. A surge of power came up his back and buzzed his neck.

The gap closed to ten feet, and then five.

Brent was close now. He could smell his sister's perfume. Brent took the gun out of his pocket, matching her stride for stride. And then a single voice in the crowd told him to stop. It pierced through the fog.

The voice, however, wasn't calling for mercy. The voice told him that she needed to pay him first. He needed to get his sister's money before she was killed. He needed the money, just in case he survived the final confrontation.

CHAPTER SIXTY SIX

G add's approach changed during the second morning of testimony. Rather than ask Vatch to comment on each individual document, Gadd offered documents in bulk.

"Agent Vatch, have you reviewed what has been previously marked as Exhibits 27 through 50?"

Gadd pointed at a stack of documents on the prosecution's table, and Vatch responded that he had reviewed them all and that they were all documents received from various banks through the course of his investigation.

"Very well." Gadd nodded. "Without any objection, the United States would now offer Exhibits 27 through 50."

Judge Husk looked at Quentin, and Quentin stood.

"We have no objection, Your Honor."

"Good. Exhibits 27 through 50 have been offered and are now entered into evidence."

A smile formed on the edges of Judge Husk's mouth as he accepted the stack of documents. It was an expression of satisfaction. His lecture the previous afternoon had worked. Gadd was no longer going to offer each exhibit individually. Therefore, there was now a higher likelihood that he would live long enough to hear the jury's verdict.

###

The rest of the morning moved as quickly as the first ten minutes. Brenda Gadd offered several batches of exhibits, and each time they were admitted without objection or further testimony. The pace of the trial was now in a full sprint, and by the mid-morning break, Brenda Gadd had finished her direct examination of Agent Vatch.

Judge Husk nodded, and looked at the jurors.

"We'll come back in twenty minutes. The prosecution has completed its initial inquiry. Now counsel for Defendant Collins will have an opportunity to question Agent Vatch. When he concludes, Ms. Gadd will ask follow-up questions and so on and so forth until we are done and move onto the next witness."

Judge Husk looked away from the jurors and out into the courtroom. There were fewer people on the second day, but it was still more of an audience than in a typical criminal case. He raised his hand, slowly.

"Please rise as the jurors exit."

Michael and the others stood and watched the jurors get up, stretch, and amble out of the courtroom. They were more relaxed than during jury selection, and Michael saw that they had started to form several internal groups. Friendships were forming. People of similar ages and education levels had gravitated toward one another. It happened every time.

Quentin waited a second until he was sure that they were all gone. Then he turned to Michael. "We should talk."

###

It took a few minutes for Quentin to make it through security, but eventually he was allowed into the back. On each floor there was one secure conference room where attorneys were allowed to meet with clients who were in custody.

Quentin came through the door. He had a notebook and pen, ready to work.

He put his hand on Michael's shoulder, gave it a squeeze, and then sat in a chair across the small table.

"Any ideas?" " Quentin asked as he wrote the date on the top of the notepad.

"Have you talked to Andie?" Michael asked.

Quentin shook his head. "No. She and Kermit have been running around, but I haven't interfered." Quentin paused. He pushed his glasses back up the bridge of his nose. "They're obviously up to something, but I don't want to know."

"That's for the best."

"So I've prepared my cross, but is there anything you want me to ask?"

Michael nodded.

"You need to suggest that they haven't disclosed all the information. You need to suggest that there are more documents out there."

"Are there?" Quentin doubted. "We've been killed with documents. My computer crashed a couple times because the files they sent over were so big."

"Just create some doubt," Michael said. "You need the jury to leave today wondering whether or not the government is hiding information. That this was all a smokescreen."

Quentin's eyes narrowed.

"Is there something specific I need to know? The judge might call me up to the bench and ask."

"Just say the situation is developing. That you believe in good faith that there are additional documents that have not been disclosed." Michael leaned in. "You've made an external record of all your written requests over the past two months, now we need to do it in there. Every witness needs to be asked about the other documents that were not disclosed."

Quentin nodded.

"Okay." Quentin stood. "But Michael, whatever is developing needs to develop soon." He walked toward the door. "We're in deep trouble out there."

The doubts that Quentin expressed in private were gone in the courtroom. His early stumbles during opening arguments were over, and now Quentin projected confidence.

"Tell me about Agent Pastoura."

"She was my partner." Vatch remained steady, suppressing his inner asshole.

"She was more than that." Quentin came back at him. "She was a good friend. True?"

Agent Vatch didn't take the bait. So Quentin continued without asking the judge to force Vatch to answer his question.

"You both were there on the night that Joshua Krane was murdered, correct?"

"Yes."

"And you are not claiming that Michael Collins is at all involved with that murder, right?"

"He has not been charged, but I don't know."

"I'm only asking about what you know." Quentin interrupted. He stopped Vatch before Vatch could do any real damage. "And as you sit here today, you have no specific evidence that Michael Collins was involved."

"Depends on what you mean by specific." Vatch enjoyed himself, and Quentin realized that his whole line of questioning was a mistake. It was one thing for Michael Collins to be a thief.

It was a totally different thing for the jury to think Michael was a murderer.

Quentin changed course. He decided to stop digging himself further into a hole.

"Other things happened that night, didn't they?"

Brenda Gadd rose to her feet.

"Objection, Your Honor, vague."

"Sustained." Judge Husk rolled his eyes. "Get to the point, counsel."

"You agree that other people were injured the night that Joshua Krane died, correct?"

"Yes."

"Krane was killed, true?"

"That's what I said and that's what happened." Agent Vatch's harder edges started to reveal themselves.

"My client, Michael Collins, was also shot that night, correct?"

Agent Vatch looked at Michael Collins.

"That's right."

"And Michael Collins could have died?"

"Yes," Vatch said. "But that doesn't mean —"

Quentin cut him off. "Thank you, Agent Vatch, that answers my question. And then there was a chase?"

"Yes."

"You and Agent Pastoura were in a car, and Agent Pastoura got out of the car to chase the shooter."

Agent Vatch didn't respond.

"Can you answer the question, Agent Vatch? Did Agent Pastoura get out of the car and chase the shooter?"

Agent Vatch nodded his head. "Yes, but I don't see the relevance."

Gadd rose to her feet again. "And neither do I, Your Honor. I object as to relevance."

Quentin looked at the jury and shook his head, and then turned back to the judge. "It shows bias, Your Honor. Agent Vatch's assessment and investigation of my client has been clouded by his own personal involvement with what happened that night."

Judge Husk closed his eyes, thinking.

"I'll overrule the objection, but you need to get to the heart of it, Mr. Robinson."

"Yes, Your Honor." Quentin turned back to Vatch. "There was no time to get you out of the car and into your wheelchair, correct? And so she ran after the shooter by herself, true?"

"Yes." Vatch's jaw stiffened.

"Then she was tragically killed in a shootout with this assailant, and you blame yourself?"

Agent Vatch stared at Quentin, locking eyes.

"Of course," he said. "But the more —"

"That answers my question," Quentin said. "And so you've spent years tracking down, Michael Collins, true?"

"Yes."

"You've worked on this case in the evenings and on the weekends, despite orders from supervisors to back off?"

"I've worked evenings and weekends," Vatch said. "And supervisors had wanted me to work on other investigations, but this was my case."

"Of course, it was your case. It wasn't the government's case. It was your case, personally, because you blamed yourself for Agent Pastoura's death."

Gadd was back on her feet.

"Objection, Your Honor."

"Sustained." Judge Husk bit his lower lip. "Next question."

"You've gathered all these documents, but there are still more documents out there, correct?"

Vatch wasn't sure how to respond. He hesitated, and that was all Quentin wanted. Michael felt the seed of doubt had been planted.

A moment too late, Vatch responded, "We've disclosed what we're required to disclose. We've disclosed all the documents that we have that are relevant and material."

"Required? Relevant? Material?" Quentin shook his head, and then continued. "You've buried us with a mountain of paper, but as you sit here today, there are more reports, bank accounts, and other information that have not been offered into evidence by Ms. Gadd and the government, true?"

"I guess I don't understand."

"There are documents that you've produced to me, as part of discovery, but have not shown the jury, correct?"

Vatch looked at Gadd, hoping for a lifeline. None came, and so Vatch turned back to Quentin.

"I guess that's right."

"You guess," Quentin confirmed. "Exactly. You guess. You've shown the jury only things that *you* think are required and *you* believe are material. But that means there might be a lot of information *I* think is required and *I* believe is material. True?"

"Objection." Gadd was on her feet.

Quentin Robinson waved her off.

"The question's withdrawn, Your Honor. I'm done with this witness."

CHAPTER SIXTY SEVEN

The ride back to the MDC was not a happy one. Michael tried to adjust his position. He tried to get comfortable, but the seats in the U.S. Marshal's transport van were stiff and unforgiving.

There were four other men riding with him. Their street clothes were in storage for the night. All of them were back in their prison jumpsuits. Their hands and legs were cuffed. This was what innocent until proven guilty looks like, thought Michael.

He stared out the tinted window. Michael forced himself to look at the people and the places. He had to pay attention and remember it all, because it was likely that there wouldn't be too many more opportunities to see the outside world again.

Quentin had done his job. He had planted a seed of doubt, which was all that Michael had asked of him. But Michael knew that Quentin's cross-examination was not enough to overcome the evidence. When the trial ended and the jury went into deliberations, the first thing that they would do after selecting a foreperson was review the exhibits, one by one.

Jurors didn't trust lawyers. When cases got complicated or legal arguments got confusing, the only thing that a jury trusted was paper. As Judge Husk had said, "the documents speak for

289

themselves." And in Michael's case, the documents all said the same thing: He was guilty.

He needed the documents to say something else, and, for that, he had to trust Andie and Kermit.

CHAPTER SIXTY EIGHT

B rea arrived about an hour late. The Bowery was one of the latest boutique hotels to open in a formerly crime ridden and depressed area of New York City. It was a twelve-story, red-brick building surrounded by slightly smaller buildings in various states of gentrification on the edge of the East Village.

Brea walked through the crowded lobby, which looked somewhat like a rich, eccentric grandmother's parlor, past the reception desk, to the elevator.

She rode to the top floor and got out.

The hotel room door was open, and so she went inside.

"Hello?" Brea unbuttoned her jacket, and poked her head around the entryway. "Tad, where are you?"

The lights were dim. Candles were burning, and champagne was chilling in a bucket of ice on the dining room table. Brea smiled, picked up the bottle, and popped it open. The cork hit the ceiling, and she quickly picked up a champagne flute to catch the bubbles.

Giggling, Brea called out to Garvin, again.

"Tad, should I pour you a glass?"

Brea took a sip, walked back to the bedroom, and saw the French doors to the balcony were open. Tad Garvin sat in a chair, reviewing a contract and squeezing in a few more billable hours before bed.

"Nice place." Brea walked through the bedroom and out onto the balcony.

Tad finished marking the document, set his pen down, and turned to her.

"The owner of this place is a client," he smiled. "I was a little surprised by your call."

Brea came to him, and kissed Tad on the head. "Just wanted to see you tonight. That's all."

"Well, I'm glad I could break away." He put the papers and pen down, and then motioned for Brea to come sit on his lap. He knew that Brea Krane was going to ask him to do something. That was just how it worked, but he appreciated the fact that Brea would wait. It made their relationship seem less unseemly.

"Told the wife I had to leave a day early for this conference in Boston, making a presentation."

"Bet she was heartbroken."

Garvin laughed as Brea walked over and sat down. She put an arm around him, and took a sip of champagne.

"So what's the emergency?" Garvin asked.

Brea shrugged, playing coy.

"Just a little lonely." Her hand edged up Tad Garvin's thigh.

Garvin felt a rush. Usually Brea made him work harder for it. He thought that he'd have to spend at least a couple hundred dollars on a dinner first.

Brea had other plans.

Having sex with a doughy, middle-aged lawyer was not what Brea wanted to do, but it was a sacrifice that she was willing to make. For the money in Michael Collins' accounts, she allowed Garvin to paw at her for about nine minutes, thrust for five, and then finish with a grunt.

She watched him as he got up out of the bed and walk to the bathroom. It was what she had expected, automatic. Every time that they had sex — which, mercifully, was not very often — Garvin would immediately go to the bathroom and take a shower. Perhaps he didn't like sweat. Perhaps he was trying to rid himself of DNA evidence related to his extramarital affair. Perhaps it was psychological. Regardless, it was something Brea had anticipated.

She feigned sleep when Tad Garvin emerged from the bathroom in a white terrycloth robe. He removed the robe and got back into bed. He kissed Brea on the cheek, and she pretended that he woke her up.

"Hey." Brea's voice was soft. "What time is your flight tomorrow?"

"Early," Garvin said. "Probably be gone by the time you get up."

"And you'll be gone for two days?"

Garvin nodded.

"You could come and visit me, if you want."

Brea smiled. She rolled over, and pressed her naked body against him.

"I'll think about it," she lied.

He kissed her, and Brea decided that now was the time to make the ask that they both knew was coming.

"Have you ever established any new trusts in the Cook Islands?" Brea smiled.

"No." Tad Garvin shook his head. "But I can learn."

Brea giggled.

"I bet you can." She lifted the sheet over them, crawled underneath and sealed the deal.

CHAPTER SIXTY NINE

Michael It was late. Kermit Guillardo knew that he couldn't delay. He knew what he had to do.

Kermit stood naked. Candles, big and small, covered every open surface of the small bathroom. Incense burned. Marijuana was smoked, and "I Will Always Love You" as sung by Whitney Houston blasted from his mini JamBox.

Kermit sang along with the Diva Whitney, hitting and holding the high notes until his breath ran out. He turned the electric razor on, and he felt the surge as the subatomic particles of the room blended into one cosmic ball of energy.

Nothing was solid. Nothing was separate, undivided. They were all connected. The world was chaos, and in the end, what was hair? He wasn't a man. He wasn't Kermit Guillardo, and he certainly was not a beard or dreadlocks. He was an aberration of interconnected nanocompounds, which could mutate and re-form.

Kermit ran the razor across his cheek. The blades caught in the knots a few times, but within a few minutes the beard was gone. Then he picked up a scissors and began to cut off his dreadlocks, one by one the bosons fell away.

He held them in his hands.

"I will always love you."

CHAPTER SEVENTY

Tad Garvin was gone before Brea woke up in the morning. Brea, then, rolled over. She got out of bed and picked up the silk robe that was draped over the arm of a nearby chair. Brea put on the robe, and then went to her bag and opened it.

She removed a thin laptop from the bag, set it on an ornate Cherrywood desk, opened the screen, and turned it on. It took a moment to connect, but she was patient.

Brea went to the website for Capital Asset Security Bank in the Cook Islands. She clicked the "online banking" tab at the top of the page, and then entered the information about Michael Collins' first account.

The screen flashed, and the password was accepted.

Brea reviewed the account information. She smiled at the balance remaining. She had complete access. She pressed another button and changed the password and security settings to something that only she would know. Then she checked the second and third accounts, and Brea did the same.

It would take Tad Garvin a few days to set up a different series of trusts and accounts in the Cook Islands. Once the money was transferred, that's when Brea would be content. In the meantime, hopefully the new passwords would be enough to keep Michael Collins and Andie Larone from accessing the accounts and taking the money back.

She logged off, and went to her purse. Brea removed the disposable cell phone that was her connection to Andie Larone. She pried off the cheap phone's plastic back, removed the SD card, and then broke the small blue card in half. She put the remnants of the broken SD card in her purse, and then tossed the rest of the phone in the garbage.

As soon as she found a garbage can on the street, the SD card would be gone as well. And when Andie called to discuss her testimony later that day, nobody would answer.

CHAPTER SEVENTY ONE

Before trial resumed for the third day of testimony, Quentin looked over at United States Attorney Brenda Gadd. She was shuffling through a stack of paper, preparing for her next witness.

"How many do you think you'll get through today?" Quentin asked as he glanced at the door where Judge Husk would slowly emerge at any moment.

Gadd looked up and over, also glancing at the door. "Probably three, the main forensic accountant and a couple of bank people."

"And then?"

Gadd shrugged.

"Depends. Probably another investigator and then the daughter."

Quentin looked at Michael, and then back at Gadd. "Any further disclosures you need to make?" Quentin asked the question largely to pacify Michael. Every break they took, Michael wad pushed Quentin to be tougher on Gadd and make it clear that they needed every document. Quentin figured that it might shut Michael up, if Michael actually heard the exchange.

Gadd smirked, puzzled by the question.

"Not that I'm aware of." She looked down at her sheet of paper, jotted a note, and then looked back up. "Is there something in particular? I could ask for it."

"No." Quentin shook his head. "Only making sure I've got everything."

The accountant tried to make his work sound exciting. His testimony, however, was just a more detailed summary of the general testimony Agent Vatch had provided on the first days of trial. The accountant explained the delay in obtaining records from foreign banks. Then he traced the money from six accounts and ultimately to Michael Collins' purchase of the Sunset Resort and Hostel.

Of all the decisions that Michael had made over the past five years, that was likely his biggest mistake. Purchasing the resort when Andie was in financial trouble was the key link to him. It cost Michael his relationship with Andie, which had never fully recovered, and now it may cost him his life.

After the prosecution ended its direct examination, Judge Husk called a mid-morning break. Quentin requested that the marshals escort Michael to a meeting in the small conference room. They didn't really have anything to talk about, but Michael preferred the conference room to the windowless holding area in the courthouse basement.

CHAPTER SEVENTY TWO

Brea Krane was never aware of their actual plans. That was by design. She was a very expensive backup plan. She had merely agreed to "do or say whatever they wanted" in exchange for the money. The details were supposed to be worked out later.

But now, Andie's phone calls to Brea Krane had not been returned. Andie had left a dozen messages, but Andie knew that Brea Krane was never going to answer. She wasn't surprised. Michael had warned Andie all along, but the sudden silence made it real. It increased the pressure. They would only have one chance.

Andie waited in the living room.

"You're going to have to come down at some point."

"No," Kermit whimpered. He peeked around the corner at the top of the stairs. "You're going to laugh at me."

"I'm not going to laugh." Andie got up from the couch and put her hands on her hips. She had tried being gentle for the past half-hour, but now they needed to go.

"We have work to do this morning." She looked at the clock. "And we don't have much time."

"Time is all relative. Time is simply a human framework to make life more ..." Kermit's voice trailed off, faltering. His heart wasn't into it and he wondered if his power of speculative philosophy would ever return.

Andie, however, wasn't going to let him off.

"Time is very real and I know we don't have much of it left. All we know is that Tad Garvin is on the panel from 10:30 to 11:30 today. That's our best time to do this. It's an hour when we know Tad Garvin is going to be unavailable for phone calls. Hopefully he won't be checking his messages in the middle of his speech," Andie's voice rose. She started to panic.

"I don't know," Kermit sounded weak. "Maybe you should do it by yourself."

Andie shook her head.

"That's not the plan." She walked over to the bottom of the steps. "You told me that you would do anything for Michael. Well, this falls into that broad category."

There was another moan from upstairs, and then nothing.

Andie wondered whether she could actually execute the plan alone. Then Andie heard a creak on the top step, and then another. She was afraid to look. Andie was worried that eye contact with Kermit would scare him back to his room. He was a feral cat.

Andie kept her eyes averted until Kermit had come all the way down the stairs. Then she looked at him. She was careful to keep her expression neutral, but it was hard to withhold comment or to prevent her jaw from dropping.

Kermit Guillardo was unrecognizable.

His hair was gone. He was bald. Kermit's ratted beard was shaved, and Andie saw, for the first time, Kermit's chiseled features and strong chin. He was almost handsome.

Kermit's baggy clothes and tie-dye T-shirts were replaced by a navy blue suit, a dark green and blue bow tie, and a pair of calfskin, Cole Haan wingtips.

"You look the part." Andie looked him up and down. "You really look the part."

Kermit shook his head. "Feels like I'm in shackles." Then he lifted his new leather briefcase in the air. "Complete with the ball and chain."

Andie and Kermit sat on the park bench, staring at the glass skyscraper across the street. It was narrow, but the top ten floors flared out and curved back into a tip. "Kind of looks like a dude's ding-a-ling." Kermit tilted his head to the side, still staring. "The architect definitely took his inspiration from the topography of the lower extremities. Agree?"

Andie looked at it.

"Could be a candle with a flame," she shrugged. "But probably a ding-a-ling."

Kermit clapped his hands and laughed.

"Genius." Then he scanned the skyline. "Although I suppose the same could be said for all the skyscrapers in this city — a hundred or so men lying on their backs with —"

"Let's stay focused," Andie interrupted. "Why don't you make the call?"

Kermit nodded.

"Can do." He reached into his pocket and removed a cell phone and a torn slip of paper with a phone number written on it.

"Here goes." He punched in the number. Two rings, and the receptionist answered. "Franklin and Uckley, how may I direct your call?"

"Yeah, this is Uptown Couriers, I need the number for Mr. Benjamin Howe." Kermit winked at Andie and gave her the thumbs-up.

There was a pause as the receptionist typed the name into the law firm's electronic directory. Franklin and Uckley had over a thousand attorneys in their New York office and thousands elsewhere in offices around the world.

"I'm sorry, sir. I don't seem to have that number."

"Well, he wants me to deliver this thing ASAP." Kermit pretended he was mad. "And the address Mr. Howe gave me is no good."

"Well, I'm sorry, sir," the receptionist said. "I'm afraid I don't have a Mr. Howe listed in our directory. Are you sure he's at Franklin and Uckley?"

"He is," Kermit said. "Now what's your name, so when I call back I know who to talk to?"

"Helen."

"Okay, Helen," Kermit said. "I'll call back in ten minutes when this gets sorted out." Kermit punched off the phone. He nodded, proud of himself.

"You get that?"

Andie nodded. "Helen." She repeated the name, again, and then stood.

Kermit handed the box of documents to her.

"Godspeed, Ms. Larone."

"Godspeed," she said back. "Hope this works."

Andie started walking across the street. When she had made it to the other side, Andie looked up, one last time, at the top of the skyscraper before going inside.

The law firm of Franklin and Uckley occupied the very top floors.

F U

CHAPTER SEVENTY THREE

A ndie Larone wore a dark Anne Klein suit, cream blouse and sensible heels. Her hair was pulled back into a tight bun. She also wore a pair of small glasses with silver rims. Andie looked serious and educated, as well as thin and attractive. In other words, Andie Larone looked like every other young female associate at the firm.

The only thing that Andie lacked at the moment was confidence and security credentials.

She tried not to bite her nails as she waited in the lobby. Time passed slowly. Andie watched the minute hand of a large silver clock above the security desk move from one notch to the next.

Seven minutes after Kermit's initial phone call, Andie proceeded to the elevators with the box of documents. If the timing was right, Kermit should be screaming at the receptionist about the same time as she attempted to sneak past.

Andie focused on the job. The elevator shot up to the top floor of the office tower in seconds. Then it was time for the show.

The elevator bell rang. The doors opened, she walked through the large modern reception area without hesitation. Andie saw the flustered receptionist talking on the phone and

305

typing frantically on her keyboard. Andie didn't know what Kermit was saying, but the receptionist looked like she was in pain. She was trying to apologize, but Kermit seemed to be interrupting her.

There was no direct eye contact. Andie saw a door behind the receptionist. She walked toward it with purpose. She never stopped. Andie acted as if she belonged there.

Then, just a few steps from the door, Andie allowed the box to slip a little in her hands. As she struggled to keep it from falling, Andie said, "Helen, can you please buzz me in?"

Andie had said the receptionist's name with a sharp tone, like commanding a dog to sit. Then she softened. "My hands are full. I'm sorry. I'm in a hurry."

Distracted by Kermit's continued tirade, the receptionist took notice of Andie for the first time.

"Yes. Of course." After years at the firm, Helen was obedient. She reached a button on the side of the receptionist's desk and pressed it. It was obvious that the person making the request was an employee, probably an attorney, and to require them to set down the document box and produce identification or swipe a magnetic card would risk the attorney's wrath.

The door clicked and buzzed. Andie pushed it open.

"Thanks." Once inside, she didn't break stride. She kept walking.

Down one hallway and then another, Andie finally stopped. She saw several legal secretaries chatting near a coffee machine.

"Excuse me," Andie said. "I'm a new associate and I'm supposed to have these documents numbered, scanned, and served. It's a rush."

The chubby legal secretary looked at the skinny legal secretary and then back at Andie.

"Of course, dear, it's always a rush," she forced a smile. "You're looking for Legal Support. They're two floors down."

"Can you show me where?" Andie looked at a clock on the wall. "I'm afraid I'm just going to get lost again. This place is so big."

The chubby one set down her coffee mug, and then looked at the skinny one.

"We'll talk later." Then to Andie, "Follow me."

The support staff was there to serve. Whether the person asking was a senior partner or a junior associate, the support staff at Franklin and Uckley were trained in the same manner as the receptionist at the front desk. They knew that they could never say no and to keep their ideas to themselves.

"Just give me the box."

"No, that's okay." Andie wasn't going to give up the box of papers that Michael had spent months printing.

"Okay," the assistant said. "I'll just lead the way. We're just going down here."

The assistant pressed her card against the black security panel. The light switched from red to green and the stairwell door unlocked. Then she opened the door for Andie and held it open.

"Thanks," Andie said. "I really appreciate this. I don't think Mr. Garvin wanted me to come back to him with a lot of questions."

The secretary shook her head.

"They never do, sweetheart. They never do."

Kermit assumed that Andie had made it inside. Now it was his turn. He crossed the street, trying to control his inner rhythm, and entered the tower of Franklin and Uckley's New York office.

He had come up with a rather simple plan, and Andie couldn't think of one that was any better.

"Simplicity is the key to life."

Kermit found a fancy wooden bench with a white leather cushion near the elevators in the building's large open foyer. Kermit walked over to the bench. He unlatched the buckle of his briefcase and removed a copy of the Wall Street Journal, then he pretended to read as he waited for the right group to arrive.

Kermit watched three older businessmen and a token woman enter the building and walk toward the elevators. Kermit didn't think that was the right combination. They could be clients. They could also be attorneys from another law firm. Then Kermit saw two young women. They looked like baby lawyers. They were dressed in the same outfit that Andie Larone had chosen. Each of them sipped some sort of expensive latte or frap-crap. Kermit decided to let the two women pass as well.

As more time passed, he started to get worried, and then Kermit saw them.

They were four young white men. Some were tall. Some were short, but they were all the same. Their hair was cut short. Their clothes were perfect. They walked with a sense of entitlement. They acted as though they had the whole world figured out, even though they were ignorant of the insignificant role they played in it.

Kermit stood, and as the young men passed him, he followed behind. In order to pull this off, Kermit needed to channel his inner douchebag.

They all got on the elevator together. The tall one pressed the button for 61st floor. They obviously hadn't worked their way up to the top floors of Franklin and Uckley, but they were trying.

When the bell rang, Kermit coughed.

"After you boys." Kermit's voice dripped with condescension, putting the younger men in their place was important.

They all turned, noticing him. They scanned Kermit, inspecting his clothes and briefcase. Because of his age and presence in the law firm's elevator, Kermit was immediately categorized as a senior partner.

The young men walked out. Because the 61st floor was not the firm's main office, there was not a large and impressive reception area. Instead, there was a small desk staffed by a middle-aged African-American woman to the right and an internal side door for employees to the left.

The young men walked to the left, and Kermit followed behind them. As one of the young men scanned his card, another held the door for Kermit as he walked inside.

"Thank you, boys. Bill this conversation to 'Admin-Mentorship.' Point-one hours."

The four young men laughed. It was unclear, however, whether they actually thought the joke was funny or whether the laughter at a superior's joke was just something that they were trained to do.

After descending two flights of stairs, the chubby legal secretary pushed open the door and led Andie down another hallway to the Legal Support Services room.

"Here you are," she directed Andie inside. "Monica, sweetie."

Another woman looked up from a table of binders.

"What is it?"

"Got a new associate with a rush job for Mr. Garvin." The chubby secretary patted Andie on the shoulder, and pointed at the empty counter.

"Just put your box down there. Monica will take care of you."

Andie did as she was instructed as her guide disappeared and Monica walked over and picked up the box.

"What's the project?" Monica brought the box over to the copier and set it down on the floor.

"Mr. Garvin needs those scanned into the system, bates numbered, and then sent over to the U.S. Attorney's Office right away."

"By courier?"

Andie nodded.

"Yes."

"What's the file number? I need to bill it to somebody. Everything needs to be billed to somebody."

"Don't know." Andie shrugged. "Can we look it up?"

Monica nodded. She walked over to her cluttered desk in the corner of the Legal Support room. Monica sat down, logged on, and pulled up a database.

"What's the name?"

"Brea Krane," Andie said. "It's for that case against Michael Collins."

"The one in the news?" Monica began to type. "Saw that in the newspaper the other day." Monica pressed enter, and the screen displayed a list of responses to her query. "Any of these look right?"

Andie looked over Monica's shoulder.

"The third one down." Andie pointed. "That's it."

"Okay," Monica jotted down the client number on a small sheet of paper. "I'll number them, scan the documents into the database for this file, and then courier them over to the U.S. Attorney's Office. Anybody in particular?"

Andie nodded.

"Yes. Brenda Gadd. They should be sent to the attention of Brenda Gadd."

"Great." Monica wrote down the name and title. "Cover letter?"

Andie had hoped that she wouldn't ask that question.

"No," Andie said. "Mr. Garvin doesn't have the time. He says that they're expecting them."

"Well," Monica's face tensed. "Don't like sending things without a cover letter. Can't you just sign it for him?"

Andie's heart skipped. "I'm new and I really don't …. um … and Mr. Garvin just wants them out, and he's traveling."

Monica looked at the box and then back at Andie. She considered her options.

Kermit found an empty office with no name plate on the door. There was a narrow window that ran along the side of the door frame. He closed the blinds so that nobody could see him from the hallway, then Kermit closed and locked the door.

He walked around to the desk. He sat down in the large leather chair and waited. Kermit had been told that if nothing happened in thirty minutes that he should leave. Andie had hoped that they would just take the box and send it, but she wanted him there in case something went wrong.

Kermit sat for a long time staring at the wall. Then his phone vibrated.

He looked up at the clock on the wall, and he knew that something had happened.

Kermit looked back at his vibrating phone. It was a text from Andie. They needed a cover letter and Tad Garvin's electronic signature inserted into the document.

Kermit sighed. He texted Andie back: HOW

He waited, and then Andie responded back:

FIND LGL SECRETARY
GARVIN HAS ELECTRONIC SIGNATURE IN SYSTEM
SHOULD BE TEMPLATE LTR
EMAIL DOC TO MONICA IN LGL SUP

Finding a woman to bedazzle with his charm was ordinarily a task that Kermit felt confident to perform, but Kermit was off. His energy level was low. His color field was blue. He was naked without his hair. He was weak.

Kermit got up from the big leather chair. He took a step toward the door, but stopped. Kermit instinctively went to touch one of his long dreadlocks for power, but the dreadlocks were gone. Instead, Kermit ran his hand along the top of his bald, shaved head.

Kermit closed his eyes. He thought about the centillion subatomic particles floating around him. He felt their magnetic energy try to enter his body, but unable to find the connection. The dreadlocks were gone. His beard was shaved. He had no way of channeling his power.

But he needed it. Andie needed it. Michael needed it.

Kermit took off his suit jacket. He removed his bow tie. The shackles that had bound him fell away, and Kermit felt a tingle at the base of his spine. He walked over to the door and peeked out the drawn shade. Nobody was around.

Then Kermit turned off the lights. He unbuttoned his shirt and removed it. He kicked off his fancy leather shoes. Then he unfastened his belt, unzipped his pants, and let them drop to the ground. The tingle grew stronger. It worked up his back. He felt the receptors allowing the energy to enter him, but Kermit was still confused as to how it was happening.

The energy propelled him. It was hope. He took off his socks and tight white underwear. Then Kermit was totally naked in the office. He had never felt so alive.

He closed his eyes. He took a deep breath, then swept his arms overhead and crouched into a sun salutation. Kermit performed a series of his favorite yoga positions. From sun salutation, he went into a downward facing dog, then a crescent pose, then to warrior.

Kermit's breathing became heavier, and he repeated the sequence. Each time through the various poses and contortions, his energy level grew higher. After ten minutes, a film of sweat glistened on his body. His color changed from blue to green to a dazzling yellow.

That was when he realized that he had made an error in focusing only upon his dreadlocks. His dreadlocks were simply the obvious receptors. He had been distracted by them, and ignored the millions of other tiny receptors on his body.

Kermit spread his arms wide and began spinning.

"Why too much hair down there?"

Terminal and vellus hair populated his entire body.

Why hadn't he seen it before? Why was he so ashamed? Why limit the power to a beard and dreadlocks? He had tiny hairs, some visible and others clear, all over his body.

Kermit opened himself up. He spun around. He felt his erector pili muscles contract, raising the small hairs higher to bring in heat and power into his soul.

He continued to spin in place, faster and faster, willing the power and energy of Franklin and Uckley to transform around him.

CHAPTER SEVENTY FOUR

The computer dinged. The document arrived in Monica's email, and Andie felt a wave of relief as Monica opened the attachment.

"Here it is." They both looked at the letter from Tad Garvin to Brenda Gadd. At the bottom of the letter, there was an image of Garvin's signature.

Monica clicked print. A letter on thick, expensive paper with the Franklin and Uckley logo rolled out of the laser printer and into the tray. She picked it up, and then turned to Andie.

"Documents are all scanned." Monica looked at the box. "I'll just pop this in there and it'll go out the door."

Andie smiled. "Thank you." She shrugged. "Sorry I hung around. Didn't mean to hover. It's one of my first big assignments."

"You ain't the first one."

Monica got up and walked toward the box. She took off the lid, put the letter inside, and then sealed the box with packaging tape.

"You want me to e-serve the documents over to Gadd as well?"

Andie thought about it.

"Sure."

"Well, okay then." Monica went back to her computer. She logged onto to third-party vendor that provided the law firm with secure e-service capabilities. Monica typed in her code, and then served the documents on Brenda Gadd. The vendor transmitted the documents and kept an electronic record of the time, date, and specific documents that had been transmitted.

"That should do it."

Andie shook her head in disbelief.

"It's done."

Kermit was now fully clothed, although his bowtie had been removed. He sat on the park bench across the street from the office tower. The world was more vibrant. A new energy radiated around him.

When Kermit saw Andie emerge, he stood. She had a huge smile on her face. He could see it, even though she was on the other side of the street. Andie ran toward him. She dodged a couple of taxis, made it onto the sidewalk, and then jumped into Kermit's arms.

"Can you believe it?"

Kermit laughed.

"Senorita, I do declare that anything is possible in this chaotic world."

"We have to let Michael know." Andie hugged Kermit, again, and took a step back. "Brea Krane should be testifying soon."

"You gonna tell her what's going on?"

Andie shook her head.

"Nope." They started walking down the street toward a taxi stand at a nearby hotel. "Even if I wanted to, she's not answering her phone at the moment."

Kermit shook his head.

"Figures. Got the money. No loyalty among thieves."

"But we don't need her." Andie walked up to the first taxi in the line. The driver opened the door for her.

Before Andie got in, she turned to Kermit.

"If we didn't get the documents served, we were going to get her to do it through Garvin, but it's better this way." Andie smiled. "The surprise will be real."

Kermit clapped his hands. "You know, I don't care what the judge says, I'm watching that go down, my lady. I'll even wear my suit. I've got to see it."

Andie, still dressed as a young associate, undid the top three buttons on her blouse and approached the blue coat standing in the hallway outside the courtroom.

"Excuse me," Andie smiled. "I'm an associate attorney with Quentin Robinson." She nodded toward the door. "He's the defense attorney with the ponytail and glasses."

The federal marshal's eyes drifted down toward Andie's chest as she talked. He caught himself, and then focused on maintaining eye contact with her.

Andie saw him struggle not to be a pervert, which gave her some power in the conversation.

"I don't want to disrupt the proceedings inside. Would you mind passing him a note?" She took a folded piece of paper out of her pocket. "It's nothing secret, just a note reminding him about supplemental disclosures."

The blue coat took the note from her, unfolded the piece of paper and read it. What Andie told him was the truth. The note simply said:

THE DOCUMENTS ARE READY

"Please," Andie smiled sweetly. "If it's not too much trouble."

The blue coat liked the attention, and so he agreed to give the note to Quentin. He turned, opened the courtroom door, and then walked down the center aisle to counsel tables.

Gadd continued her questioning and Judge Husk didn't give the old federal marshal a second look.

The blue coat leaned over a wooden railing, tapped Quentin on the shoulder, handed Quentin the note, and walked away.

Quentin opened it, trying to read the note while still listening to Gadd's questioning. He raised his eyebrows, a little confused. Then Quentin put the note down on the table and slid it over to Michael.

Michael read what was written on the small piece of paper, suppressing a smile. He turned around and looked for Andie in the courtroom, although he knew she wasn't allowed inside. Then he closed his eyes in a quiet, silent celebration. He thanked Andie and Kermit, and he told Father Stiles that he just might be a believer, maybe.

CHAPTER SEVENTY FIVE

Gadd finished her questioning of the accountant, and Quentin took the rest of the morning with his initial cross-examination. There was a break for lunch, and then Gadd proceeded with a redirect and Quentin followed with additional cross-examination. The witness was finished by mid-afternoon.

Judge Husk let out a heavy sigh, and then turned to Gadd.

"Next."

Brenda Gadd stood.

"Yes, Your Honor." Gadd looked at the back of the courtroom. "The United States calls Brea Krane to the stand."

At the mention of her name, the jurors perked up. This was going to be the first female witness, and so the men hoped that she might be attractive. This was also going to be one of the first witnesses who was probably not going to talk about bank accounts, electronic fund transfers, and the service of subpoenas upon foreign corporations.

Brea Krane walked down the center aisle. She was poised and confident, paying no attention to Michael. Brea walked up a few steps to the witness stand, was sworn to tell the whole truth and nothing but the truth, and then sat down.

Gadd's initial questions were general: schools and hobbies. Then Gadd ventured into Brea's relationship with her dad and her family. Quentin could probably have objected to the questions as irrelevant, but she was the victim's daughter. He didn't want to come across as insensitive.

Eventually, Gadd elicited testimony about how her father's death had affected the family and Brea told a few stories, which may or may not have been true, and she even managed a tear.

The reality was that Brea barely knew her father because he was either working, managing various mistresses in multiple cities, or squeezing in a bribe to this government employee or that congressman. But because of all the lawyer shows on television, the jury expected some tales of love and sorrow. Brea Krane obliged.

The direct examination ended, and Judge Husk brought down the gavel. The jury was dismissed for the evening. Brea Krane's testimony would continue in the morning. This time it would be Quentin's turn to ask the questions.

Michael leaned over.

"We need to talk."

"About the note," Quentin looked at the folded piece of paper still in Michael's hand.

"Yes," Michael said, "and some other things." He nodded toward Brenda Gadd. "Ask her again for any supplemental discovery. Tell her that you know she's winning, but that you need more to work with."

Quentin scrunched up his brow, rubbing his chin.

"I don't think that's a good idea."

"Just do it," Michael was impatient, but was too happy to get upset.

"I've already badgered her every day, sometimes twice a day, for weeks."

Michael put his hand on Quentin's shoulder and gave it a squeeze.

"Trust me."

Michael waited in the small attorney-client conference room, just off the back entrance to the courtroom and next to the secure elevator that led to the holding area. In his hand, Michael held fifteen typewritten pieces of paper.

There was a quick knock on the door, and then it opened. Quentin came inside the room and immediately saw the paper in Michael's hands.

"What've you got?"

Michael looked down, and then handed the paper to Quentin. "I've been working on this for awhile. It's Brea Krane's cross-examination."

Quentin glanced at it. "I know you're trying to help," he said. "But I think I can handle her cross-examination."

Michael shook his head.

"No, Quentin. Things are changing."

"Do I want to know how?"

"Not really," Michael said, "but you're going to need to be prepared."

"For what?"

Michael smiled. He started to answer, and then he stopped himself.

"Read the questions and you'll understand."

Michael closed his eyes and thought of leaving New York forever, going back to the Sunset and his beloved ramshackle hut. He dreamed of falling asleep on the Point with Andie in his arms. He dreamed about being free, once and for all.

"Just read it, and we can talk tomorrow if you want before the start of court."

"Anything else?"

"These questions only make sense if Gadd produces the documents." Michael nodded. "I know she's got them now. She just needs to dump them on you. That's what I'm counting on."

Quentin shook his head.

"How do you know this?"

Michael took Andie's note out of his pocket.

"Because this says so."

They both stood up, and Michael gave his attorney and friend a hug. He finished with two man-slaps on the back and pulled away.

"It's time, my friend. It's time."

CHAPTER SEVENTY SIX

Gadd returned to the office after a quick dinner. She threw her suit jacket over the simple "guest" chair in her office, and then she saw the box. Gadd shook her head and muttered a few expletives to herself.

Walking around the desk to the other side, she pulled the box toward her. Gadd looked down and saw that the return address for the box was from Tad Garvin at Franklin and Uckley.

FU, she thought.

Then Gadd found a scissors, cut the tape, and opened it. Inside the box, there were probably a thousand sheets of paper. She closed her eyes, too exhausted to think, and then removed the cover letter. She was hoping it was for another case, but Gadd knew that it wasn't.

The letter was from Tad Garvin, and the documents all related to Michael Collins and Joshua Krane.

Gadd put the lid back on the box and pushed it away. Then she sat down at her desk, logged on, and checked her email.

There was a message from an administrative assistant at Tad Garvin's law firm. Attached to the email was a zip file, an electronic duplicate of the box of paper.

Gadd leaned back. In the olden days, she would have just ignored it. She wasn't calling any more witnesses. She had submitted all of her exhibits. She wasn't going to use anything in the box, because she didn't have to.

In the olden days, she'd have pretended that it was never received and if somebody asked about it, Gadd would dismiss the paper as irrelevant (which it probably was) and duplicative of all the other documents that Tad Garvin had provided the government through the course of its investigation of Michael Collins.

Gadd leaned back in her chair. She stared at the box, rubbing her eyes.

She had a slam-dunk case. Michael Collins' attorney hadn't put up much of a fight, but Quentin Robinson had been persistent. He'd asked about additional disclosures consistently before the trial and during.

Gadd stood. She removed the first piece of paper of supplemental discovery. It was a six-year-old SEC filing related to a Krane Construction subsidiary. Gadd put the piece of paper back in the box, and then pulled another at random. It was a similar corporate disclosure. Then she pulled another and another. They were all the same.

Gadd sat back down. A jury trial was a grind, and she was getting old. She needed sleep, and she didn't want to spend the night reviewing documents.

Gadd picked up the phone, punched in a series of digits, and waited.

After a few rings, there was an answer..

"It's Brenda Gadd." She took a deep breath, and then she did what any United States Attorney does: she exerted her power to make a subordinate's life miserable. "Got served with a bunch of new disclosures in the Collins case. I need them reviewed so that I can disclose them in the morning. There's probably nothing there, but it needs to be done. I'll send them over."

Gadd pressed a button on her computer while she listened to Agent Frank Vatch complain. When Vatch paused to take a breath, Gadd continued. "Since you're so excited to get to work, I'm forwarding you the electronic file right now."

Gadd forwarded the email she had received from Franklin and Uckley to Vatch.

"Call me if there's a problem. Otherwise, I'll send them to the defense early tomorrow."

###

Vatch pressed the "end" button on his cell phone, shaking his head. He knocked on the Plexiglas separating himself from the cab driver in front.

"Turn around up here."

Vatch knocked on the Plexiglas again.

"Gotta go back to where you picked me up."

"You going back to work?" The Indian driver shook his head and tut-tutted. "No good."

Vatch shoved the cell phone into his pocket and glared out the window.

"Got that right."

###

Vatch flashed his card at the security guard and rolled toward the elevator bank. After thirty-five years, Vatch was familiar with the "my dick is bigger than your dick" game that was pervasive among the federal law enforcement "partners."

In public, they were all on the same team. High-level elected and appointed officials populated inter-agency task forces with the goal of cooperation and information-sharing. They spouted platitudes about how they all had the same mission to protect the public.

But in private, nothing was done for a bureaucracy that had a different scramble of letters: FBI, ATF, CIA, NSA, TSA, UST, DOJ. You only belonged to one tribe.

There was really only one exception: United States Attorney Brenda Gadd. When she called, there wasn't much choice. Despite being a woman, she had a bigger dick than almost anybody. She had the power to send Vatch to the file room for the rest of his career if he disobeyed her. It didn't matter that she was DOJ and he was FBI. Everybody worked for Brenda Gadd.

Vatch reached out and pressed the elevator button. The doors slid open. He rolled inside, and they slid closed. A short trip up a dozen floors, and Vatch emerged into the deserted hallway. A motion sensor clicked. The office's fluorescent lights flicked to life.

Vatch rolled past the cubicles to his small office. He spun around to the other side of his desk and turned on his computer.

He pressed a few buttons and opened his email. The message from Brenda Gadd waited for him. He clicked the attachment and the computer froze, thinking about how to handle the massive file.

A few seconds passed, and then the computer flashed. A list of six hundred separate, imaged documents popped up, over a thousand pages.

Vatch clicked the first one and started to work.

CHAPTER SEVENTY SEVEN

V atch was about thirty percent through the documents after two hours. He had to admit that he wasn't looking particularly closely at any of them. They were all mostly SEC disclosures or some other corporate report. Once Vatch reviewed the first page, he'd quickly scan through the rest and move onto the next.

There was nothing new.

Vatch had seen most of the documents before. They appeared to be duplicates of past disclosures. Perhaps Tad Garvin had merely sensed the end of the case and wanted to squeeze out a few more billable hours by making up some work for his law firm.

Vatch clicked to the next file. A new document popped up on his computer screen, and then his cell phone rang.

He dug into his pocket, got the phone, and answered.

"Yeah."

He had half-expected it to be Brenda Gadd, checking on him. But it was Anthony's mom. She rarely called unless there was trouble.

"Slow down," Vatch listened. "Is he hurt?"

She rambled. Anthony's mom sounded drunk or high or both.

"Wait a second," Vatch closed his eyes. He tried to be patient as Anthony's mom talked in circles. "Listen to me, okay? Slow down. Where is he?"

She strung a coherent answer together. Vatch nodded. His chest tightened. It was the phone call that he had been expecting for months.

"Well, I can't do anything for a few more hours. I'm still at work."

She cried harder and screamed at him, something about losing her baby boy.

"Just wait." Vatch turned off the phone, put it away, and tried to refocus on the documents.

He reviewed another three. They were more of the same. Then he looked at another half-dozen, and then finally he couldn't take it anymore. He couldn't concentrate.

For nearly five years Vatch had hunted Michael Collins. He had stayed with the case, even when others had told him to stop.

When Agent Pastoura had died in an alley, she didn't have backup because of him. Vatch couldn't get out of the car on his own to help her, and so he had to pay off that debt, make amends. Now the Collins case was over. He needed to move on. He needed to care for himself and the only other person that meant anything to him.

Vatch took out his cell phone. He pressed the "call log" button, and the phone number from Anthony's mother was listed at the top of incoming calls. He pressed another button, and waited for her to answer.

"It's me." Vatch looked at the computer screen. He shook his head, clicking the document viewer closed. "Be there in fifteen minutes. Don't answer the door unless it's me. Don't talk to anybody else. Don't let Anthony call or talk to anybody. Nobody. Don't do anything. Don't let anybody inside without a warrant."

Vatch ended the call. Then he logged off and shut the computer down.

###

There was confusion and too much activity in the neighborhood. Vatch stared out the window of the cab as the cab driver wound his way around police detours. There were small crowds of people — huddled and sharing gossip.

Two NYPD cruisers blocked an intersection near his apartment. The street corner was lit up by large, temporary lamps on poles, like the kind that photographers use on photo shoots. Vatch, however, knew what these lamps illuminated. He knew what the cops were all staring at, even though he couldn't see it.

"Doesn't look good." The cab driver pointed. He pulled over in front of the apartment building.

Vatch took out a twenty, handed it to the driver, and then waited for the driver to get out of the cab and fetch his wheelchair out of the trunk.

The cab driver unfolded the wheelchair. He put the brake on, and then opened the back, passenger door. "You need any help?"

"No." Vatch grabbed the rubber handle above the door. "I got it."

Vatch pulled himself up and out, lowering himself into the wheelchair. He took another quick glance down the street, and then rolled inside his apartment building, unsure of what he was going to do.

Anthony wasn't a little kid anymore.

Vatch had clung to the idea that Anthony would remain the little boy who had crawled through his window to talk and play chess. Even though Vatch had resisted the idea that Anthony would grow up, he had seen the change. Anthony was definitely not an innocent boy, but that didn't mean he should be thrown away.

Vatch knocked.

"It's me." He shouted at the door and knocked again. There was movement on the other side, some rattling. The deadbolts and chain were unlocked and undone. Eventually the apartment door opened. Vatch rolled inside.

"Where is he?"

Anthony's mother didn't say anything. She looked away, and Vatch rolled past her toward the back bedroom.

Vatch didn't hesitate at the door. He opened it, went inside, and closed the door behind himself.

Anthony sat on the bed, staring at the floor. He had his headphones on, some monstrosity of molded plastic and foam. The headphones were supposedly designed by a 1990s rap star. Vatch heard the drum beat, and he was thankful that he couldn't understand the rhymes.

"Anthony," Vatch rolled closer to the bed. "Anthony."

He reached out and shook Anthony's leg.

"You need to talk to me."

Anthony's movements were slow. He looked up from the floor, turning to Vatch. Anthony had been crying. His eyes were puffy. He was scared.

Anthony pressed a button on his iPhone. The music stopped. He took off his headphones.

"What did you do?" Vatch stared at him.

Anthony bit his lower lip and looked away. It was all that Vatch needed to know. He rolled over to the window and looked outside. There was the fire escape that Anthony had used to come up to Vatch's apartment in the past.

Vatch had to make a decision. He hesitated, but not for long.

"Take off your clothes." Vatch turned around. Anthony looked confused, and so Vatch repeated his command. "Take off your clothes," he said. "You want to live? You want to stay out of prison? You want a second a chance? You need to listen to me. Now take off your clothes. All of them."

CHAPTER SEVENTY EIGHT

Vatch tossed Anthony a towel. The boy wrapped the towel around his waist.

"Listen to me, Anthony," Vatch rolled toward him, holding the boy in a hard stare. He wasn't yelling, but his voice was sharp. "You've got about five minutes, maybe less."

Vatch paused. He studied Anthony.

"I'm trying to save your life. Understand?" Vatch waited for Anthony to agree, and then continued. "But now I'm going in deep with you. So you have to listen to me. We're in this together."

"I will," Anthony nodded.

"Go to the bathroom and clip your nails as short as possible. There can't be any dirt, blood, or anything else underneath. Then take a hot shower, use soap, and scrub every part of your body, especially your hands."

Anthony looked a little confused and Vatch started to explain about gun powder residue, but stopped. There wasn't enough time.

"When you get out of the shower," Vatch said. "I want you to pick out an outfit that is exactly the opposite of what you were wearing tonight. If you were wearing baggy clothes, find something tight. If you were wearing a white shirt, find something black. Understand?"

Anthony, a little shocked, understood.

"You're not lying to anybody. You're not saying anything to anybody. Do you understand? If they want to know your name and date of birth, give it to them. Tell them the truth about that, because if you say you're somebody else, they'll charge you with obstructing legal process or giving a peace officer a false name or some other bullshit charge. You should cooperate with that information, but that's it. Then you ask for a lawyer. Ask for a lawyer over and over. Do not say a word, not one word beyond your name, date of birth, and asking for a lawyer. No matter what they say or how much they threaten or how much evidence the cops say they have, do not say a word. Don't speak. You want a lawyer. Say you want a lawyer."

"I got it," Anthony said, but there was hesitation and Vatch pounced on it. At this point, he had too much at stake for Anthony to mess up.

"No, Anthony," Vatch shook his head. "You need to be confident. You have to do this." Vatch spun his wheelchair around and saw a garbage can in the corner near Anthony's closet. He rolled his wheelchair over to the can, dumped the small amount of paper out onto the floor, and removed the plastic liner.

"Put your clothes in this." Vatch handed Anthony the plastic bag. "And your shoes and socks, everything."

Anthony picked his clothes off the floor and filled the bag. Then he went to his closet, picked up a pair of red Adidas, and put the shoes in the bag, too.

Vatch followed him. He took the plastic bag from Anthony and started to leave. Then he stopped. "What's on your cell phone?" he asked.

"Cell phone?" Anthony was confused.

NO TIME TO HIDE | 335

"Any texts, any emails about this?"

Anthony told Vatch that there weren't any.

"Give me your cell phone anyway." Vatch held out his hand. "Don't tell them your cell phone number, don't tell them anything. Just ask for a lawyer."

Anthony went to his bed, disconnected the iPhone from the headphones, and gave it to Vatch.

"Okay," Vatch took a deep breath, still thinking about where he would search and what he would do if he was running the investigation. "I think that's it. Go get in the shower. Then when you're done, climb up the fire escape to my apartment. You're going to sleep on my couch tonight." Vatch decided to clarify, just in case Anthony didn't understand. "I'm your alibi. You were in my apartment the whole night."

"Okay," Anthony turned. He took a few steps and stopped. "Frank?"

"What is it?"

Anthony looked away. "There's one more thing." He walked back to his bed. Anthony lifted up the pillow. He picked up a 9 millimeter Smith & Wesson. It was Ms. Finkel's gun. "Gotta get rid of this too."

CHAPTER SEVENTY NINE

Vatch watched a rookie patrolman in the alley below through his window. The patrolman put on a pair of gloves, and much to the delight of the older supervisor, the patrolman climbed into a dumpster. His assignment was to pick through the garbage and find evidence. It was evidence that wouldn't be found, because Vatch had it all in his little plastic bag.

They had come for Anthony about thirty minutes after Anthony had finished his shower, changed his clothes, and climbed up the fire escape. He was already gone, and his mother had lied. She told the police that she didn't know where he was and that she hadn't seen Anthony all night. She let them search the apartment, and then they had left.

Vatch turned away from the window and looked at Anthony, sitting on his couch and watching his television. Vatch felt sick. He worried about Anthony, and he also worried about himself. If either Anthony or his mother said anything, he could be charged with a crime. For the first time in his life, Vatch wasn't the chaser. He could be the person being chased.

The only positive was that the victim was a gang-banger. Anthony had shot him in the small, nearby park. Nobody was around.

337

It was questionable how much effort the New York Police Department would actually put into the case. Dead black kids didn't generate a lot of news coverage in New York City or much demand for accountability and justice.

Vatch looked down at the plastic bag in his lap. He needed to get rid of it. He rolled over to his closet. He found an old, empty backpack. He stuffed the plastic bag inside and zipped the backpack closed. His plan was fairly simple. He would dump the clothes at one of the large metal Salvation Army donation bins on the other side of the city. The cell phone would be smashed and put in a dumpster far away, and the gun would be wiped clean, taken apart, and tossed into the Hudson River.

"Anthony, you need to sit tight," Vatch started toward the door. "I'm going out for a little while. Don't answer the door for anybody."

Vatch was almost out of the apartment when his phone rang. He rolled back over to his desk. His cell phone had been charging. He disconnected the cord and picked up the phone.

Vatch looked at the caller ID. It was Brenda Gadd, and he figured that he didn't have any choice. He had to answer.

Vatch pressed the "receive call" button.

"This is Vatch." He listened, and then, "Yeah I looked at it all. It's reviewed."

Vatch took a breath and lied in response to a series of other questions.

"It actually went pretty quick," he said. "Mostly securities documents, federal filings, stupid stuff that I thought we already had."

Gadd complained about Tad Garvin and the last minute document dump.

"Well it's taken care of," Vatch said. "It's good to go. Just send it over to Collins' lawyer and go to bed. That case is done."

Vatch hung up the phone, and he realized how much he didn't care anymore. He had obsessed about Michael Collins for years. He had lost sleep. He had hunted Michael Collins as if it was the only thing that mattered in his life. And now ...

Vatch looked down at the backpack in his lap. Then he looked over at Anthony, and Vatch decided that Michael Collins didn't matter so much.

CHAPTER EIGHTY

The testimony resumed with the same formality and rituals that had occurred over the previous days. People stood as Judge Husk was led carefully to his chair by his loyal law clerk. The jurors returned to the same seats that they had occupied over the past week, and Michael and Quentin waited for Judge Husk to begin.

"Good morning," Judge Husk smiled at the jurors with a hint of sympathy. "I hope you got the coffee and doughnuts that I brought in this morning. If not, they should be waiting for you in the jury conference room at our first mid-morning break."

The jurors nodded. The judge, at this point, had become their wise grandfather, another flock of converts to the Cult of Husk.

The judge turned back to the attorneys.

"We are back on the record in the United States versus Michael Collins. As you all may recall, we took a break yesterday afternoon at the conclusion of Ms. Gadd's direct examination of Ms. Krane. Now it's time to give the defense an opportunity to ask its questions."

Judge Husk nodded toward Quentin. Then the judge looked past the attorneys to the people in the gallery, scanning for Brea Krane.

"Ms. Krane," Judge Husk said a little louder. "Ms. Krane, if you could return to the witness stand, we shall continue."

Brea Krane sat in the back next to Tad Garvin.

Tad Garvin watched her as she stood and walked up to the front of the courtroom. The Cook Island accounts had been created for her. Garvin assumed that she had received the money transfer from Michael Collins and Andie Larone, because she told him that her flight out of the country left later that evening.

He was anxious for his afternoon reward. She had promised him that. One little gift before she left, and he hoped that he'd also get an invitation to come along.

Brea sat down in the witness stand. She had changed her outfit. It was a dark blue dress, not quite black but almost. It was conservative, so as not to offend the women on the jury, but it still showed off her form for the male jurors.

Once she had settled, Judge Husk continued.

"Ms. Krane, you are still under oath and still obligated to tell the whole truth. Do you understand?"

"I do," Brea Krane nodded her head, and Michael noticed a very slight smile.

Then Judge Husk motioned for Quentin Robinson to begin.

Go slow, Michael thought. He stared at Quentin, wishing that he could do it. He didn't want to be the client. He didn't want to be the person being defended. He wanted to the be the attorney, but it was out of his control.

His freedom was in the hands of Quentin Robinson.

Please don't mess it up.

Quentin stood at the podium. He looked down at the notes and questions that Michael had prepared for him along with some of his own. Quentin's heart pounded and he wondered if others could hear it as well or maybe see his hands tremble. It was nerves.

This wasn't his first jury trial. He'd represented hundreds of people as a poverty lawyer. Quentin had hustled deals. He had walked the fuzzy ethical line that all defense attorneys walk. But this was different. The stakes were higher. Michael wasn't a homeless man accused of public urination. Michael Collins was a friend who was about to get away with stealing over $500 million and he, defender of the poor, had helped him in exchange for a roll of gold coins.

"Everything okay?" Judge Husk tilted his head to the side, wondering why Quentin hadn't started his inquiry.

"Yes," Quentin nodded. He took a deep breath, trying to catch himself. He turned to Brea Krane.

"Good morning, Ms. Krane. As you know, I'm Quentin Robinson. I represent Michael Collins in this matter."

"I know who you are." Brea Krane provided the requisite hostility.

"Very well," Quentin looked down at his notes again. "I'm not exactly sure why the prosecutor, Ms. Gadd, called you in her case in chief." Quentin glanced over his shoulder at Brenda Gadd, and then back to Brea Krane. "Because you're *my* star witness. Did you know that?"

Gadd was on her feet before Brea Krane could respond.

"Objection, Your Honor."

Judge Husk perked up. The old man had been getting bored. This was starting to get entertaining.

"Grounds?"

"Irrelevant, speculation, badgering." Gadd shook her head. "I could go on."

Judge Husk looked at Quentin, a sparkle in his eyes. Michael could tell that Judge Husk would give Quentin some room, if for no other reason than for sport. The trial had been so lopsided up until this point that the jury would've likely only deliberated for five minutes before returning a guilty verdict.

"Overruled. I'll allow counsel to present its defense. But let's get to the meat of the matter, shall we?"

"Yes, Your Honor." Quentin bowed his head slightly. "I'll withdraw the question."

He turned his attention back to Brea Krane, who now looked slightly uncomfortable.

"You're my star witness, because you know that Michael Collins did not steal this money, true?"

"Are you kidding?" Brea laughed. "I think the documents ..."

Quentin held up his hand, interrupting her.

"You didn't answer the question." Quentin took a step to the side. His nerves were under control now. He'd found a rhythm, and, as he paused, Kermit and Andie snuck into the back of the courtroom to watch the show.

Quentin looked at the jurors, scanning their faces, adding to the drama of the moment. This was what jurors expected defense lawyers to do, and he was going to exceed their expectations.

"Let me pose the question another way." Quentin scratched his chin. "Michael Collins never admitted to you that he stole the money, correct?"

"That's correct."

"And you don't dispute that your father worked with Michael Collins and other attorneys at Wabash, Kramer and Moore, true?"

Brea Krane didn't answer, and she didn't have to.

"Lowell Moore and Michael Collins were the lead attorneys for your father, correct?"

"That's true."

"And Michael Collins was there with your father on the night he was killed. He was likely the last person to see your father while your father was still alive —"

"Object, Your Honor." Gadd was on her feet. "This is speculation. Ms. Krane can't testify to this. She wasn't there."

Quentin turned to Gadd, pointing.

"Exactly!" he shouted before Judge Husk could rule. "I withdraw the question, and I'll ask this." Quentin turned back to Brea Krane. "You weren't there the night your father was killed. Isn't that right?"

Brea Krane nodded.

"Correct." She tried to force some tears in order to slow Quentin down, but Quentin wasn't going to stop. She didn't know where this was headed, and Brea now regretted her decision to stop talking with Andie Larone.

"And you weren't there in the meetings between Lowell Moore, Michael Collins, and your father, true?"

"What does this have to do with anything?" Brea Krane looked at Michael. "He took my money."

Quentin paused. He shook his head and looked at the jurors, and then back at Brea Krane.

"Whose money?"

Brea started, but stopped herself.

"Perhaps the court reporter could read that last bit back to us." Quentin looked at the court reporter. He nodded at her, directing the court reporter to read back the exchange.

She took the narrow roll of paper that fed into her stenography machine, and then brought it toward her to read:

Question: You weren't there the night your father was killed. Isn't that right?

Answer: Yes.

Question: And you weren't there in the meetings between Lowell Moore, Michael Collins, and your father, true?

Answer: What does this have to do with anything? He took my money.

Quentin nodded and thanked the court reporter.

"In your mind, it's your money. Isn't that right?"

"It's my family's money," Brea tried to recover.

"And you want it, right? Who wouldn't want a half-billion?"

"It's my family's money," Brea repeated, avoiding the question.

"As a family member, you've had meetings with the prosecution and the investigators throughout this case. Isn't that right?"

"Yes."

"You've been kept apprised of the progress of this case. Isn't that right?"

"We have," Brea nodded, nervous.

"You are represented by Mr. Tad Garvin. He's an attorney at Franklin and Uckley, is that right?"

Brea hesitated, and then answered.

"Yes."

"He represents your family and he has provided corporate documents and other information to the government, on behalf of your family, to the government. Right?"

Brea shrugged. She looked at Tad Garvin for direction. He nodded, and so she answered. "Yes. That's correct."

"And you sent Mr. Garvin down to Mexico, where Michael Collins has been living openly over the past few years, isn't that right?"

"I don't know anything about that," Brea said.

"Are you denying that Mr. Garvin went down to meet with Michael Collins on your behalf shortly before this indictment was issued?"

Michael was going to provide a complete story. He didn't want a hung jury. He wanted a not-guilty verdict. He needed double jeopardy to apply, a complete bar toward the government prosecuting him again. And he didn't care if Brea Krane was damaged in the process.

He watched as Brea's mood changed, now looking concerned. It wasn't an act.

Brenda Gadd had stood and objected, the objection was sustained.

Judge Husk looked at Quentin.

"She testified that she didn't know," Husk said.

"Fine," Quentin waved it off. "But if I were to say I have a security video of Tad Garvin at the Sunset Resort with Michael Collins just a few weeks prior to his arrest." Quentin held up a silver DVD, as if to prove that the video existed. "You don't dispute that, correct?"

"Objection," Brenda Gadd rose, again, with a little less confidence this time.

"Overruled," Judge Husk turned toward Brea Krane and nodded. "You can answer."

"If you have a video, I don't dispute it, but I can't verify it either."

"Right," Quentin nodded, preparing himself to drop the bomb. "And at that meeting, Michael Collins explained to your attorney that he would not release the money in the trust account to you, correct?"

"Objection, Your Honor. She wasn't there."

Judge Husk's eyes narrowed.

"Sustained." He bit his lower lip, and then looked at his law clerk. The judge was about to call for a recess, but Quentin didn't let him. The older judge's reflexes were a little too slow to cut him off.

"Michael Collins is the trustee for a trust that your father created, correct? A lawful trust to which he was and still is the administrator."

Brea shook her head.

"That's ridiculous."

"You were frustrated because, as the trustee of this account, Michael Collins would not release the money to you, correct?"

"I don't know what you're talking about," Brea looked, again, at Brenda Gadd, her eyes begged the prosecutor to stop the questioning.

"And so, you sent a lawyer to reason with him, and Michael refused to deal with you, and in retaliation, your brother went down to the Sunset Resort and tried to burn it down?"

Gadd was on her feet now, screaming an objection. Murmurs and whispers rolled over the courtroom.

"And then you tried one last time to intimidate Mr. Collins and his friends —"

Judge Husk pounded his gavel.

"Okay, Mr. Robinson. That's enough." The courtroom was silent, waiting to see how Judge Husk would react.

The judge remained cool. He closed his eyes, never raising his voice. The silence held the courtroom still. Then he broke the peace with a calm suggestion.

"I think it's time for our morning break."

Judge Husk opened his eyes and looked at the jurors.

"Remember your oath and instructions. You are not to discuss this case or any aspect of this case at this time. This court stands in recess."

Judge Husk placed his hand on the bench, and pulled himself up. "All rise for the jury as they exit."

The jurors filed out of the courtroom. They all watched, and then once the jurors were gone, Judge Husk turned his attention back to the attorneys and sighed.

"Looks like we have something to talk about. Mr. Robinson is now going to explain to me why we don't have a mistrial on our hands."

CHAPTER EIGHTY ONE

Judge Husk sat behind his desk. He had taken off his robe and he somehow seemed even smaller than in the court-room. He sat with his wrinkled hands folded on the desk. His tiny wrists were dominated by a pair of silver cufflinks.

The law clerk led the attorneys into chambers.

Gadd sat down in one of the open chairs. Quentin occupied the other empty chair while the judge's law clerk remained standing.

"Well," Judge Husk looked at Brenda Gadd. "Looks like we've had a development."

His eyes twinkled with mischief. This was the part of his job that he loved, and it was the primary reason he would likely die before he retired.

"Your Honor," Gadd edged up in her seat. She glanced at Quentin with a flash of anger, and then back at Judge Husk. "I've been sandbagged." She pointed at Quentin. "Sanctions and contempt would be too nice. Mr. Robinson has disrupted a major trial. He obviously knew his client was going to lose, and now he is trying to get a mistrial."

Quentin shook his head.

"I don't want a mistrial, Your Honor. I want the jury to hear my client's side of the story. It is totally appropriate for the defense to offer alternative explanations for what has —"

"Alternative explanations," Gadd shook her head and rolled her eyes. "The cross-examination needs to be in good faith. It needs to be rooted in the truth. You can't just lie. You need to —"

Now it was Judge Husk's turn to interrupt. He held up his hand.

"I think we get your point." He took a heavy breath, and then turned to Quentin. "Perhaps it would be best to explain."

Quentin lowered the tone of his voice. He wanted to match the judge's calm demeanor, which was easy in this situation. He had all the leverage.

"Your Honor, my client has told me all along that he was a trustee for a legal trust created by Joshua Krane prior to his death. It was a secret trust with a very specific confidentiality clause."

Judge Husk narrowed his eyes, focusing his attention on Quentin and trying to understand the implications.

"Which means?" he prompted.

"Which means," Quentin continued, "that the money that Michael Collins consolidated, transferred and disbursed was not stolen. He was lawfully managing the money on behalf of a trust created by Joshua Krane prior to his death. The charitable contributions and the purchase of the resort were expenditures and investments within the sole discretion of the trustee. There was no wire fraud because Michael Collins was acting within his legal authority to —"

Gadd stood.

"This is ridiculous, Your Honor. We've been investigating for years. Michael Collins could have just told us this story and the

NO TIME TO HIDE | 353

investigation would have likely ended or this trust would be debunked, but instead, he takes it to trial."

Quentin raised his hand.

"Your Honor, if I may address that issue?"

Judge Husk nodded. "Please."

"Thank you." Quentin smiled, sheepishly. "To tell the truth, Your Honor. I didn't believe him. That's why nothing was said. Michael Collins said he had proof, a copy of the trust agreement, but that it was destroyed in the fire at the resort where he had been living. A fire we believe was started by Brent Krane, the witness's brother."

"There's no proof of that. There's no proof of any of this." Brenda Gadd folded her arms across her chest and sat back down. She was flustered and irritated.

"I don't know, but I'm sure that the United States Attorney's Office can check the TSA's database and see whether or not Brent Krane was in Mexico at the time of the fire."

"I can't believe we're listening to this." Brenda Gadd threw her hands up in the air. "We are in the midst of a jury trial, and now we're getting last-minute conspiracy theories."

"It was a theory," Quentin said. "Until early this morning." Quentin opened his briefcase and took out a copy of the trust agreement that had been disclosed to him by the United States Attorney's Office.

"I had been harassing Ms. Gadd for many weeks, if not months, to supplement her disclosures, because Michael Collins had insisted. I was annoyed with my client, and I'm sure Ms. Gadd was annoyed with me. Nothing further was provided, until this morning. Finally, she sent over another batch of documents from Franklin and Uckley related to Joshua Krane's business dealings. In those documents, the trust agreement was disclosed."

"Let me see that." Gadd snatched the pieces of paper from Quentin Robinson's hand. She started reading.

Quentin sat back and let her read. There was nothing she could do.

CHAPTER EIGHTY TWO

A rmstrong stuck his head into Agent Vatch's office.

"Hey Frank," He knocked on the door as he walked inside. "Is your phone on? Brenda Gadd is trying to reach you."

Agent Vatch turned.

"My phone is on." He picked it up off of his desk and showed the lit screen. "I'm just not answering at the moment."

"Well, things are falling apart." Armstrong was confused by Vatch's reaction, but he continued, hoping further explanation might get Agent Vatch to move. "We need to check out Brent Krane. And she wants to know whether you remember some document that was disclosed to Collins' attorney. She said it was a trust agreement or something. It was in the stuff that you reviewed last night."

Vatch shook his head. He was tired. He had spent the night disposing of any physical evidence linking Anthony to the shooting. He still hadn't gotten the whole story, but somehow Anthony got sucked into one of Spider's feuds. It wasn't an honorable crime. Vatch had hoped that Anthony felt threatened in some way. He had hoped that it could be loosely rationalized as a form of self-defense, but that wasn't true. It was murder. That was all.

355

"Frank, seriously." Armstrong came into Agent Vatch's office and closed the door. "Gadd is flipping out. She needs you on this."

"Sorry, kiddo." Vatch took a breath. All the venom that had driven him for years was now gone. He had helped a murderer escape. "You do it."

"What do you mean? This is your case." Armstrong didn't want to get into a ship that was sinking.

Vatch turned back to his computer and clicked the print button. The printer underneath his desk hummed, and then spat out a letter that he had written that morning. Vatch took it off the tray, and then handed it to Agent Armstrong.

"This is a copy." Vatch's face knotted up. "Submitted the real one to HR this morning along with the forms."

Armstrong scanned the first few sentences.

"Early retirement?"

"I'm done."

"When?"

Vatch took a breath. "Effective immediately."

CHAPTER EIGHTY THREE

The people in the hallway started to file back into the court-room. Brea Krane had already gone inside and retaken her place on the witness stand. Tad Garvin remained on the wood-en bench, thinking about what Brenda Gadd had just told him and trying to understand how a box of documents had been sent from his office without his knowledge.

Of course, he admitted to nothing. He had a reputation to protect. Admitting that he was sleeping with a client was not an option, admitting that he had, in fact, visited Michael Collins in Mexico shortly before the indictment was not an option, admit-ting that he set up a series of off-shore accounts for Brea Krane was not an option, and further admitting a security breach at the mighty Franklin and Uckley was also not good for anybody.

He had remained as calm as he could while being verbally attacked by Brenda Gadd. Even though he felt the walls closing in on him, Tad Garvin had merely promised Brenda Gadd that he would look into the situation and that was what he was going to do.

Garvin stood. He didn't need to hear the rest of Brea Krane's testimony. He had seen the copy of the trust agreement. It was a disaster.

Garvin began walking toward the elevators when he heard a familiar voice.

"How much did you know?"

Garvin turned around and looked at Brent Krane.

"Look, Brent, this really isn't the time or place to have this discussion. Why don't we —"

Brent cut him off.

"I've got something that you need to see."

Garvin shook his head.

"I need to go back to the office and figure this out, Brent. I don't have time."

"Work with me," Brent said. "And I can help you out of this." Brent walked closer to Garvin, and Garvin could see that Brent didn't look right. Brent hadn't showered in weeks. His hair was disheveled. He smelled. "I need to talk to you right now."

"I'll talk to you later," Garvin turned away, but Brent grabbed his arm.

"I know everything," Brent said. "And what I know can get you disbarred from the practice of law. What I know can probably get you tossed in jail for witness tampering and obstruction of justice and a bunch of other stuff. So don't mess with me. We need to be a team."

Garvin's eyes widened. He understood the threat.

"What?" Brent Krane twitched, staring at Garvin. "Didn't think I knew big words? Did my sister tell you I was crazy? Well, I've done some research. I know enough about what you and my sister are doing to know that it's illegal." Brent looked at the door to the courtroom. "Maybe I should just go in there right now and put a stop to this whole game."

Brent let go of Garvin's arm, and walked past. He was a few feet from the door, when Garvin caved.

"Okay, Brent," he said. "You win. Let's not do anything rash. I'm sure there's a way to accommodate you. To be a team."

"I'm sure there are ways." Brent's eyes narrowed and the crowd inside his head went wild. They wanted Garvin dead, too.

CHAPTER EIGHTY FOUR

The testimony of Brea Krane continued. Quentin Robinson was now firmly in control. Judge Husk had chastised Brenda Gadd for constantly interrupting with objections, and now Quentin had a clear path.

Michael watched Quentin Robinson introduce the trust agreement into evidence, and then listened as he walked through each term of the trust agreement. Quentin had Brea Krane read aloud for the jury the agreement's confidentiality clause. He highlighted the specific prohibition to disclosing the trust agreement to any government agency absent a court order.

Quentin pointed out the dates of Michael Collins and Joshua Krane's signatures. Then he carefully parsed the paragraphs related to Michael Collins authority as trustee.

"Do you see paragraph five of the trust agreement?" Quentin held his copy in the air and pointed to the text halfway down the second page. He waited for Brea Krane to nod her head.

"Now could you read this first part? Slowly."

Brea stared hard at Quentin, but she had no choice.

"The trustee, in the trustee's sole discretion and judgment, may invest any assets of the trust, in whole or in part, in any stocks, bonds, mutual funds, real estate, real property, or any

361

other venture the trustee deems appropriate." Brea Krane put her copy of the exhibit down.

"Now, Ms. Krane, we've heard a lot about the purchase of the Sunset Resort and Hostel by Mr. Collins through corporations that he established to maintain the confidentiality of the trust and himself. You'd agree that the Sunset Resort and Hostel is a business and also a piece of real property, true?"

Gadd stood half-heartedly.

"Objection, calls for a legal conclusion."

Quentin turned to the judge.

"The witness is a Harvard MBA, Your Honor, and she can answer based on her own understanding. I'm not asking for a legal opinion."

Judge Husk nodded.

"Overruled. The witness shall answer, and Ms. Gadd, I'm sure that there will be a series of these questions. I'll interpret this objection as a standing objection to this whole line of inquiry." Judge Husk took a deep breath, clearly annoyed. "So please stop interrupting."

"Very well," Brenda Gadd forced a tense smile. She nodded and sat down.

Quentin turned back to Brea Krane.

"Now, if you could answer the question. Is the purchase of the resort a real estate investment?"

Brea Krane hesitated, and then nodded.

"Arguably."

It was an answer that evaded the question, but Quentin got what he needed and moved on.

"Now looking at paragraph five, sub-part B. Can you read that?"

"I can read it," she responded, but then didn't actually read the paragraph. Brea was trying to being smart by only answering the question, but the jury was not amused.

"Of course." Quentin shook his head. "I know you are literate and can read. Now, I'm asking you to actually read this sub-part aloud for the jury."

"The trustee, in the trustee's sole discretion and judgment, may make charitable contributions to any non-profit organization recognized as a 501(c)(3) corporation in good standing by the United States Internal Revenue Service and located within New York, New York. Charitable contributions cannot exceed 3% of total trust assets as of the formation date of said trust." Brea Krane sighed, and put the exhibit down. She knew what was coming and Quentin delivered.

"Now, in this trial, we have also heard about a contribution to a Catholic church. It is a parish that is located here in New York City. Based on your own life experiences and knowledge, you must agree that the Catholic Church is a non-profit organization, true?"

This time there was no objection, and so Brea Krane answered.

"I suppose."

"You suppose." Quentin nodded, as Michael Collins sat silently, watching it unfold.

It was a complete and utter fraud upon the court. It was all theater.

Quentin Robinson played the role of the zealous advocate. Although he certainly knew that Andie and Michael were scheming, his job was not to question his client. His job was to win. He was provided a trust agreement directly from the United States government, which was given to them directly from the

Krane's attorney. Quentin Robinson broke no ethical rules by using it.

Brenda Gadd played the role of self-righteous prosecutor. Judge Husk played the role of supervisor and referee. It was not his job to second-chair the prosecution or the defense. If attorneys made mistakes, they were forced to live with them.

The trust agreement was properly disclosed to the defense as exculpatory evidence. The mistake was not a legal one. The mistake was rooted in the investigation and government's apparent hubris.

And finally, Brea Krane played the role of an attorney's worst nightmare. She was a liar. She was a witness that self-destructed on the stand. The only thing that she did not testify to was the transfer of money to her Cook Island accounts. Michael didn't want to go there.

It ended with a whimper. After Brea Krane stepped down and exited the courtroom, Brenda Gadd stood. It was not how any prosecutor wanted to end her case in chief. It was, however, her only choice at the moment.

"Your Honor, the prosecution has no further witnesses at this time. It rests. I do, however, reserve the right to call rebuttal witnesses."

Judge Husk nodded. His expression did not betray his neutrality. Even though everyone in the courtroom understood that the dynamics of the trial had completely changed in one morning, he remained calm and businesslike.

"That being the case," he said, "the Court needs to talk about some logistics with the attorneys, and so I'll excuse the jurors for lunch. I'll also remind the jurors of their obligation not to discuss this case or witnesses among themselves or anyone else, because the trial is not over and deliberations have not begun."

Judge Husk turned away from the jury box, and then looked out at the courtroom full of spectators. "Please rise for the jury as they exit the room."

The people in the courtroom stood and watched the jurors leave.

Michael put his hand on Quentin's shoulder, gave it a squeeze, and whispered "thank you" in his ear. Michael knew that the jurors were watching, and he hoped that it would make it clear to the jurors that their job had just gotten easier.

When the side door leading to the jury room closed and all the jurors were gone, Judge Husk continued.

"Mr. Robinson, how would you like to proceed?"

Quentin stood.

"First, Your Honor, we would ask this Court for a directed verdict. In light of the testimony just received and the disclosure of the Trust Agreement, there is no need to continue this trial. The prosecution has failed to satisfy its high burden to prove wire fraud beyond a reasonable doubt and it is unnecessary for this trial to continue."

Judge Husk offered no reaction. He, instead, turned to Brenda Gadd.

"Response?"

Brenda Gadd stood.

"Yes, thank you." She paused, weighing her words carefully. "Obviously this case changed this morning, but nothing this morning absolves Michael Collins of guilt. The government remains confident that Michael Collins stole Joshua Krane's money, and we believe, just as Ms. Krane believes, that the trust document is a fraud."

"But it came from her family's attorney," Judge Husk said. "And it was produced to the defense by you."

"I still believe that it is a fraud, and I would respectfully request a continuance to investigate the document and offer such evidence in my rebuttal."

Judge Husk tilted his head to the side, and then looked at Quentin. He raised his hand, directing Quentin to stand and respond.

"A continuance is highly unusual in the midst of a jury trial. These jurors have already made a huge sacrifice in being here, and they deserve to receive the evidence, deliberate on that evidence, and go home. The government has had five years to investigate. They are now claiming surprise about a document produced by the attorney for one of their own witnesses, which they produced to me."

"As for the rebuttal?"

"Judge Husk, there shouldn't be a rebuttal. This case should be done." Quentin looked over at Michael, and then back. "But ultimately, if you don't grant my motion for a directed verdict, then Ms. Gadd can put up whatever rebuttal evidence she wants. That's her right, but there shouldn't be a delay and we can address whatever issues exist with the rebuttal testimony as it comes."

Judge Husk nodded.

"Very well." He looked over at his law clerk, and then back at counsel. "The motion for a directed verdict is denied. Although counsel for Mr. Collins is correct, that the testimony this morning significantly undermines the government's case. I believe there are clearly facts in dispute, and that is for the jury to resolve. So I'm not willing to stop the trial and declare a winner."

Judge Husk looked at Brenda Gadd and his expression hardened.

"As for a continuance," he shook his head. "That request is denied. This case is going forward, and Ms. Gadd, you have all the tools and resources of the government at your disposal. Certainly, you can prepare your rebuttal in a timely matter. The jury has been sworn. The trial has begun. Double jeopardy has attached, and you cannot change the rules of the game simply because things are not going your way."

Judge Husk then turned to Quentin Robinson.

"Anything else?"

"Yes, Your Honor, assuming that Ms. Gadd stipulates to the trust agreement as an exhibit for the defense and it is accepted as an affirmative defense, then we will call no witnesses. The defense would rest."

Judge Husk turned from Quentin to Michael.

"And Mr. Collins, you have been informed of your right to testify in this trial?"

Michael Collins stood.

"Yes, Your Honor. And I choose to exercise my right to remain silent. The trust agreement speaks for itself regarding my actions and authority as well as my obligations to keep the trust confidential."

Brenda Gadd rolled her eyes and shook her head.

"Your Honor, I respectfully ask you to reconsider your ruling."

"Why?" Judge Husk asked, daring Brenda Gadd to answer him. "Nothing has changed in the last sixty seconds that would require me to reverse this decision." He folded his hands in front of himself. "Now, in light of defense counsel's request, I anticipate that you will not waste the Court's time by requiring them to lay the foundation for a document that you yourself produced to the defense. True?"

Brenda Gadd didn't respond. She didn't want to agree to anything, but she also knew that the trial was going to continue and that further irritating Judge Husk was not going to help. "That is true, Your Honor, we will stipulate."

"Fine. Then that is settled." Judge Husk nodded. "We'll come back after lunch. Mr. Robinson will offer the trust agreement as affirmative evidence of its defense. He will rest, and we will break for the day. Tomorrow morning, Ms. Gadd will offer any rebuttal testimony that she may have, and then we will go straight to jury instructions and closing arguments."

Judge Husk took a breath and steadied himself.

"I think the afternoon is plenty of time for us to wrap up this trial, for Ms. Gadd to fashion her rebuttal, and for both the prosecution and the defense to draft their closing arguments."

Judge Husk nodded at the bailiff and his law clerk and both stood.

"Court is now adjourned."

CHAPTER EIGHTY FIVE

Agent Armstrong left Vatch. Armstrong had spoken to Brenda Gadd briefly before she returned to court that afternoon. She had given him a list of questions that he needed to answer in the next four hours. The case had fallen apart. The only way to salvage it was by lighting a fire.

Armstrong dispatched one agent to find Brent Krane. A record check confirmed that he had, in fact, traveled out of the country during the purported fire at the Sunset Resort. It was just as Michael Collins' attorney had alleged. It was a good fact for the defense, but it might also give the FBI some leverage during questioning.

Another agent was sent to find Tad Garvin, and Armstrong assigned himself the task of breaking Brea Krane. He wanted to be the hero.

Armstrong checked the address, again. Then he took a left on 2nd Avenue and a right to Brea Krane's condo. He found it, but there was no parking in front. Armstrong circled the block twice, and then he saw a Toyota Prius leaving a meter a half block from the front door of Brea Krane's building.

370 | J.D. TRAFFORD

###

Brea Krane walked into her front foyer. The lights were on, and she knew that she wasn't alone.

"Hello." She placed her keys on a small table and walked further inside. She called out, again, and this time, there was an answer.

"We're in here."

Tad Garvin sat on the couch in her living room. Her brother sat in a chair across from him. Brent was, as always, pale and a little dirty. What concerned her, however, was the gun in his hand.

Brent glared at her. There was a darkness in his eyes.

"Wondering when you'd show up."

"Put that away." Brea gestured toward the gun. She decided to push away her fear and be the big sister. She needed to control him, just as she had always controlled him. "I thought you were still up in Montauk."

The crowd didn't like his sister's attitude, and Brent didn't like it either.

"Been back long enough. Long enough to see you meet with Michael Collins' girlfriend." He looked at Garvin. "Long enough to hear about the money and the new accounts that our lawyer has set up for us." The crowd grew impatient, and Brent lost his train of thought in the noise. "Then we've got this scheme. ... A fake trust agreement." Brent shook his head. "Brilliant."

"I didn't know anything about that," Brea said, but her brother ignored her.

"I saw you in court today. Didn't know you were such an actress."

"Listen, brother, you need to put the gun away so that we can talk."

"I've had enough talk." Brent shook with anger. Brea saw his trigger finger twitch and his other fingers tighten around the gun's grip. He said, "I'm tired of you talking."

"Brent, you're obviously not feeling too well." Brea walked toward him. "How about we —"

Her brother jumped out of his seat. "Not another step." Brent stood in front of her. Brea stopped. Her arms in the air, surrendering.

"I know what I'm doing." Brent pointed the gun at her, and then directed Brea to the couch. "Sit next to your beloved lawyer."

She did as she was told. Brea sat down on the couch.

"While we were waiting for you, I was just discussing life with our boy, Tad. Isn't that right, Mr. Garvin?"

Brea turned to look at Tad. She watched him nod his head. His hands trembled. She noticed a fresh bruise on the side of his face and a few drops of blood on his collar.

She tried again to calm her brother.

It didn't work.

Brent made a sudden move toward Garvin. He raised his hand, as if to strike with the butt of the gun. Tad Garvin flinched, and Brent laughed. The crowd appreciated Brent's dominance.

"I think I'll spare you for now." Brent lowered the gun, and then pointed it back at his sister.

The crowd liked the power, and encouraged him to continue.

"So, at some point, you talk with Michael Collins and concoct a plan. He turns himself in, and you start working with Collins' girlfriend. Am I right so far?"

"If you would just let me explain why?" Brea's tone had changed. She couldn't keep the fear away anymore. She was pleading.

"I know why," Brent snapped back at her. "Money. It's always about the money. But what about honor and pride and family?"

Brent took a step closer to her. "Just let me finish," He pointed the gun at Brea's head, inches away. "You sleep with our boy, Tad, and then get him to send the bogus trust agreement to the government. You get the money in exchange for the magic evidence that's going to set Michael Collins free."

"Please, Brent," Brea was crying now. "Please. I wasn't ever going to help Michael Collins. I was just shaking him down."

Brent ignored the explanation. "I figure you didn't let Tad know about everything. Just enough. You were just using him. Right?"

"Brent, that money was for you," she lied, but it was the only thing that she could think of.

"False," Brent took a step back. "It wasn't for me. It was all for yourself. Nothing is ever enough for daddy's princess. You needed a little more. And you couldn't handle the government and all those supposed victims taking it away from you."

"You're too emotional, Brent. I couldn't let you in on the plan. Especially after you went down there, lighting fires and taking unnecessary risks."

The crowd didn't like his sister's accusations. The crowd wanted her to plead for her life again.

"I was exacting revenge for what Michael Collins took away from me." Brent tried to get the power back. "You got the trust fund. I got nothing. The horde of lawyers and government bureaucrats clawed it away from me. I was a laughingstock at school. I was harassed. I was hated. Then I had to leave because our family couldn't afford it." Brent cocked his head to the side, thinking. "But you could afford it. You could have kept me in school. You had some money."

Brent walked toward Brea. The crowd pushed him closer, urging him to finally be rid of her. Now the crowd didn't want any of the tainted money. There was no reason for it. Everybody knew that they weren't going to survive the day.

Brent felt his heart pound. Adrenaline shot through his body, making him feel taller, stronger, better. He put the muzzle to his sister's forehead.

Brent closed his eyes.

"Goodbye, sister." Brent pulled the trigger, and just before the gun fired, he felt his arm jerk away. The shot missed his sister's head and blew a hole into the living room wall.

His sister screamed. Tad Garvin was on top of him, wrestling him to the ground and trying to get the gun.

Agent Armstrong heard the first shot when the elevator doors opened. He and the building manager ran down the hallway toward Brea Krane's condominium. Armstrong wanted to call for backup, but there wasn't time.

They sprinted toward Brea Krane's door. The building manager got out his master key, as Armstrong drew his own service weapon.

The door unlocked, and Armstrong burst through the doorway just as a second shot fired. He threw himself to the ground. Armstrong was unsure about whether he was being shot at or whether anybody even knew that he was inside.

He pulled himself up to his knees.

"FBI," he shouted. "Put your hands above your head. You're under arrest." Armstrong rounded the corner. He saw Tad Garvin on the ground. His chest was painted red, and then he saw Brent Krane charging him, screaming.

Brent Krane fired three wild shots. Armstrong heard the building manager scream in pain from behind him. Then Armstrong returned the fire.

The first shot went through Brent Krane's shoulder. It didn't slow him. He kept charging. The second shot hit his neck, and spun him around, and the third hit Brent Krane in the head. He fell backward, into a glass coffee table. Brent was dead before his body touched the floor.

Armstrong fell back onto his knees. He turned around and saw the building manager. The building manager was on the ground, bleeding, but he was still alive. Then Armstrong stood and surveyed the living room.

Tad Garvin was lying on the floor. Brent Krane was just a few yards in front of him. Half his skull was gone.

Then Armstrong saw Brea Krane in the distance. She looked like she was sitting on the couch, frozen.

Armstrong took another step forward. He called out to her, but Brea Krane did not respond. That's when he noticed the red dot on her shirt. The first shot that had gone through her brother's shoulder had continued. It had struck her in the heart.

Armstrong heard the sirens coming. He turned back to the building manager. "Help is here." He was breathing hard. "You hang on."

Then Armstrong walked over to the wall and sat down on the floor. He pulled the phone out of his pocket. He found Brenda Gadd's phone number in the directory. He knew that he had to call her, but, first, he needed to figure out how he was going to explain that all three of their witnesses were dead.

CHAPTER EIGHTY SIX

Brenda Gadd's fight was replaced by bitterness. She had been wronged. She knew that she had been cheated. She knew that a guilty man was going free, but there was little that she could do.

"I'm going to make a promise to you," she leaned over to Quentin Robinson, checking to make sure that the judge had still not arrived. "I'm going back and reviewing everything. I'm investigating everything you did in this case. I'm investigating all the correspondence. I'm figuring out how you got paid. I'm looking at everything, and if I discover any evidence that you conspired to illicit false testimony or interfered with our investigation, you're going to jail."

Quentin closed his eyes. He wasn't going to be baited. He wasn't going to be drawn into an argument, especially in a judge's chambers. He decided to keep his mouth shut and wait.

"Good morning." Judge Husk entered the room, and then tottered around Brenda Gadd and Quentin Robinson's chairs to his desk. "Quite a trial we've had."

Judge Husk slowly lowered himself into his chair. Then his dutiful law clerk pushed him and the chair closer to his desk.

"Now," Husk nodded, settled. "My clerk tells me that there have been developments since we adjourned yesterday afternoon." Husk's tone when he said the word "developments" indicated that he knew that such a description of recent events was an understatement.

"Yes, Your Honor." Brenda Gadd tried to put on a strong front. "After the morning's testimony, I sent several agents out to talk to Brea Krane and her attorney. There were serious questions after yesterday's testimony regarding how that trust agreement had been disclosed, why it had been delayed until the end of trial, and why nobody informed me of its existence. As you know, Your Honor, I maintain that it is a fake." Brenda Gadd clenched her jaw.

"I know what you believe, Ms. Gadd, but that is not the critical issue at the moment." Judge Husk looked at Brenda Gadd with a certain amount of pity. "Please go on."

"Well a confrontation occurred when one of our agents arrived at Brea Krane's condominium. A shot had been fired. The attorney was dead when our agent entered the premises. More shots were exchanged, and when the episode concluded, the building manager had been wounded by a stray bullet and Brea Krane and her brother, Brent, were dead."

Judge Husk rubbed his chin, thinking. He obviously had opinions, but he kept them to himself.

Gadd continued. "And so, needless to say, our investigation was halted and we have been unable to fully develop a rebuttal argument."

"You could call the investigator or agent. He could testify as to what he saw. He could testify related to the wire transfers and your belief that the document is a fake." Judge Husk made the suggestion half-heartedly. He knew there was little to be gained. In fact, telling the jury that there were three people now dead would only bolster the defendant's theory. Michael Collins and his attorney were arguing that Brea Krane and her brother were trying to extort him, pressure him into giving them control of their father's trust. The fact that they both met such a violent end suggested that this theory was true.

"I'd rather just make the argument in closing, Your Honor." Gadd looked at Quentin. "But we all know this stinks, and I will investigate it. There has been a fraud committed upon this court."

Quentin looked at the judge. "I disagree," he said softly. "The questions aren't ever going to be answered, but as an officer of the court, I swear that I simply listened to my client, built my defense, and argued the evidence that I had. Keep in mind that the trust agreement didn't come from one of my witnesses. It came from the government. It was Brenda Gadd who sent it to me after her agents reviewed it."

Judge Husk raised his hand.

"I think I've heard enough." He took a breath. "You can save it. The trial will continue."

CHAPTER EIGHTY SEVEN

Michael Collins listened to Brenda Gadd's closing argument with pity. He kept waiting for Brenda Gadd to do something amazing or brilliant. He kept waiting for her to magically repair the damage that the trust agreement had wrought upon the government's case against him.

But nothing came.

Her Mother Hubbard smile was gone. The veneer of folksy wit had worn away. Instead of reframing her case in a new light, Brenda Gadd was sarcastic and condescending. She acted superior to everyone in the courtroom. Then she ended her closing argument with a bizarre warning to the jurors.

"Don't be fooled by the smoke and mirrors," Gadd pointed at Michael and Quentin. "Don't be fooled by a fantastic story, when the truth is so clear."

She sat down, and Judge Husk nodded toward Quentin.

It was the defendant's turn, and Quentin Robinson approached the podium like a man who knew he had the winning lottery ticket.

"Remember when this trial started?" Quentin rocked to his toes, and then back again. A spring in his step. "Remember when you were all picked as jurors, and you were sworn in, and you sat right here in this courtroom, and Judge Husk told you that the attorneys would now present their opening statements?"

Quentin nodded, making eye contact with each member of the jury.

"I remember it. I was nervous. I dropped my paper on the floor. I looked pretty foolish." Quentin put his hands on his hips. He allowed the jurors to remember that rocky start and laugh with him. It was as if they were all good friends now.

Quentin then stepped directly in front of the jury box. He looked down, as if collecting his thoughts, and then looked back up.

"I remember two other things about that day. First, I asked you all to keep an open mind. I asked you all to wait until all the evidence was in. In fact, that is also exactly what Judge Husk asked you to do, and you swore, under oath, to uphold his rules."

Quentin paused, making sure everyone remembered the same thing. He wanted them all on the same page before moving forward. In that way, he was the exact opposite of Brenda Gadd. Quentin was not condescending. He didn't act superior. He was a helper and a friend. He was gently guiding the jurors.

"The second thing that I remember was what Brenda Gadd said. The government told us that, and I'm quoting here, 'the documents do not lie. The documents speak for themselves.'" Quentin nodded. "I agree."

"The document is the trust agreement. It was signed by Joshua Krane and my client, Michael Collins. It authorized him to make investments and make charitable contributions, which he did. And it also required him to maintain confidentiality. Now you may not agree with the investments that my client made with part of the trust assets. You may also not agree with the charitable contribution, which went to the church where Michael

Collins attended as a young man. But the plain language of the trust agreement gives Michael Collins "sole discretion" to make the decisions on behalf of the trust. Sole discretion means, simply, it's his call. He can do what he thinks is best, despite Brea Krane or her brother's opinion."

Quentin took a step back and pointed at Brenda Gadd.

"She said the documents do not lie. She said the documents speak for themselves. And here we have the document that explains what Michael Collins did and gave him the legal authority to do it."

Quentin put his hands on his hips.

"Agent Frank Vatch testified that Michael Collins was a thief. He said, essentially, that Michael Collins saw an opportunity to get rich and took it, but the documents do not lie. There's no evidence that Michael Collins took all the money and spent it on himself. Most of it still remains in the accounts frozen by the government. What is missing are the investments and charitable contributions that Michael Collins had the complete authority to make. And if you look at the very bottom of the agreement, which is in evidence and you can review during your deliberations, it allowed Michael Collins to pay himself a reasonable amount for his services, which he did. He used trust assets to lease a little hut and gave himself a little extra to live on."

Quentin walked back to the podium.

"So, we now have a decision to make. The government must prove beyond a reasonable doubt that Michael Collins took money that he was not authorized to take and committed wire fraud. Now what is "beyond a reasonable doubt"? It is the standard of care and confidence that you would need to make one of the most important decisions in your life. The care and knowledge you would need to choose to have a major operation or get married."

Quentin paused. He shook his head.

"It isn't here. Given the existence of this trust agreement, I wouldn't trust the government to have that operation or get married. There is just too much doubt. There is too much doubt, because we all know that Michael Collins didn't take any money. He acted in accordance with his agreement with Joshua Krane."

CHAPTER EIGHTY EIGHT

Michael Collins did not even get out of the building. Notice came down to the holding area in the basement of the courthouse just an hour after Quentin had finished his closing argument.

The jury had reached a verdict.

Michael followed the U.S. Marshals into the elevator. He watched the doors slide close in front of him, and Michael knew that this was going to be the last time that he'd see the inside of a jail. He knew that he wasn't going to be coming back down that elevator or see the inside of Pod 3 at the MDC.

He knew that he was going to walk into the courtroom, hear the verdict, and then walk out the main courtroom door and never come back.

A bell rang. The doors slid open and the Marshals led him toward his seat at counsel's table. Michael shook hands with Quentin. Ordinarily, a quick verdict was good news for the prosecution, but not this time.

Michael glanced over his shoulder. He saw Andie and Kermit sitting in the back row. Michael almost didn't recognize Kermit without his dreadlocks, but Kermit's broad smile and bobbling head gave him away.

Judge Husk was led into the courtroom by his clerk, who helped him up a step and lowered the old man into his seat. The strength and spark that Judge Husk had shown throughout the trial was now gone. He looked tired.

"Bring the jury in." Judge Husk instructed the court clerk. She obliged.

"Please rise." Judge Husk raised his hand and everybody in the courtroom stood.

The jurors filed in and walked to their seats. The judge directed everybody to sit down, and then he cleared his throat.

"Ladies and gentlemen, we are back on the record in the United States versus Michael Collins." Judge Husk turned to look at the jurors. "Members of the jury, have you selected a foreperson?"

The jurors all nodded their heads, and then a man in the back row stood.

"I was selected the foreperson, Your Honor."

"Good," Judge Husk nodded. "And have you reached a verdict?"

"We have, Your Honor."

"And what say you."

The foreman turned away from Judge Husk and looked directly at Michael. For all Michael's confidence, a moment of doubt crept in and he felt his heart stop as the verdict was pronounced.

"We, the members of the jury, find the Defendant, Michael John Collins, not guilty of all charges."

"Very well," Judge Husk smiled. "You may be seated." He looked at Brenda Gadd. "Ms. Gadd would you like the jurors polled?"

"Yes." Brenda Gadd stood. "I would ask that the jurors be individually polled, Your Honor."

"Fine. Starting with you," Judge Husk looked at a woman in the first row at the bottom left corner. "Will you rise and state your decision, and then we will go down the row."

Each of the jurors stood and declared that Michael Collins was not guilty of all charges. Then Judge Husk gave them a final word of thanks and dismissed them from the court. Michael rose and watched them leave, and then he remained standing as Judge Husk released him from custody.

"You are free to go, Mr. Collins, and good luck to you."

"Thank you, judge." Michael turned and gave Quentin a hug, and soon they were joined by Kermit and Andie.

Michael took Andie into his arms. He squeezed her and kissed her.

"It's over," he said. "I don't have to hide anymore." Michael closed his eyes and thought about getting on a plane back to the Sunset Resort. He thought about Hut No. 7. He thought about drinking a beer on the Point, and then he thought about Brea Krane, her brother, and her lawyer.

He was found not guilty, but nobody would say that he was innocent.

CHAPTER EIGHTY NINE

Michael stared out at the blue Caribbean water. It never got old. He was never tired of sitting. The waves rolled past the rocky peninsula and onto the shore. The view was never boring.

He took a sip of Corona, and the sun cooked away the white paste that had developed after three months in custody.

"This place isn't exactly handicap accessible."

The sound of the voice sent a shiver up his spine. Michael Collins had to remind himself that he was safe. It was all in the past. "Francis," he said, knowing that Agent Frank Vatch hated the name Francis. "Wondering when you would pay me a visit."

"Just wanted to see where all the misfits and losers hang out." Vatch rolled his wheelchair forward. He stopped at the edge where the stone path ended and the beach began. "I also figured you missed me."

Michael Collins shook his head.

"Not so much." He set down his beer on a small wooden table next to his chair. Michael then stood, picked up the chair, and brought it back to Vatch.

He set the chair down next to Vatch, and then sat.

389 | J.D. TRAFFORD

"This is better. No wait ..." Michael got back up and re-claimed his beer, then sat down again. He took a sip and nod-ded. "Now that's better."

The two enemies sat together side-by-side for about five minutes. Michael was in no hurry, and so he waited. Eventually, Vatch broke the silence.

"It's nice here." Vatch looked out at the water, and then took in a deep breath of air. "Except for the fact that you're not in compliance with the Americans with Disabilities Act, but other than that, it's nice here."

"Yep," Michael agreed, and he resisted the temptation to point out that the Americans With Disabilities Act doesn't apply to resorts in Mexico.

"So this is home?" Vatch asked.

"I wish it was." Michael took a sip of beer. "Took the civil law-yers about two minutes before I got served with all sorts of civil lawsuits and garnishments. Looks like they're going to sell this place, divide the proceeds, keep me out." Michael took another sip of beer. "But I've got some time. I'll fight it."

"Lawyers," Vatch said it with such disgust that Michael could only laugh.

"Why are you here, Francis?"

"Got nothing better to do," Vatch looked at Michael. "Took early retirement."

"Congratulations," Michael said. "I'll buy you a beer whenev-er our server notices us."

"I'd appreciate that," Vatch rubbed the back of his neck. "It was time for me to go. The good guys and the bad guys weren't so easy to distinguish anymore."

"Well, I'm a bad guy, just in case you were confused." Mi-chael looked over at Frank Vatch. The two made eye contact, and Vatch's eyes narrowed.

"I wasn't ever confused about you," he said. "But after five years, I was done. And after your trial, it seemed like I'd be sent to the mailroom for my foreseeable future."

"So you're not here on business," Michael thought for a moment. "No point in harassing me anymore. All the trust assets are frozen. The resort is on the auction block. You're on permanent sabbatical. The government is barred from prosecuting me, again." Michael finished his beer. "So what gives?"

"Just wanted to see it." Vatch looked out at blue water. He watched the seagulls chase each other. "I just wanted to see it. See if this was really worth it."

"You're welcome to stay," Michael said as Vatch turned his wheelchair around and started back down the path.

"No thanks," Vatch waved his hand. "I got what I was looking for."

"Good," Michael leaned back. He looked at the clear expanse of peaceful water. Then he looked at the wedding ring on his finger and closed his eyes. "That makes two of us."

Thank you for reading "No Time To Hide"
Feel free to contact J.D. Trafford at JDTrafford01@gmail.com

Printed in Great Britain
by Amazon